The Guesthouse at Autumn Lake

AUTUMN LAKE BOOK 1

BECKY DOUGHTY

BraveHearts
Press

First edition 2023

ISBN: 9781953347510

1
Penny

"THERE'S SOMETHING RATHER... *EUPHORIC* about pulling into a place that feels like home after having been away for ten long months." Even as she said the words aloud, Penny knew they made little sense, even to her. Not only was this place not her home, but these next two months were, in fact, her time *away* from home, not the other way around. Eventually, she'd have to return to her own life and pick up the pieces of everything she'd left behind.

But until then, until July wound down and August reared its responsibility-laden head, she wouldn't think about that.

In the air-conditioned comfort of her car, while her road trip playlist piped out another Ranae song, Penny gave herself a stern look in the rearview mirror. Then, she placed a hand over her heart and declared, "I, Penelope Eva Anderson, do solemnly swear that I will leave my worries at home where they belong, and that I will wake up each morning in this beautiful place with a spirit of gratitude and hope and anticipation for whatever the day will bring."

The vow was one she made to herself every summer before she set foot out of her car in the lovely little town of Autumn Lake.

She took a deep breath and let it out slowly, forcing her shoulders to relax and the spinning plates she always seemed to be balancing in her mind to drop.

Outside the car windows, the late-morning sun shone warmly down on the lush front lawn of the bed-and-breakfast Penny would call her home away from home for the next two months. Flowerbeds awash in early summer color pooled whimsically around the base of the wraparound porch, a telltale sign of the green thumb who resided at the property.

Behind the house, sprawling out from the back door like rainbow rays, was the rest of the garden Hazel Poleman tended so meticulously. Penny could hardly wait to make her way back there so she could revel in the ordered chaos of flowers and vegetables cohabiting the space so beautifully. There was also a small orchard of stone fruit trees, their branches aggressively pruned to hang low for easy picking, and several apple and pear trees espaliered against a south-facing brick wall to make the most of the space. She itched to get her hands dirty, to bury her fingers in the rich, dark soil that was the foundation of Hazel's gardens.

Just as she reached down to turn off the ignition, Taylor Swift's "Shake it off" riffed out through the speakers. Penny laughed gleefully and turned up the volume. She popped the trunk latch from her key fob and scrambled out of her seat, leaving the car running so the song could play loud and proud. It would be her summer anthem, she decided, and she let herself shimmy-shimmy-shake-shake to the catchy rhythm of the song.

Eyeing the basket of groceries—nonperishables she'd keep stashed in her room for late-night reading binges—and the bag of her shoes in her back seat, she realized she'd have to make at least two trips. She left the driver's side door wide open so she could hear the music and bopped her way around to the back of the car. Singing along with the words she knew far too well for someone her age, she shook her backside as she unloaded her small suitcase of clothes and personal items, followed by her much larger duffel bag loaded with the books she'd brought with her. Most of them she'd already read over the last school year; she'd donate those to the Autumn Lake Library when she paid the place a visit in the next few days. But there were several she hadn't been able to get to, and she was determined to do so before she made her way to The Cracked Spine in town to restock her to-be-read pile. She had a whole new list of books to pick up from Claire Maitland, the owner of the bookstore on Dahlia Drive, so the pressure was on, as the proprietress would say, to get to cracking spines. Book spines, of course.

It had always struck Penny as a bit of a morbid name for a bookstore. Claire acknowledged that it did sound more like a chiropractor's office than a bookstore, but she didn't care. "It's my life's work to get people reading, and that means cracking some spines. I want them to love books so much they all but fall right into them." With her waist-length blonde hair, her porcelain features, and her willowy figure, Claire looked like she'd stepped right out of a fairy tale herself.

Penny hoisted the heavy bag of books onto her shoulder, then closed the trunk lid, still singing along with Ms. Swift. It was a little harder to shimmy and shake all loaded up the way she was, especially since her old suitcase had a broken wheel that kept getting stuck sideways. But she still managed a little jiggle-jiggle as she dragged her suitcase toward the front steps of the old waterfront guesthouse where she would be staying for the next two months. The wraparound porch beckoned her already, and she couldn't wait to fill a Mason jar with Hazel's homemade lemonade and settle into one of the comfortable old patio chairs with a brand-new romance novel.

She managed to lug her things up the wide steps to the front porch, and although the privacy screen door prevented her from seeing inside, she already knew that the heavy front door stood wide open to allow the cooling breeze from off the water to circulate through the house.

She rapped gently on the screen door, then pulled it open, not waiting to be invited in. There were no formalities at The Garden Gate Guesthouse.

The front parlor sat empty, but that wasn't unusual, especially this early in the season. Come July, though, when the summer temperatures hit their peak, especially in the middle of the day, guests were much more likely to head inside and make good use of the comfortable furnishings just to stay out of the worst of the midday heat.

"Hazel?" Penny called out, smiling as she heard banging coming from down the hall.

Hazel, the delightfully eccentric proprietress of the bed-and-breakfast, had a bit of a reputation for being a wannabe Rosie the Riveter. She'd fearlessly tackle repairs around the place, only to have to give in and ask for help, often after she'd exacerbated the original problem. The septuagenarian claimed to love being self-sufficient, but sometimes, especially in the last couple of years, Penny got the feeling that Hazel wouldn't mind having someone around to help her with keeping up with the house and property. The woman had mentioned as much on more than one occasion to Penny.

"For whatever reason, the good Lord didn't see fit to surround me with a husband and children of my own. Instead, He gave me this house and told me to open up its doors. Sometimes, I admit, it seems more than I can handle on my own, but then, without fail, He sends just the right help my way, and I somehow manage."

Penny would love nothing more than to be 'just the right help' for Hazel, but she knew that was an impossible dream. Her help was desperately needed elsewhere.

Back at home.

But she wasn't going to think about that.

She left her suitcase and bag of books in the parlor and headed toward the sounds coming from the direction of the stairwell that sat just around the bend at the other end of the hall. She let her fingertips drift over the pattern of the vintage wallpaper, relishing in the familiarity of the kitschy décor. Her footsteps were muffled on the thick wool carpet runner under her feet. Nothing had changed about the place in so long, and as far as she was concerned, that was what made it feel so much like home to her.

Then she heard the buzzing shriek of a saw blade. "Oh, Hazel," Penny murmured in trepidation. "What on earth?" In a surge of panic, she quickened her pace and rounded the corner, only to stop in surprise at the sight that greeted her.

A curtain of opaque painter's plastic hung to the floor from where it was taped to the ceiling, closing off access to the stairs. The whir of the saw quieted momentarily. "Hazel, what are you doing?" she called out carefully, not wanting to startle the woman, lest she sever a thumb. Or worse. "No morbid thoughts while on vacation, Penster," she chided herself.

When there was no response, Penny fumbled her way around the plastic enclosure until she found an opening and drew it back. The aroma of fresh-cut wood washed over her, and once again, she pulled up short.

"Oh!"

A man stood with his back to her, his shoulders and arms speckled with sawdust, his t-shirt damp with perspiration, and clinging to his torso. He leaned over a makeshift workbench constructed of a thick piece of plywood resting across two sawhorses. On it was the chop saw he'd just been using. He wore protective eyewear and a pair of chunky headphones, presumably sound protection, Penny surmised, since he clearly hadn't heard her. He lifted an arm to grip the back of his neck, the motion tightening the muscles in his back and making his biceps bulge.

"Oh," Penny said again, a little breathier this time, a flush warming her from head to toe. She fanned her face with one hand. *It's the heat in here. Of course, it's the heat.* It had to be a good fifteen degrees warmer inside the plastic-draped space.

Penny suddenly had no idea what to do. Should she make her presence known? Should she go back down the hall and make more noise so he would know she was coming? Should she run?

"Um, yes, Pen. Run!" It came out much louder than she'd intended, just as the guy pushed the headset away from his ears.

A sound that probably shouldn't come out of a man—ever—came out of him. A shriek, not unlike the sound the saw had just been making. He spun on his heels, the headphones clattering to the floor behind him, his fists clenched at his sides, his mouth and eyes open wide in surprise.

Penny, in turn, let out a scream of her own, and she lurched backward, with the plastic sheeting still clutched in one hand. To her dismay, a few feet of the curtain pulled free of where it was taped to the ceiling.

The next sound that emanated from the guy was much manlier. A snarl. No, a growl, Penny decided. His eyes darted from her face to the plastic in her hand, up to the ceiling, and back again in quick succession.

"Sorry!" She let go of the sheeting and lifted both hands at her sides in the universal sign of I-mean-you-no-harm-don't-hurt-me. "I'm so sorry," she repeated. "I—I didn't know you were in here."

He narrowed his eyes and clamped his jaw shut as he glared at her. His chest—she was doing her best not to notice his very broad chest—rose and fell rapidly. His fists were still balled up, but he'd lowered them. That had to be an encouraging sign, right?

"I mean, I figured *someone* was in here. I just thought you were Hazel." Like that didn't make her sound a little crazy? Why on earth would Hazel be enclosed in a plastic bubble using power tools? Penny was pretty sure that the woman wouldn't have bothered with the dust containment. No,

Hazel would have wielded her power tools right out in the open for all to see.

What had she been thinking?

And why wasn't the guy saying anything? Hadn't she just apologized?

She lifted her chin and gave him as disdainful a look as she could muster. "Look, I said I was sorry, okay? I didn't mean to scare you into letting out that man-scream." He flinched at her choice of words to describe the noise he'd made, and she wanted to raise a triumphant fist. *Good one, girlie.* But then she immediately felt remorse. She wasn't unkind by nature, and she didn't like that this snarling, glowering man was goading her into saying things out of character for her. "Besides, you surprised me, too, you know. I—I thought—."

"You thought Hazel was in here using power tools," he finished for her, as though he'd read her mind. His tone, however, made it clear that he didn't believe a word of it.

"Where *is* Hazel?" Penny asked, not liking his sarcasm. But at least the guy had found his voice. She crossed her arms and glowered back at him. "And who are you?"

"Who are you?" he shot back, crossing his own arms in what she could only assume was a mockery of her stance. So rude.

"I'm a guest here. Where is Hazel?" she demanded again, this time a bit more adamantly.

"She's not here." He thrust his chin at her. "And you're not supposed to be here, either." He bent over and scooped up his headphones, brushed sawdust off them, then set them beside the saw on the makeshift table.

"Uh, yes, I am," Penny declared indignantly. "And who did you say you were, again?"

"I didn't say," the guy retorted as he busied himself doing something with a pencil and a tape measure. He had his back to her, so she couldn't see what the project was, but curious as she might be, she wasn't about to poke the bear even more by trying to sneak a peek around him.

Besides, she wanted a name. Someone she could put on her '*Who to Avoid this Summer*' list. A list that consisted mostly of men Hazel and her friends had tried to set her up to have summer romances with. They tried every stinkin' year, no matter how often she insisted she wasn't interested in such a thing.

She didn't even have to wait for someone to suggest this guy. His name—at least, once she found out what it was—was going on her list immediately.

"Name's Ward," he tossed over his shoulder at her.

Penny blushed; *could* he read her mind? Was that even possible? And was Ward his first or last name?

He turned around again and leveled an impatient glare at her. "Hazel said no one would be here this morning. Said I'd have the place to myself at least until noon."

Was he sulking? Penny had to fight the urge to roll her eyes. *Hazel said…* He sounded like one of her second graders. She glared right back at him. "Oh, I'm sorry. Did I interrupt your you-time?"

"No. You interrupted my work time." He pointed at the ceiling where the plastic had come away from the tape, thanks to her. "You going to fix that?"

"Excuse me?" she spluttered.

"Are you going to fix that?" He said each word a little slower, like he thought her half-witted.

"I heard you the first time. And no. You can fix it yourself, bubble boy." It was time to go. She'd just come back later when, hopefully, this rude, sweaty man wouldn't be here.

As she spun on her heel, her foot tangled in the edge of the drooping plastic. Ward let out another strangled sound of warning, but it was too late. With her first angry step, she brought down the rest of the sheeting, and the whole thing drifted down around them like a billowy cloud.

Penny froze, her hands coming up to cover her mouth. "Oh, no," she groaned behind her fingers.

"Are you kidding me?" Behind her, Ward's voice rang with frustration.

Dreading having to face him again but knowing there was no avoiding it—she couldn't just run, no matter how badly she wanted to—Penny slowly turned back around, not even bothering to disentangle her foot from the plastic. "I am so sorry," she murmured. "I really did not mean to do that."

Ward stood with his hands propped low on his hips. His head was bowed, but she could see the muscles in his jaw bunch with restraint.

"I—I can help you put it back up, if you..." Her voice faded to silence as he lifted his head to glare at her. Her chin went up again, even though she felt a little sick over the chaos she'd just brought down around him. Literally. "Or I can just leave now."

"You know, I think that's a good idea."

He really was awful, Penny decided. It had obviously been an accident. It wasn't like she'd meant to tear down his work bubble. "Fine. Leaving. I'll come back this afternoon when I'm *supposed* to be here," she added, making air quotes around the word with her fingers.

He wasn't wrong. She *was* early, and technically, check-in time wasn't until three p.m. She'd tried to call Hazel to let her know she'd be arriving sooner than she'd expected, but the calls had just gone to voice mail. She'd gotten on the road several hours earlier than she'd originally planned, and she'd made remarkably good time, having avoided the worst of the morning traffic by leaving the city before rush hour. Hazel had never seemed to mind her showing up before check-in in the past, and Penny had just assumed today would be no different.

"You do that." Ward was already turning away from her, stalking toward a ladder that was propped up against one wall.

In the silence that followed, Penny could hear the faint strains of music wafting down the hall toward them. She smacked herself in the forehead. "My car." She'd left the thing running this whole time. She quickly disentangled her foot from the plastic and headed back the way she'd come. She only felt the tiniest bubble of shame at the state she was leaving him in, but that was because she was a nice person. In fact, if he had been even the tiniest bit nice, himself, she would have insisted on staying and helping. She may not know a whole lot about construction, but she worked with children. She was a master at taping.

Penny paused in the parlor for a moment, wondering if it was safe to leave her things there until she returned. She decided she'd better take them with her, just in case Bubble Boy harbored grudges. Who knew what he might do to her belongings if given the opportunity? Just because he was doing work for Hazel—she obviously trusted him enough to leave him alone in her house—didn't mean Penny should blindly trust him.

She couldn't take the stuff upstairs to her room, either, thanks to him blocking the stairs. "Technically," she mused, darting a look back down the hall, a capricious grin tugging at the corners of her mouth. "Thanks to me, the stairs are no longer blocked."

But no, it probably wasn't a good idea to drag her things through his demolished workstation just now. For all she knew, he'd close off the stairs while she was up in her room, and then she'd be stuck there until he left. And she was hungry.

Sighing loudly, she hoisted the duffel back up on her shoulder. Holding the screen door open with her rear end, she backed out, dragging her wobbly-wheeled suitcase over the threshold.

"Let me get that for you," a male voice said from right behind her, and suddenly, the resistance of the screen door was gone, making her stumble backward.

For the second time that morning, Penny screeched in surprise. And then a third time, when the bag of books slipped off her shoulder and landed on her toes. Her suitcase, too, hit the floor, but thankfully, she managed to dodge that one.

The man on the porch sported a light blue t-shirt over a pair of cargo shorts, and on his feet were well-worn work boots. His backward baseball cap held his shoulder-length hair away from his face, and Penny couldn't miss the far too amused grin he flashed at her as he watched her perform her hobble-in-circles dance. She had a sudden violent urge to throw something at him.

"Are you kidding me?" she snapped out, sounding a little too much like Ward, which only stoked her irritation. "There's another one of you?"

The guy still held the screen door wide for her, but he slowly shook his head, his grin growing even bigger. "Far as I know, there's only one of me." He winked at her. "The world couldn't handle more than one of all this." With his free hand, he made an all-encompassing gesture at himself.

Granted, he was ridiculously good-looking in a casual construction worker kind of way. But so was Ward Whatever-His-Name-Was, which only proved her point.

Ward, who decided, at that moment, to make another surprise appearance, burst out of the house and onto the porch, tripped over her bag, and barely caught himself from careening into her.

Penny managed to hold in her squawk of surprise this time, although she forgot all about the throbbing pulse in her toes when he stopped barely a foot from her.

"What? What happened?" Ward made a quick assessment of the situation, obviously coming to some kind of—probably wrong—conclusion, then turned to her and barked, "What is it now?"

That was the last straw. Penny bent to snatch up the strap of her bag, but the ball cap guy started forward at the same time. She hesitated. She wasn't about to get between the two monoliths. "I just—can you please...." She waved her hand aggressively between them. "Back off, both of you, so I can get my bag."

Ball Cap stepped back, arms up in surrender. But Ward just stood there, practically straddling her books, still glaring at her. "I heard you scream. Are you alright?"

"Of course I'm all right. But no thanks to either of you." She scowled at him, frustration at feeling so vulnerable warring with her bruised pride. She wasn't usually so clumsy. In fact, she wouldn't consider herself clumsy at all. "You scared the living daylights out of me," she said, turning with the same dark expression to Ball Cap. "I mean, where did you even come from?"

"Sorry, little lady," he said, reaching up to snatch the hat off his head. He shook his hair out, the sun-bronzed locks tumbling loose and messy around his face. Even to Penny's not-so-experienced eyes, it was obvious that he expected her to go all gushy at the move. "I was just trying to be a gentleman and hold the door for you."

But come on. Little lady? Did that still go over well with anyone these days? And just who was he calling little?

Penny had always been admittedly a bit too sensitive about her petite stature, and although she'd made peace with the fact that she sometimes still shopped in the junior clothes department, every once in a while, a comment like that could make her feel... well, *small.* Especially when it came from someone significantly larger than she was.

Ward cleared his throat, drawing their attention back to him. "What took you so long, Alex? We're even further behind schedule now," he said churlishly, shooting a scathing look at Penny.

"Really?," Penny said, planting her hands on her hips and returning his glare. "I said I was sorry. I offered to help. You kicked me out."

Alex, that stupid grin still lighting up his face, bounced his gaze back and forth between Penny and Ward, clearly entertained, and not at all intimidated by Ward's reprimand. "What's going on here?" he asked, openly curious.

"Nothing," they both retorted in unison.

"She was just leaving," Ward added, then bent for her duffel bag. Penny winced at his surprised expression when he picked it up. "What's in here? Bricks?"

She gave in and rolled her eyes. "Wow. And you're funny, too." But she wasn't smiling. She held out her hand toward the bag. "I read, okay? They're books. Give it to me." It was so full that she hadn't been able to close the zipper all the way, and she didn't need him judging her about her reading material. So, she liked romance novels. Especially romantic comedies that also made her cry.

But guys, she had discovered firsthand, didn't really understand that.

"I see." But Ward didn't hand the bag over. Instead, he looped the strap over his shoulder, then peered down into the unzipped opening, cocking his head as he studied the contents. After a moment, with his face showing a rather surprising lack of judgment, he asked, "Where do you want these? Back seat or trunk?"

Alex picked up her suitcase, then the two of them stood there staring at her, waiting for her to tell them where to cart her things off to.

Penny was momentarily at a loss. Partly because the situation was so awkward and weird, but also because... well, because there were two offensively handsome men holding her things and awaiting her beck and call.

"Um..." She bit her bottom lip, then stopped immediately at the way Alex's eyes widened appreciatively at the sight. She shook her head. "I can take them. I got them this far by myself."

Ignoring her completely, Ward, followed closely by Alex, hauled her things right past her and down the steps toward her car. Apparently, the guys could hardly wait to get her loaded up and out of their way. "Okay, then," she snipped, trying not to be offended. "The trunk will do."

Penny reached inside her car to turn off the music, but she remained standing in the open driver's side door.

"That it?" Alex asked, one hand still on the open trunk lid. Ward, however, gave her a barely there nod and started back toward the house.

"That's it," she confirmed, her jaw tight with indignation. She didn't actually have to thank them, did she? Weren't they, for all intents and purposes, all but booting her off the property?

Would Hazel be okay with that?

No, Hazel would not. Indeed, Penny couldn't wait to tell her about this morning's encounter. Ward the Builder had better prepare himself for a comeuppance. The thought brought a little levity to Penny's insulted heart.

"Alex, by the way." Alex closed the trunk, then circled the car toward her and stuck out his hand.

She hesitated only a moment, reminding herself that if these guys were working for Hazel, that meant they couldn't be all bad.

Although, she had yet to hear as much out of Hazel's mouth.

In fact, she hadn't heard from Hazel since last Friday.

Hopefully, Hazel was, as Ward had said, out and about, and not locked in the basement in the dark.

Okay. Wow. That spiraled quickly. No morbid thoughts, remember? Penny cleared her throat. "I'm Penny. I'm supposed to be staying here at the guesthouse." She shot a withering look at Ward's back just before he disappeared inside. "I mean, not yet, according to your buddy, there. But starting today. This afternoon. Once I check in."

"Thanks for clarifying," Alex said with a wink. He was just teasing her, she knew, but she felt her hackles rise. She tugged her hand free and waved it in the general direction of downtown.

"Okay, I'm going to...." She trailed off; it wasn't any of his business what she would do while waiting for Hazel's return.

Alex nodded good-naturedly. "If you're hungry, stop in at Juno's Coffee. Uh, Juniper's Coffee Bar," he corrected himself. "She'll take good care of you. Best coffee in town, too."

"Um, thank you." She'd been planning on doing just that, especially since it was right next door to The Cracked Spine. "That's where I was going for lunch."

"Great! Tell Miss Juno that Alex says 'hello', will you?" He paused, almost like he was trying to decide whether he should say the words on the tip of his tongue. He added, "And don't mind Ward. He's a good guy. I can vouch for him. He's probably just having a bad day."

Penny snorted and slid into her driver's seat, rolling her window down so she could say, "Yeah, well, thanks to him, I'm having a bad day now, too."

Alex nodded, but he didn't try to assuage her. The muffled sound of hammering started up from somewhere inside the house, and they both turned toward the noise. Alex saluted her with two fingers to his forehead, then launched himself up the front steps and headed inside, the screen door snapping shut behind him with a loud thwack.

This was *not* how Penny had envisioned her two months of rest and relaxation would begin.

2
Ward

WARD KNEW HE WAS scowling because of the way the sweat pooled between his brows and dripped down the bridge of his nose to burn his eyes. He had a list a mile long from Hazel containing a myriad of little things to fix around the place, and he'd given himself until noon to finish up. That would allow him just enough time to pack up here, grab a bite to eat, and still make it around the lake to his next job.

Which was why he'd called in the favor Alex owed him from back in February when Ward had helped pull his truck out of the ditch. Alex had dozed off at the wheel for what he claimed was only a moment, but it had been one moment too long to stay on the road. The truck hadn't been badly damaged—just some dings and scratches that could be buffed out with the right tools. But the embankment down which he'd careened was just steep enough, and the truck was lodged at the right angle, that he couldn't get enough traction, even with the four-wheel-drive, to get the beast out without help. Ward had driven by at the opportune time and had helped haul him out, no questions asked.

"I owe you one, man," Alex had repeated multiple times as he worried the bill of the baseball cap he was rarely without. "Any time. You just call."

Alex hadn't been injured, either, but he'd been shaken up by the accident, and Ward had tried to reassure him with a friendly clap on the shoulder. "You'd do the same for me."

Alex had insisted, though, and rarely a week had gone by since then, that he didn't remind Ward about it.

So when Ward called him early that morning to see if he had any time he could spare, Alex had jumped at the chance to return the favor. He had been sitting on Hazel's porch steps, armed with his loaded tool belt, a crate of power tools, and two cups of coffee from Juniper's Coffee Bar, when Ward pulled up at seven AM.

Hazel, of course, had chided them for spending their money on the "foofy" coffee when she had perfectly good coffee right there in her kitchen. Alex had charmed her with his crooked grin and compliments about how pretty her hair looked that morning, and she'd practically force-fed them some of her apple cinnamon muffins. By the time she'd climbed into her big old Chevy Suburban and lead-footed it out of her driveway, the morning was well underway, and Ward was feeling the pressure of his precious time slip-sliding away from him.

So to have Miss.... He shook his head, realizing she'd never told him her name. Whatever her name was, she'd walked into the middle of the already chaotic morning, scared whatever that sound was out of him, then ripped down his dust protection plastic, all in a matter of a few minutes. Well, he just didn't have time for that.

Hazel had told him that her first guest of the summer was arriving that day; hence, the pressure to get the inside work wrapped up that morning. But she'd assured him that no one would be there until sometime mid-afternoon, long after he'd be gone for the day.

If he'd known guests would be arriving early—it had to be an attractive, female guest, of course—he'd have made the railing repair first thing in the morning instead of leaving it until last. He could've been cleared out of the hallway by ten and then would have avoided that whole confrontation—because that's what it had quickly become—with the woman in the fluttery sundress.

Ward had seen the expression on her face when he'd turned around. She'd looked downright horrified at the sight of him, her nose upturned, eyes wide, her cheeks pink. What was up with that? Had she never seen a working man before? Did she have an aversion to sweat?

He pulled the collar of his shirt open and took a whiff down the front of it. He didn't stink; at least, not that he could tell.

So maybe she was just trying to hold back a laugh at the sound he'd made. "What was that?" he muttered to himself. Man-scream, she'd called it. He cringed, his gut tightening with embarrassment at the memory. He hadn't known it was possible for him to produce that high of a note without injuring himself.

"Who you talking to?" Alex said, coming around the corner from the kitchen where he'd replaced two cupboard door hinges and fixed a broken drawer.

Alex had been a godsend that morning. He'd already reinforced the front porch railing and replaced two of the deck boards that had succumbed to water damage this last winter. The whole thing needed to be pressure-washed, sanded, and resealed, but Hazel said that was something she'd have to put off doing until after she'd built up her house repairs account from her paying summer guests. Ward had sent Alex on a quick run to the hardware store for parts, but he'd been back in no time—not late at all, in fact, which only made Ward feel pettier about calling Alex out. And in spite of the disruption caused by Hazel's guest, they'd gotten right back to work the moment she was gone.

Ward didn't meet Alex's eyes, a little embarrassed at being caught talking to himself. Nor did he bother answering the question. "How's it going in there? Ready for something else?"

Alex made a sound that might have been a chuckle, but he just nodded and said, "Doors and drawers are working smooth as butter. What else you got for me?"

"There's a window with a broken latch in the bathroom on the right upstairs. I set a new part on the vanity, if you can replace that."

"I'm on it, boss." Alex started up the stairs, but he paused to admire Ward's work. "Nice. This sure is a sweet old house, isn't it?"

"If you like money pits," Ward grumbled with a noncommittal shrug. He pulled the used piece of twenty-grit sandpaper from the disc on his sander and tossed it into his trash bucket. He hadn't bothered taping the plastic dust protection back up, deciding it would probably take less time to clean up what little mess he had left to make. "Most of what we're doing is cosmetic, just to get her through the season."

Alex nodded agreeably. "Think the structure is sound, though? The foundation?"

"I don't know." Ward shook his head. "I'd be afraid to investigate. Let sleeping dogs lie, you know? And I don't even want to know what the plumbing and electrical look like. Half the outlets in this place are still the old two-pronged version, and I have a feeling the three-pronged ones aren't actually grounded."

Alex patted the cordless drill in the holster attached to his tool belt. "Good thing I came with my batteries fully charged."

"Good thing." Ward turned to put the sander back in its case, but Alex wasn't finished.

"Speaking of fully charged."

Ward stilled, somehow knowing what was coming.

"Penny, hm? She's something else."

Penny. So that was her name. Somehow, it suited her. Not in any obvious way, he supposed. She didn't have copper curls or brown eyes. No, her chin-length hair was a pale blonde that he'd seen a whole lot of on his Southern California beach clientele. But if he were a betting man, he'd wager that Miss Penny hadn't spent a single penny on getting hers that color. She was... well, the word that came to him was *shiny*. She sort of sparkled, in spite of her sass—or maybe because of it—in that spirited girl-next-door way that some people seemed born with, and Ward had found it difficult to look away from her. "Yep. Something else," he echoed with another shrug.

"I've seen her around town before, but never up close and personal." Alex seemed oblivious to Ward's reticence to continue the conversation. "Honestly thought she was a kid last summer. Cute, but too young to take note of, you know?"

Ward didn't even have to look at Alex to know he'd find that half-cocked grin on his face, the one that could win over even the hardest of hearts. He felt himself bristling at his words, and he didn't like that it bothered him to think of Alex ogling Penny.

"But up close and personal?" his friend continued. "And fully charged like she was?" He let out a low whistle, one that made Ward straighten. "Not a kid, after all. She's a little ball of fire, yeah? I wouldn't mind putting out that —"

"Hey." Ward cut him off, shooting a steely look up at him. "She's Hazel's guest, man. Cool it."

Alex grinned and lifted his hands at his sides in a show of innocence. "*I'm* cool," he said, then headed up the stairs, taking them three at a time.

Ward stood glaring after the guy, feeling as if he'd just been duped. Exposed. Like he'd just inadvertently admitted to something, but he had no idea what. He snatched up the nozzle of his shop vac and kicked on the power button at the base of the canister, then hosed up the sawdust that had settled since he'd stopped sanding. With a clean tack cloth, he wiped down the railing, then soaked another rag in mineral spirits to make sure the surface of it was clean of any residual dust before applying the polyurethane.

He ran his hand down the sleek curve of the century-old banister and smiled with satisfaction at a job well-done. In spite of what he'd said to Alex, this old house was a beauty. A beauty in much need of a thorough renovation, perhaps, but from what Ward could tell, she still had good bones.

Built right on the lake, the eight-bedroom Cape Cod-style home had been in Hazel's family for generations. When Hazel's young husband had been thrown from a horse and died only two years after they were married, she'd moved back home with her parents. She'd cared for her mother and father into their golden years, and when the house came to her after their passing, she couldn't bear the loneliness in the great, echoing rooms. So she had opened the home as a bed-and-breakfast, calling it The Garden Gate Guesthouse at Autumn Lake. From May through September, she took in as many summer lake vacationers as she had rooms available, and fed them spectacular breakfasts made up of produce from her abundant gardens, eggs from her happy chickens, and locally sourced bacon and sausage.

The town center sat about two miles down the road, at a part of the lake with a broad, accessible shoreline where boat and water sport rentals, restaurants and cafes, and kitschy tourist shops lined a boardwalk. There was even a small fairground with well-maintained rides, a miniature golf course, and a vintage merry-go-round with fantastical creatures of all kinds.

Around the turn of the millennium, however, the town of Autumn Lake had been featured as "a hidden gem vacation spot" in one of the popular travel magazines. As a result, the area had experienced a surge of attention, and seemingly overnight, businesses catering to wealthy summer vacationers started popping up all around the lake shore, including fancy bed-and-breakfasts, rental cottages, and even floating cabins for people who wanted to be lulled to sleep by the rocking of the water.

Autumn Lake had thrived on the influx of money coming in, and although it had lost some of the appeal that had made it the hidden gem it once was, most of the changes had been beneficial to the locals.

So when Ward moved back last fall, he'd been taken aback by the state of Hazel's grand old house just across the little inlet from his childhood home. In fact, it seemed to have deteriorated noticeably right alongside its owner, who had also—quite suddenly and rather shockingly, at least to Ward's eyes—started looking her age.

The home's décor felt outdated rather than vintage, the garden seemed much smaller than he remembered it and in bad need of some attention. Although the waterfront property had a sturdy old well-maintained dock, Hazel no longer kept even a skiff boat for puttering around the lake or fishing.

"Oh, I've still got my daddy's old johnboat, but it's put up in the barn out back. I can't afford the insurance required to have one available to my guests," she'd told him when he'd asked about it. "Katy Lawrence just got sued by a guest last year, did you hear? The man insisted he knew how to operate her little bowrider, then he rammed it into her deck, and caused significant damage to both the boat and the dock. To add insult to injury, he then had the audacity to sue poor Katy because he broke his nose on the windshield when he smashed his face into it."

Ward had heard all about it. He'd been the one to repair the boat, as well as Katy's dock, shortly after he'd moved back to town. Katy had been devastated, both emotionally and financially, and she'd closed up her little studio apartment over her garage, no longer willing to take in lodgers.

It didn't help matters that across the lake, the new Carpe Diem Resort with its all-inclusive amenities, was packing in the wealthy out-of-towners—WOOTS, as the townies referred to them—who used to spend their summers in the bed-and-breakfasts, bungalows, and lake cabins owned by the locals.

"Hey, Ward," Alex called out, interrupting Ward's meandering thoughts. "I've got a few more mornings I can give you between now and the end of the month." He appeared at the top of the stairs, a concerned frown furrowing his brow. "Have you seen the roof outside this bathroom window? I think you should come take a look."

"Yeah, I know." Ward wrapped the cord around his orbital sander and shoved it into its canvas bag. The whole roof needed replacing, but it was another job Hazel claimed she needed to put off until after her summer guests were gone. "Hazel asked if I could just do whatever I needed to do to make it last another few months. I plan on getting up there with a fiver of O'Henry next week sometime and seal up the worst of it."

"A good summer storm could make quick work of a patch job." Alex's frown deepened.

"I know," Ward said again. A good summer storm could wreak havoc with any roof, old or new, if it came in off the water the right way. "But I promised Hazel I'd do my best to get her through until the fall. If you're interested, I could use a spotter." The roof wasn't pitched too extreme, but any time Ward was up more than a few feet off the ground, he preferred knowing there was someone near at hand in case anything should happen.

"Absolutely. You let me know when."

Ward would talk to Hazel about scheduling a day to work on the roof. God forbid he should have another run-in with a guest like the one he'd had today. With Ms. Penny in particular. "Will do. Thanks."

Alex didn't return to the task he'd been working on, but instead, remained at the top of the stairs.

"Was there something else?" Ward asked.

Alex was no longer frowning. One side of his mouth crooked up in a half smile. "So, do you think that shiny Penny will still be here next week?"

3
Penny

THE CRACKED SPINE SAT on the corner of Dahlia Drive and Camellia Court, with its double glass doors painted to look like the covers of an open book. Pushing through those doors gave one a sense of stepping out of reality right into a book, which was exactly what Claire had intended. Just inside the front doors, the foyer walls were covered in vintage handwriting wallpaper. Adding to the ambiance, in a three-dimensional wire tree that looked to be right out of a Tim Burton movie, was perched an iridescent purple Cheshire Cat grinning down out of its bare, claw-like branches.

It always gave Penny such a thrill to step through that transformational passageway into the otherworldliness of the bookstore. Granted, much of her anticipation had to do with seeing Claire again after so long. Penny already had her book wish list out of her purse—she'd been adding to it all year—and she made a beeline for the counter, not allowing herself to look left or right until she'd dropped off her order.

Claire, too, looked forward to Penny's visit every year, and would practically snatch the list out of her hand just to see what was on it. It would then take Claire some time to gather all the titles, giving Penny the opportunity to wander the delightful little shop and peruse the display racks and wall-to-wall bookshelves to her heart's content.

Today, however, Claire wasn't in her usual spot near the front door. Instead, a smiling teenager with heavily made-up eyes greeted Penny with a warm, "Hello! Welcome to The Cracked Spine."

Penny returned the smile and greeting, but when she asked after Claire, Tina, according to her name tag, said she was out of town for a few days. "She'll be back on Monday, though," Tina offered brightly.

Disappointed, Penny wasn't sure whether she should go ahead and give Tina her list or wait for Claire. Several titles on it would need to be ordered, and the sooner those orders got processed, the sooner she'd get them. But she still had several books to read from her visit last year, she reminded herself. She could wait another few days and return with her list when Claire was back.

Tina gave her a quick explanation of the layout of the shop, which genres were where, what the week's special promotions were, and then left her to roam around on her own. "Just holler if you need anything, okay?"

Penny made a beeline to the back of the shop, then slowly worked her way toward the front, mostly just scoping things out. Claire rearranged things on a regular basis, and every summer, Penny felt a little like she was visiting a brand-new place. She couldn't resist picking up a few of the titles from her list as she came across them, but she was selective. She didn't want to ruin the fun for Claire.

Near the front window, on a fancifully decorated table, was a display pyramid of books by an author Penny had never heard of; one Destiny Baudelaire. Romance novels, at least by the look of the covers, and if that wasn't a pen name, the author was just born lucky.

"Destiny Baudelaire," Penny murmured under her breath, giving the last name as French an accent as she could muster. She could almost taste the rich and heady essence of it as the name curled over her tongue. She picked up one of the books and said again, "Destiny Baudelaire."

"Have you read any Destiny Baudelaire?" Tina asked from where she stood at the checkout counter nearby. Penny felt her cheeks grow warm and hoped the girl didn't think her too crazy, standing there muttering the author's name over and over.

She set the book back down on the table. "I haven't. I've not heard of her before."

"Oh, she's wonderful. She writes the perfect blend of romance and humor. Claire says they're categorically contemporary romance, but Ms. Baudelaire has a way of finding the humor in even the most mundane bits of life. But she'll also make you cry, so fair warning."

Wow. Tina the teenager with her ghoulish black eye makeup spoke with insightful eloquence.

"That sounds right up my alley. I'm a sucker for push-me-pull-you books." Penny picked up a different title by the same author and flipped it over to read the back cover. "That's what I call books that make me laugh and cry in equal measures."

Tina nodded agreeably, her chin-length messy curls bouncing. "Totally."

Ah. Eloquent, maybe, but still a teenager.

"You should read her," Tina said with a hint of authority in her voice. "Start with *Lace it Up*. You can thank me when you come back for the next one in the series."

Penny laughed out loud at the girl's confidence in her recommendation. "You're on. I think I will."

"She's one of Claire's new favorites," Tina added. "She can't get enough of Destiny Baudelaire."

"All the more reason for me to read her." Penny's curiosity about the author grew with each passing moment.

"Yeah, well, if Claire were here, you wouldn't have been able to leave without at least one of those books. My boss practically forces one on every single person who comes through that door."

Penny set her short stack of books down on the counter in front of Tina. "Sold," she said, tapping *Lace it Up* where it sat on the top of the stack. "I hope Claire knows how lucky she is to have you on board."

"Thank you," Tina returned politely, her cheeks turning pink at the compliment. "I'm lucky to be on board. I love this job."

Penny paid for her books, then headed around the corner to Juniper's Coffee Bar. It was just before noon, so not too early for lunch. She could use an iced coffee and one of Juno's braised beef and roasted pepper sandwiches. She'd visit with Juno at the counter while she ate her sandwich, then curl up in one of the squishy armchairs at the back of the café and dive right into Destiny Baudelaire's book. Wouldn't Claire be surprised when she showed up already having read it?

"Penelope Anderson!" Juno's rich, melodic voice rose above the clinking of dishes and whirring of espresso machines as she called out a greeting the moment Penny set foot inside the bar. "Get over here, woman, and let me kiss your face."

Penny did just as she was told, her relief at finally seeing someone she knew far greater than she'd have expected. She plopped her pretty paper bag of books and purse on the bar, then turned to give the proprietress a tight hug. The familiar earthy fragrance of Juno's cornrows—like cocoa butter and coconut oil and a hint of tangerine—brought with it a rush of emotions, and Penny clung to her a little longer than necessary.

When she stepped back, Juno cupped Penny's face in her hands. She studied her for a long moment, then kissed her on both cheeks. "You doing all right, hon?"

Penny nodded and dropped onto a barstool before she responded. "I'm just so glad to be back at the lake," she said. "I've missed this place so much."

Juno ducked back around the counter and washed her hands before picking up the knife she'd been using to slice fresh strawberries behind the bar. "How's Hazel this morning?"

"I haven't seen her yet," Penny said, sounding more disgruntled than she actually felt. She hadn't given much more thought to Ward and Alex, at least not once she got distracted by all the treasures at Claire's bookstore. But now that the conversation had so abruptly circled around to them, Penny couldn't get the image out of her mind of the two of them hauling her luggage off Hazel's front porch. "There was a construction crew doing some work at her place this morning. I guess Hazel was out running errands or something."

"A construction crew?" Juno continued slicing the fruit into a large container, but she eyed Penny curiously. "I thought she had Ward St. James over there working for her."

"Ward. Yes. That was one of the guys' names. The other was Alex."

Juno's fingers stilled just for a moment, and if Penny hadn't been watching her skilled hands at work, she might have missed it. "Alex Frampton?"

"I don't know. They only told me their first names. The Alex guy is big. I mean, really big."

"Everyone is big to you, honey," Juno teased her, and for some reason, it didn't bother Penny at all coming from her.

"Like several inches over six feet. Longish hair. Really great smile and pretty eyes with laugh crinkles." Penny made a sweeping gesture with her fingers at the corners of her own eyes. Ward hadn't offered her even a hint of a smile, so she had no idea if he even had any laugh lines.

"Baseball cap?" Juno asked, an odd look in her eye.

"Backwards. Yes."

Juno lifted her knife to point at Penny. "You watch out for that one, Miss Penny. He'll take your feet right out from under you before you even know he's heading your way. That smile of his could charm a cat out of its cream."

Penny nodded slowly, studying her friend a little more closely. There was a twinge of something more than just a friendly tip in her voice. Was she talking from firsthand experience? "Gotcha," she said. "Thanks for the warning."

"And speaking of cream," Juno said, adroitly changing the subject. "What will you be having today? Your regular iced coffee with cinnamon cream?"

"Please. And one of your beef and pepper sandwiches, too. I've been craving that thing for the last week while packing and closing up the condo for the summer."

"You know just what to say to make a girl smile," Juno said. "I'll make your sandwich myself, just for that." She handed off the coffee order to a young man named Tyler who was already working the espresso machine like a pro. Then turned to help another customer who'd just stepped up to the bar.

Penny turned on her stool to look around, surprised to see how crowded the café had suddenly become. The lunch crowd, of course. She should have come at a time when it wasn't so busy, especially if she hoped to visit with her friend a little. One of the overstuffed armchairs in the back corner was empty. If she didn't act fast, it wouldn't last. "Hey, Juno," she said, catching her friend's attention before she could take yet another customer's order. "I'm going to snag that chair and read for a bit. You do your thing—we can catch up later."

Juno nodded. "Sure. I'll bring your sandwich and coffee to you shortly."

Out of the corner of her eye, Penny saw a woman enter the café and shoot a quick glance over at the vacant chair before heading to the counter to place her order. Penny snatched up her things and made a beeline for it, dropping into the chair before chancing another look at the customer who had obviously hoped to land the spot for herself. But the woman had taken Penny's vacated bar stool and seemed perfectly content, which made Penny feel quite a bit better about snagging the chair the way she had.

An hour later, her stomach full and her mind buzzing happily with the effects of the caffeine and Destiny Baudelaire's brilliant storytelling, Penny happened to glance up over the top of her book toward the door to find none other than Ward St. James pushing through it.

"What is *he* doing here?" she muttered under her breath. She narrowed her eyes at his back as he made his way to the counter. Had Alex told him she'd be here?

But that was silly. Ward had certainly made it clear that he had no desire to be anywhere near her.

Wait. Did him being here mean that Hazel was back from her morning outing? "Does this mean that I'm allowed to go home now?" One of the teenagers at a nearby table glanced over at her with a wary expression, and Penny realized she'd asked the question a little too loud. She smiled brightly, hoping to relay to the girl that she wasn't crazy. Not really.

Ward greeted Juno with a wave and settled onto one of the stools at the bar. They chatted briefly, then, to Penny's horror, Juno pointed in her direction, and Ward turned to look over his shoulder at her. It was all Penny could do not to duck behind her book. She held her head high, though, and when he did that chin thrust thing at her by way of greeting, she pressed her lips together in a grim line. Did he have any idea how antisocial jerking one's chin at people was? And without even a hint of a smile? She wasn't his bro, after all. Giving him a taste of his own medicine, she mimicked the motion back at him, not cracking a smile, either.

Even from all the way across the room, she saw his prominent eyebrows hitch up in surprise, then furrow in question. Clearly, if his bouncing brows were any indication, he'd expected a different response from her.

A fluttery-fingered wave? A giggly coo? Ha.

Penny shifted in her chair so that she was sitting sideways, no longer facing the bar, one leg bent under her. She all but hung up a 'Do Not Disturb' sign, just in case Mr. St. James got any notion in his head that she was interested in his attention. She wasn't.

She skimmed the open pages of the book on her lap to find her place. Reaching for her near-empty cup of coffee, she took a slurpy sip through the straw and picked up the story of Ewan Hunter and Wendy Brandt where she'd left them. They'd just had their first real argument, and the two of them were now cautiously circling each other in the book, heated emotions held in check for fear of getting hurt. She was less than a third of the way in and already deeply invested in the couple's bumpy journey toward happily-ever-after.

A few pages later, the sound of a throat clearing nearby drew her attention away from a rather tender and hopeful scene between Ewan and Wendy. "Uh, Penny?"

So engrossed had she been in her book, she hadn't heard him approach. She turned to look up at Ward, who stood far too close for comfort. At least for *her* comfort. She caught a whiff of a pleasantly male scent made up of fresh cut wood and soap or aftershave. She ducked her head, hoping he hadn't seen her nostrils flare, then looked back up again. Apparently, he was perfectly at ease with the close proximity. She sat up a little straighter in her chair. "Yes?"

He held out a plastic cup toward her. "Juno said you like your coffee cold. With cream."

For a moment that seemed to last far longer than moments were supposed to last, Penny sat frozen, just staring at the proffered drink. Finally, she stammered, "You—you got me a coffee?"

"No. No. It's from Juno," he said, his voice gruff. "Not from me. I'm just delivering it for her."

Penny cringed inwardly at his adamant clarification. Why did his words bother her so much? Of course, the coffee wasn't from him. Why on earth would he do something so nice?

"You work for Juno now?" she asked, hoping her flippant tone would mask the mixed emotions behind her thoughts. She reached up to take the coffee from him. "Thank you. And tell Juno thank you for me, too." Then she turned back to her book, not waiting for a response from him.

But when he remained there, not speaking, she lifted her gaze to meet his, lifting the cold drink between them. "What? Am I supposed to tip you for this?" Ugh. She was being so rude. What was it about this guy that brought out the aggressor in her?

"No," he said, drawing the word out in a long-suffering tone. "I brought it as a peace offering."

"But it's from Juno. You don't get to take credit where credit isn't due." She lifted the cup to her lips and took a slow swig of the smoky, creamy cold brew. It took every ounce of willpower she had not to close her eyes and moan at the decadence of it. That first sip of one of Juno's coffee concoctions always had that effect on Penny.

"Right," Ward said, his brusque tone shaking her out of her momentary bliss. He gave her another one of those dumb chin nods. "You're right."

She waited for him to continue. Did he want her to argue with him?

"So, yeah." He cleared his throat. "Just wanted to let you know that Hazel is home now."

She set her drink on the little occasional table beside her, wondering where he was going with this rather awkward conversation. When he remained silent, she narrowed her eyes up at him. "Does that mean I'm allowed to go back there now? Did you come find me here just to tell me that?"

His lips pressed together in a thin line, and Penny wanted to snap at him, tell him to spit it out, whatever it was he came to say. He squared his shoulders and said, "I was rude this morning."

Penny's eyes widened, surprised he'd admit his bad behavior, but also wondering if he was actually apologizing, or just stating a fact. She waited, wondering what would come next.

"Hazel was not happy with me for sending you away."

"I can only imagine," Penny muttered, having surmised as much would be true, once the woman heard the story. Should she give the guy a break and assume the best about him, that he'd been having, as his buddy had insisted, a bad day? "Look, I did try calling Hazel about me coming early—"

Ward spoke at the exact same time. "You shouldn't walk up behind a guy using power tools, not without some kind of warning, at least. It's dangerous, you know."

She clamped her mouth shut as his words sunk in. He was going to blame her for his bad behavior? Wow. She straightened in her seat, then made a show of checking the time on a nonexistent watch on her wrist. "Oh, hey. Look at the time. I'd better get going." She tucked a clean napkin into the book to mark her place, then slipped it into the paper bag with her other new books and stood. "I have someplace I was supposed to be hours ago." She put as much edge in that last sentence as she could rally, and the jab had its intended effect; the guy stepped back like she'd thrust a dagger at him.

"I was working with a saw," Ward said, bracing his feet a little wider and crossing his arms. Was he going to try and stop her from leaving? "You surprised me."

"Really? I hadn't caught that," she retorted. "What with that cute little man-scream you let out. I thought maybe you were just singing."

"I didn't scream. Man-scream. Whatever."

Penny's eyebrows shot up as high as they could go. "You didn't?" The sound of his shriek still rang in her head, and suddenly, she had to press her lips together to hold back a chortle. It was clearly *not* the opportune time to laugh at him. "Okay. Well, I gotta go." She snatched up her coffee from the table and held it up toward him. "Thanks for delivering this."

With that, she brushed past him and headed to the bar. She didn't see Juno, so she called out to Tyler, "Best coffee I've ever had," she told him. "Every time, without fail."

Tyler beamed at her, and she shoved a few dollars into the tip jar at the counter before heading out the door.

She only allowed herself to glance back toward the shop when she was seated behind the wheel of her car. Ward still stood beside the empty chair where she'd been camped out, but now he faced the window. Yep. Watching her. Their eyes met for one brief, jolting moment, then she turned her attention to the downtown bustle and eased out onto the street.

4
Ward

WELL, THAT HAD NOT gone the way he'd planned. Ward dropped his chin to his chest as her car disappeared around the corner.

"Everything all right?"

He jumped, a frisson of irrational anger coursing through him at being snuck up on once again. "Geez," he muttered, turning to look at Juno, who had come to stand next to him. "I'm glad I wasn't holding a hot cup of coffee."

"Me, too," Juno quipped, not bothering to hide her smile. "Would have been a shame if you'd spilled any of my fine brew." She patted his shoulder. "But what on earth did you say to her? She left without saying goodbye to me."

"Nothing." He glanced down at the empty chair where Penny had been sitting, a slight indentation in the soft seat cushion the only telltale sign that she'd been there.

"Did you give her the coffee?"

"I did. And she made sure it wasn't from me before she took it."

"But it *was* from you," Juno said, giving him a bemused look.

"She wouldn't have taken it if I'd admitted as much." Ward had seen the look in her eyes, the hesitation as she stared at the cup in his hands. Like she thought he might have spit in the drink, or something. "She was quite appreciative when I told her it was from you, though." A flush warmed his neck as he thought of the delicate sound she'd made when she tasted it.

Juno nodded slowly, still studying him. "Hm."

"What does that sound mean? Why can't you women just say what you're thinking?" Because he'd bet his bottom dollar that the noise she'd made held a world of meaning in it.

The woman's chuckle rarely failed to elicit a smile from him. He liked the sound of it, the way it flowed out of her like a burbling mountain brook. But now, he frowned, something he'd been doing a lot of since his morning encounter with Hazel's guest. It was something he'd been doing a lot of since moving back to the lake, if he were being honest. "It means, my dude, that I don't know what's going on here, but I do know *something* is going on, and I'm trying to figure out just what exactly that something is."

Ward was shaking his head before she finished her sentence. "Never mind. I think I prefer the one-syllable version."

"Oh Ward." Juno gave his shoulders a quick squeeze. "Don't be such a crabby pants. I won't let you come in here if you're just going to keep scaring off my customers. I like that one, especially, too. She's good people, you know."

Ward let out a grunt, and Juno stepped back, cocking her head at him. "And what, pray tell, does that sound mean?" she asked him, her smile discrediting the censure in her tone. "Why can't you men just say what you're thinking?"

He shook his head and snorted. "Okay. I deserved that. Sorry, Juno. I'm in a mood today."

"Yeah, you are," she agreed amiably. "Want to come back to the bar so I can whip you up something that will turn that frown upside down?"

"Nah. I gotta get going. I have a repair across the lake."

"A WOOT?"

"Yep." He tried to hide his reticence, but she picked up on it without too much effort.

"What's going on with you? I mean, you're always a bit of a grump, especially since—well, whatever. But today?" Juno crossed her arms, her brows drawn down in concern. "Is it your mom?"

Ward shook his head, ignoring her "grump" jab and the slip she'd almost made. "Mom is doing okay. It's the North Shore job," he admitted. "It's a repair Dad supposedly already made a few days ago."

"Huh. That doesn't sound good," she mused.

Ward grimaced. "Yeah. And it's one of the Austin's boats." Everyone knew who the Austins were. Year-rounders, but still WOOTS by definition, Camden and Lysha Austin owned the largest of the North

Shore homes across the water, complete with its own private sand beach, large dock, and two-story boathouse that looked like a slightly smaller replica of their house. Lysha Austin sat on the Board of Directors at the resort, while Camden Austin came from old money. His job was keeping the caddies busy at the North Shore Country Club.

It was Lysha who had called about having him come take a look at her bowrider. Ward had routed all work calls to his cell phone—his father had been letting too many of them go to voicemail and then never retrieving them. "My pretty boat is making a horrific squealing sound whenever I start it up. Word around town is that you're the one to call when I need a repair," she'd purred over the phone, making Ward scowl in distaste. He didn't need her flattery to ensure he'd do a good job. His father had built his business on a reputation of good work ethic, quality service, and fair prices.

Ward had assigned the job to his dad. It wasn't an uncommon problem and should have been a straightforward fix, since the alternator belt was a part Ted kept stocked in his work van. So when Lysha had called Ward back, reporting that the boat was still making noise, he'd promised to come over that afternoon to take a look at it himself.

Lysha Austin had seemed far too pleased when he'd assured her it would be him this time and not his father. "You're the one I really wanted to see, anyway." He got an uneasy vibe from the sultry way she spoke, but he couldn't tell if she was intentionally throwing out double entendres or just naturally sounded that way.

Although he'd seen the woman several times since he'd first come home—it was hard not to run into the same folks in their small town of fewer than a thousand year-rounders—he'd only officially met her a couple of months ago when he'd gone across the lake to work on a pontoon for one of her neighbors, George Caper. She must have seen them out on the dock from her home, which sat a little higher on the bank from George's place. She'd made her way along the well-maintained boardwalk that connected the private North Shore docks along that stretch of the shore, greeted George with a warm hello, and they'd chatted briefly about her husband's golf game. Then she'd turned to Ward and introduced herself, giving him the once over as he straightened from where he'd been switching out an aluminum 3-blade propeller for a stainless steel 4-blade one that would give George a little more control over the big boat. Ward had felt a bit like a horse at auction under her bold perusal.

"So you're the St. James of St. James Mobile Boat Repair," she'd said. "I'm Lysha Austin." She didn't offer her hand, presumably having noted the state of his after putting George's motor back together.

"Actually, no," he'd corrected her. "That's my father, Ted St. James. I'm just helping out for a few months."

"But you *are* a St. James, aren't you?" She did one of those slow-blink, cocked head things women did that reminded him of a cat toying with its prey. She was quite beautiful, with her sleek black hair and ebony eyes. Her very feminine curves strained strategically at the designer outfit she wore, and her shoes, impractically high for George's dock, gave her already statuesque figure several more inches, so that she towered over her neighbor and stood eye-to-eye with Ward.

"Yes. Ward St. James," he confirmed, wanting nothing more than to get back to the job he'd been hired to do. It was late in the day, he was starving, and he still had one more stop to make before heading home. He didn't feel like being the mouse in her game.

Because he recognized it for what it was. This wasn't the first time he'd been called up to "fix a boat" for a bored North Shore wife whose husband was too busy working or at the country club to "do the repairs himself." The first time that it happened, the guys had laughed it off when Ward mentioned it over a game of Cutthroat Pool at Patsy's Pizza one night. They'd assured him that requests like that came often from the North Shore, and Alex had propped his hands on his hips. "Come mow my lawn. Clean my pool. Patch my roof," he'd said in a sugary falsetto to a chorus of chuckles and catcalls and even a few eye rolls. He'd slapped Ward on the shoulder and added, "Get used to it, man. As far as they're concerned, we South Shore locals are here to please."

Alex, Ward had discovered that night, had a reputation for taking on a few of those North Shore jobs.

It was a reputation that Ward wasn't interested in garnering for himself, and he'd gone over and above the call of duty to present himself as nothing but professional on every job. He knew what signals to watch for, and typically, it started with the once-over, like the one Lysha Austin had just all but assaulted him with.

"Well, if I ever need my boat fixed, I'm giving you a call, Ward St. James," Lysha Austin had promised that day on George's dock, before heading back down the boardwalk the way she'd come. To Ward, it had sounded more like a threat.

"Are you more worried about the woman or about your dad?" Juno's question drew his attention back to the moment. The way she asked had him shaking his head with wry amusement.

The question was valid, though. At least the part about his dad. Within a few weeks of being back in town, Ward had realized that there was more going on with the business than Ted just taking some time off to care for his sick wife. There were unpaid notices from suppliers dating back six months or more, jobs his father had done in that same time that had never been invoiced, and therefore, he'd never been compensated for, and the cargo van that was usually kept immaculate and well-stocked with parts was neither. It had taken Ward several sixty-hour weeks to catch things up in time for their accountant to file year-end taxes, and even longer to get the business back to just breaking even. He expected to be operating in the black by the end of the summer, and his plan was to hand everything back into his father's care and head home to California.

"Dad, of course," Ward admitted. With a wry grin, he added, "Mrs. Austin is pretty scary, but I can handle her."

Juno snorted. "If you say so, big guy." Then she sobered. "How is your dad? Your mom?"

"He insists he's fine," Ward said with a shrug. They'd had this conversation before. Juno knew his concerns about his dad's neglect of the business, but she also understood that Ted had good reason to be distracted these days. "Mom is doing better, all things considered. She's getting used to taking things slowly and resting regularly. Of course, she'll sigh despairingly and tell you she's resigned herself to being old before her time."

Juno chuckled softly. "I can see how slowing down would feel that way to her." His mother was one of those women who woke up ready to roll, stayed busy all day, then slept like the innocent all night long. Since being sick, all of that had changed.

Ward nodded. "Yeah. It's been tough, that's for sure. For both of them. I think Dad isn't quite sure how to handle any of it, so he just doesn't, you know? He hovers around Mom until she shoos him off."

Something had happened to his father during his mother's illness last year, and Ward wondered if either of his parents would ever fully recover from the terrible virus that had nearly taken his mom's life. Ted had been sick, too, but his symptoms had been nothing like Rachel's, and Ward felt in his gut that his father's loss of footing was a direct result of having come face to face with the real possibility of losing his beloved wife.

Rachel had come home from the hospital just before Thanksgiving, and they'd celebrated with a quiet, small feast with Hazel, who had shared their holiday table on many occasions over the years. Without family of her own, she'd taken them under her wings, and with her bed-and-breakfast closed for the season, she usually did most of the cooking, too, desperate for someone to take care of.

It was after that Thanksgiving meal, while Ted and Rachel napped, that Hazel had urged Ward to consider coming home for longer than the six weeks he'd planned.

"Your mother is your father's world," she'd said to him. "I think they both lost a little bit of themselves to that awful virus, and I'm not so sure they're going to be able to go back to life the way it was before."

She'd been right; Ward knew as much even before she put his concern into words. But he had a full life out on the West Coast, where he and his business partner, Johnny Bolton, co-owned and operated Blue Waters Boat Chartering, a company that offered fishing trips, sightseeing tours, and party charters along some of the most beautiful coastlines of the Pacific Ocean.

Ward had entrusted the care of Blue Waters into Johnny's hands—something that still made his gut churn uncomfortably, since Johnny was much better behind a desk than on the water. But they had a dependable crew, and four solid helmsmen, two of whom had been with them since the beginning, and Ward met with them via Zoom calls at least once a week. Things were running better than he could have hoped for in his absence, which made his extended stay in Autumn Lake doable.

He'd also been in a comfortable, long-term relationship with Rochelle Trebler, a much-sought-after muralist whose artwork could be found all over Laguna and the surrounding beach towns. They'd met when she'd chartered one of his boats for her father's sixtieth birthday. She'd returned the following week to pick up her jacket that she'd 'accidentally' left in the cockpit after she'd asked Ward to show her what all the controls were for.

He'd asked Rochelle to take some time off and come with him to the lake, knowing she wouldn't. She was a Southern California beach girl through and through. "You'll be back," she'd told him, her face pressed into the hollow of his neck, her tears warm on his skin. "And I'll be right here, waiting for you."

He wasn't sure if she was trying to convince him or herself of his return. But as the weeks turned to months, their good intentions of traveling to see each other kept getting blown off course, and their phone calls and emails, and then even their texts, grew fewer and farther between. They'd both been so busy once spring set in, and Ward hadn't worried too much about their flagging communication.

But Rochelle had called him one evening in April, and he'd recognized immediately that he'd let things flounder too long between them.

"Oh, baby. You shouldn't have to choose between me or your family," she'd said in that husky voice that reminded him of gentle waves washing up on the beach. "I know you're doing what's best for your parents right now, and I absolutely support you in that." She loved no one in the world more than her own father, and Ward knew she meant what she said. But he'd also thought she *was* his family. They'd been together almost three years, and although they hadn't made anything official, they'd always talked about their relationship as permanent.

"I'm coming back, Ro. I just don't know exactly when," he'd tried to tell her, but she'd stood her ground.

"If—when—you do return, then come find me. I'll be here; you know I'll never leave this place. But baby, let's give each other the freedom to live right where we are, okay? Let's not miss out on the moments we're in because we only have eyes on the moments that may never come."

He hated it when she called him 'baby'. It usually meant she was trying to placate him. He'd known then that she'd met someone else.

Juno was right; he'd been grumpy ever since that phone call. Longer than that, if he was going to be honest.

"Come on." Juno looped an arm through his and started maneuvering them back toward the bar. "You're at least going to take a goodie bag with you. Something to look forward to after you fend off the wiles of Mrs. Lysha Austin. And something to take to your folks, too."

"To give the woman the benefit of the doubt," Ward said, letting her pull him along. "It's possible that Mrs. Austin might actually just need her boat worked on."

"Hm. Is that what you kids are calling it these days?" Juno's chuckle made him grin in spite of himself, and when she handed him a brown paper bag with a sampling of her organic fruit tarts and a pint of his mother's favorite non-dairy pumpkin spice chia pudding, and then refused to let him pay, he stuffed the tip jar with cash.

Juno's crew, Tyler and Poppy, had thanked him effusively. At least he'd managed to make someone happy today.

5
Penny

"Welcome home, Sweet Pea!" Hazel Poleman called out a boisterous greeting from where she sat in the shade of her front porch.

Penny didn't bother unpacking her things again, but instead, made a beeline across the front lawn and up the steps toward her hostess.

"I'd get up, but as you can see, I'm a bit encumbered right now." Murtagh, an old Irish setter, lay belly up on the swing beside Hazel, his head in her lap, eyes half-closed, his front paws sticking up, his back legs splayed wide. Hazel scratched his belly in long, gentle strokes, and if it weren't for the tail swishing back and forth against the seat cushion, Penny might have thought the dog to be in a trance.

"I can see that," she said, then bent forward to give Hazel a quick hug. She reached down and patted Murtagh's belly, too. "Nice man-spreading, old boy." Then she flopped into a cushioned loveseat across from Hazel and glanced around. "Where's Jimbo?"

"Oh, he's in the sunroom with Delilah. After this morning's excursions, we all needed a little rest. Murtagh and I came out here for ours." Jimbo, a Jack Russel with too-short legs, had a thing for Delilah, Hazel's French bulldog, and wherever Delilah went, there was Jimbo. "I should have named him Samson," Hazel often said as she watched the little guy follow Delilah around like the lovesick pup that he was. It didn't seem to matter to Jimbo that he was half Delilah's age. He was smitten by the Frenchie's squished face and droopy jowls, her wide grin and lolling tongue.

"Well, don't let me disturb you," Penny said, starting to rise. "I'll just get my things unloaded and head to my room. You and Murtagh rest. I know my way around."

"Don't go on my account," Hazel said with a wave of her free hand. "I can't afford to fall asleep. If I take a nap now, I'll be up all night." She waited for Penny to get comfortable in her seat again. "I'd offer you something to drink, but it looks like you've already been to see Miss Juniper Thomas," she said, indicating the coffee cup Penny held.

"Yep. I'm good." She took a sip of the delicious drink as if to prove her statement.

Hazel tut-tutted, and Penny assumed she'd get on her about drinking coffee all day long, but instead, the woman began apologizing. "My darling girl, I am so sorry about this morning and those boys running you off like that. I was so set on getting my errands run, that I just didn't think about the possibility of you showing up early. Please forgive Ward for his very bad behavior. He's a lovely young man, and I can assure you, his bark is much worse than his bite."

Penny dropped her gaze to her lap. "It's fine, Hazel. Don't worry about it. I spent some time at The Cracked Spine and then got to see Juno, so it all worked out." Everyone kept telling her that Ward was such a great guy, but so far, her experience with him told her something completely different. Maybe he just didn't like her for some reason, but that didn't excuse his rudeness.

Clearly not convinced, Hazel said, "He's just had a bit of a rough patch lately. He felt real bad about how he treated you this morning."

"Hm." As soon as she made the noncommittal sound, Penny wished she could draw it back in. The last thing she wanted was to offend or upset Hazel. "I totally understand, you know? Going through rough patches, I mean."

Rough patches, indeed, she understood. Being ugly to complete strangers? That was something she didn't understand at all.

Snuffling and scrabbling claws on hardwood floor just the other side of the screen door drew their attention, a disruption Penny was grateful for. She got up to let the dogs out and was greeted with wiggly dog butts and excited yapping once they recognized her. "Hello, you goofy little things," she cooed, crouching down to their level so she could greet them properly with ear scratches and belly rubs.

"How is your mother, dear?" Hazel asked once the melee subsided.

Penny sighed and returned to her seat. Jimbo and Delilah jumped up onto the loveseat, too, and she scooted over a little to make room on either side of her for each pup. "Not great. I guess you could say that we're having our own rough patch," she said with just a hint of sarcasm. "Except it's not really a patch. Things are hard, and honestly, I don't see them getting easier anytime soon."

Penny's mother's disease had first reared its ugly head almost a decade ago when Judy had begun having trouble recognizing people and places. She couldn't remember names, or she'd get distracted and forget what she was doing. That, in and of itself, wasn't such a terrible thing, but when she started accusing her friends and loved ones of hiding things from her, or worse, stealing from her, Penny had all but forced her mother to see a specialist.

By the end of the appointment, Judy had been in tears as she'd acknowledged how afraid she was just to wake up each morning. "I feel disoriented and scared all the time," she'd admitted, clinging tightly to Penny's hand as she talked. "The other day, I went to the grocery store." She'd paused to blow her nose, and when she lifted her head again, the expression on her face had broken Penny's heart. "I—I walked out of the store with a full cart and didn't pay for anything. I just went to my car and started loading up."

"Oh, Mom," Penny had murmured from the chair beside her. "I'm so sorry."

"It gets worse," Judy had continued. "They sent security out after me, and I thought it was the police. I—I panicked, not understanding what they wanted from me, so I got in my car and locked my doors, and just sat there, crying. Finally, another customer came up to my window pushing a cart and holding my purse. I guess I trusted her, because I rolled down my window enough to talk to her. She was very nice, by the way."

Dr. Traynor had nodded understandingly. "People usually are," he said. "We forget that sometimes."

"Well, not only had I walked out of the store without paying, but I'd taken her cart instead of my own." Judy had lifted her arm to show them the bright purple lanyard she wore around her wrist. It had her house and car keys on it. "I started wearing this thing some time ago after locking myself out of my house a few too many times, so I had my keys, and I didn't even miss my purse."

At first, Penny had been upset that her mother hadn't confided in her, but as Dr. Traynor explained more about early-onset Alzheimer's—Judy was only forty-eight when she'd been officially diagnosed—and what the future held for them, she'd quickly shifted her mindset toward what they could do to make things easier for them both, rather than focusing on what couldn't be changed.

To limit the disruptions in Judy's life, Penny had given up her little apartment and moved into her mother's condo, back into the bedroom where she'd spent her teen years. Judy had brooked no argument about giving up her driver's license, and less than a year later, she could no longer continue her job as a bank administrative assistant. So while Penny was at work, Judy attended a daycare for adults that was less than half a mile from the elementary school.

It was during her second year of living with Penny that Judy started talking about taking a summer vacation at a place called Autumn Lake. "I want to take pictures of it," she said by way of explanation. "I think having photos of people and places that mean something to me will help me remember the important stuff as long as I can," Judy had said, even though Penny had never heard her mother talk about the town before. But she'd been happy to oblige, and Judy had insisted on paying for everything.

That first summer in Autumn Lake had been such a gift to both of them. Judy had seemed to regain some of her confidence and *joie de vivre*, and Penny had found herself relaxing for the first time since learning of her mother's illness. Sitting out on the dock one day, their legs dangling in the water, floppy sunhats protecting their faces, her mother had told Penny about her memories of Autumn Lake.

"I came here with my parents and another family a few times when I was a teenager. Your Aunt Jean was already married and out of the house by then," she'd said. "The family we came with were the Pontiers—I don't remember the parents' names, but there were two girls about my age, Silvia and Rita, and a boy, Hector." Judy had smiled shyly at Penny and added, "I was so in love with Hector Pontier, Penny. We stayed in the Pontier's little vacation cabin closer to town, but they knew a lot of people around

Autumn Lake, and we spent long, lazy days in float tubes or, if we were lucky, row boats, drifting up and down this shoreline. This dock was always one of our favorite stops. It was before that house was there," she said, pointing at the little bungalow on the other side of the inlet. "We'd swim in the little cove there, climb up here and warm ourselves in the sun, then head on home when we got too hungry."

To Penny's delight, her mother had relayed story after story about the summers she'd spent in Autumn Lake. It was as though being here had opened a trapdoor and let all the memories out.

They'd made the decision to spend every summer from then on at Hazel's bed and breakfast. Sadly, Judy had only come with Penny the first three years before traveling became too difficult and too confusing for her. Then, Aunt Jean, Judy's sister, had insisted Penny continue to go on her own. "Your mother set this up with me right after that first trip you girls took. She made me promise that I'd take care of her when the time came that she couldn't go, and that I'd make you go, anyway." Her mother had even thought to earmark a small savings account to be used each year to cover Penny's expenses. "It's your mother's gift to you for giving so much of yourself to her."

Penny had been coming back to the lake alone every year since.

To Hazel, she now said, "The sundowners has gotten a lot worse lately. She'll sleep for maybe an hour at a time, then get up and wander the house. I have childproof stuff on all the doors, all the appliances around the house, all the faucets—she started leaving faucets running every time she washed her hands—but I'm considering putting up some kind of a temporary partition or maybe even a pony wall with a door that can be locked to keep her out of the kitchen altogether, since cooking with her underfoot can be pretty chaotic. At least with a half wall, I could keep an eye on her while fixing our meals. She's not so easily distracted by television anymore, and I think somewhere in that head of hers, she just wants to be useful, to help."

Jimbo licked Penny's hand in commiseration, and Hazel nodded slowly. "Is she a flight risk?"

Penny shrugged one shoulder. "Not that I know of. I have cameras all over the house now—it's kind of creepy. It's the only way I can keep track of her and still get some sleep, though, and so far, I haven't seen any signs of her trying to leave the house."

"And your aunt? You mentioned that she was having some health issues, too."

Penny nodded. "That's part of it. Aunt Jean is almost twenty years older than my mom. Did I tell you that? Her arthritis is bothering her much more these days, particularly on her right side, her hip and shoulder. Her doctor says she might be a good candidate for surgery at some point, but he wants her to lose some weight and start with physical therapy first. The PT is helping a little, but she's struggled with her weight her whole life. She's trying; it's just not happening very fast, and she's super discouraged about it." Penny paused, then added, "I think having Mom is a bigger burden than she's letting on."

"Oh dear. My goodness. What a painful situation you're all in, my dear girl."

"Uncle Ron is a godsend, though," Penny said, the thought of her aunt's fun-loving husband bringing a smile to her lips. "He's great with Mom, and she responds positively to him, even though she doesn't seem to know who he is anymore, so that makes me feel a little better about leaving her to come here." She rested her head against the back of the seat and blinked rapidly against the tears that stung her eyes. She didn't want to cry, and she knew she would if she looked at Hazel. "I kinda think this may be my last time here, Hazel. At least for a while. I just don't know how much longer they'll be able to manage Mom without me around, you know?"

Hazel said nothing for so long that Penny lifted her head to see if perhaps she'd fallen asleep. But the woman was studying her with a contemplative expression, her brow furrowed, and her lips pressed together.

"What?" Penny asked hesitantly, not sure she wanted to hear what Hazel was thinking.

"I suppose I'm worried about how much longer you'll be able to manage your mother if you *don't* come here."

Penny looked down at Delilah who had shifted so that her head rested on Penny's knee. She stroked the velvety fur of the dog's ears. "Me, too," she admitted softly. "But then I just feel selfish, and that doesn't help anyone.

We do what we have to do, right? She's my mom." As if that clarified everything.

To Penny, when all was said and done, that was, indeed, the bottom line. Judy Anderson was her mother, and other than Aunt Jean and Uncle Ron, there was no one else who could or would care for her the way Penny did.

"You know I'm praying for you, Sweet Pea. And for your mama and your aunt and uncle." It wasn't a question. Nor was it news to her. Penny knew Hazel had an active prayer life, and the older woman had been blessing her with her prayers for all the years she'd been coming to Autumn Lake.

Penny sighed again and squared her shoulders. She needed to talk about something else. At least until she was settled into her room, had a few uninterrupted nights' sleep under her belt, and several hours of escape between the pages of her books. "So what kind of work are you having done around here?"

Ugh. Ward was *not* a topic she was interested in discussing, either.

"Oh, it's just minor stuff. A wobbly banister, a loose floorboard or two, a roof patch, that kind of thing. This old house is feeling her years." Hazel let out a dry chuckle. "Just like I am. We both need a little shoring up these days."

Penny shook her head. "Don't say so. You're both perfect just the way you are, Hazel. That's why I come here. I don't want some fancy shenanigans like they have across the water. I want hearth and home and cozy, creaky beds, and tranquil views of the water out my bedroom window." She gestured at the expanse of the wraparound porch. "I want to lounge in squishy chairs with a cuddly dog or two and while away the day in a good book. I want to sit on the end of the dock with my feet in the water, wishing Mom were here with me. Maybe take a swim with the dogs, because they won't judge me for wearing the same bathing suit that I've had for more than a decade. Don't ever change any of this, you hear?"

Hazel laughed appreciatively. "You are a delight to my soul, Sweet Pea."

That evening, Hazel served up a simple meal of buttery baked potatoes and a mix of sauteed summer vegetables for dinner. Even though her home was officially a bed-and-breakfast, Hazel often cooked all three meals for her guests when there weren't too many mouths to feed. Tonight, it was just the two of them and the dogs.

"Why does food always taste so much better when someone else cooks for you?" Penny asked when her plate was clean and her stomach full. "That was absolutely delicious, Hazel."

"I hope you left room for dessert."

Penny grinned, stuck out a leg, and rapped her knuckles against her shin. "It's hollow. There's room."

"Dishes first, then strawberry shortcake with whipped cream out on the front porch," Hazel said, pushing to her feet. "We can watch the sun set over the water; it's glorious this time of year."

The two of them made quick work of the cleanup, then took their dessert plates outside just as the first of the fireflies began drifting up from the lush grass of the lawn. They ate in awestruck silence as the sky turned to molten lava, the fiery hues painting the water to match, then faded to bruised purple, then inky blue. The stars pricked holes in the velvet night, and the crescent moon, come late to the party, made her grand entrance low on the horizon, while the reflection on the lake transformed the display into something otherworldly.

In a hushed voice, Penny said, "I wonder if God is looking down and seeing what we're seeing right now, and thinking, 'Wow. I did good.'"

Hazel reached over and patted her knee affectionately. "I can assure you, Sweet Pea, that He says exactly that whenever He looks at you."

Penny had to blink away the sting of tears. "Thank you," she murmured. Hazel always knew just the right thing to say. Sometimes it was hard to remember that she was precious to anyone. As her mother's condition worsened and she had a harder time remembering her daughter at all, Penny found it especially hard to remember.

On the other side of the little inlet, the windows of the bungalow across the way glowed warm with light from within, and she could just barely make out the carefully manicured shrubs that bordered the porch and marched down either side of the straight walkway that led to the driveway. So different from Hazel's whimsical style, but still lovely in its own right. She pointed at it. "Doesn't that place look like something right out of a painting?"

Just then, the front porch light of the house flickered on and off, then on and off again.

"All is well across the way," Hazel said by way of explanation. "That's Ward letting me know. He's likely sitting out on his front porch this evening, too."

"Wait. Ward? I—I thought your friends lived there. Rachel and her husband... um, Ted, right? Did they move?" She hoped nothing bad had happened to either of them.

Hazel nodded. "Ted and Rachel St. James, yes. St. James Mobile Boat Repair. They're still there. Ward is their son," she clarified, a smile in her voice.

"Ward St. James? He's your neighbor? He—he's sitting outside watching us?" She was suddenly terribly self-conscious. Had she unknowingly flashed him when she'd propped her feet up, or something else as equally awkward? Had he seen her pointing at his house and thought she was pointing at him?

"Yes, Ward lives there with his parents. For now. He's working with his dad." Hazel was chuckling softly now.

Penny couldn't blame her—she was acting kinda silly. But the thought of that awful man living just around the inlet had her way too flustered. She could see that front porch from her bedroom window. Which meant that he could see her bedroom window from his front porch.

Not that he'd be looking, of course.

"I thought he was... I don't know. A handyman? He was here doing construction stuff."

"He was here doing neighborly stuff," Hazel corrected. "And boat repair isn't such a far cry from home repair, is it?" Now she was teasing her.

Penny turned in her seat so that she was facing Hazel, no longer looking out over the water. She felt very conspicuous sitting on the well-lit porch. Ward had to have seen her pointing at the house. There was no way he hadn't. He'd flashed the lights right then. "I suppose if he has the right tools," she said in response to Hazel's question.

"Oh honey. He's got the right tools." Hazel winked at her. "You had to have noticed how handsome he is. I know you're not blind."

"Hazel!" Penny couldn't help the chortle that escaped her at the woman's tawdry remark.

"What?" Hazel shot back. "I'm not blind, either. That young man comes from good stock, too. His parents are lovely people, inside and out, and they raised him to be the same way."

Penny shook her head. "You know, people keep telling me he's this great guy. I just don't see it." She shrugged. "And no, I'm not blind, either. He might be good-looking on the outside, but at least around me, that's where it ends."

"Hmmm." Hazel made a thoughtful sound in the back of her throat. "Well, maybe you two need the chance to make a second first impression."

Her deceptively casual tone made Penny narrow her eyes at her. "Now don't you be getting any crazy notions in your head, Miss Poleman. I've already had a second first impression of him, thank you very much. We ran into each other at Juno's, too. And my first impression was accurate the second time, as well. He is not someone I have an urge to spend time with anytime soon, okay?"

Hazel shook her head. "I don't know why not. You two have several things in common, now that I think about it."

"I don't want to know what they are," Penny insisted, covering her ears with both hands. "And please stop thinking about it."

Hazel chuckled and patted Penny's knee again. "If it's meant to be, it's meant to be."

"I have no idea what you mean by that, but again, I don't think I want to know." Penny lowered her hands and drew her legs up so she could rest her chin on her knees. She smoothed her skirt down over her legs so just the tips of her feet stuck out from under her hemline. She'd painted her toenails candy apple red yesterday, and she peered down at them, smiling at how cheery her feet looked. She didn't love pedicures like every other woman she'd ever met—she was too ticklish to enjoy someone else touching her feet, for one thing, and she inevitably messed up the polish before it was dry. But she'd gotten pretty good at applying her own polish and had quite a collection of fun colors to choose from.

"Rachel—Ward's mother—almost died last year," Hazel said, ignoring Penny's protestations. "Ward came home to help take care of her and to help his father run the family business until they get back on their feet. He left behind a whole different life to be here for his parents, and it hasn't been easy for him. I think you, of all people, would understand. You might be good for each other, Sweet Pea."

"But he's a jerk," she retorted, reticent to give him a break, even though her heart twisted sympathetically inside her chest. "And I don't think he has any more interest in spending time with me than I do with him." Desperate to change the subject, she said, "Speaking of ways to spend my time here, I can't wait to do a little gardening. I can't believe I haven't been out back to see it all yet. Today has been a rather odd first day in Autumn Lake for me, that's for sure."

Hazel's expression softened, and her eyes took on a wistful gleam. She didn't speak for a moment, and Penny found that she was holding her breath. Finally, Hazel said, "Well, dear, as you know, nothing stays the same for very long, right? You'll find that's true in the garden, too."

"Is—is everything all right?"

"Of course," Hazel assured her. "Everything is just the way it should be."

Later that night, lying on her side on the comfy creaky bed in the pale peach room that she loved so much, as she peered out through the partially opened curtains into the night sky, Hazel's words came drifting back through her mind.

Hazel hadn't really answered Penny's question at all.

6
Ward

It was, indeed, a proposition that Lysha Austin offered Ward, but not the one he'd been prepared to fend off.

He'd arrived at the Austin's home nine minutes early to his appointment. Lysha had already told him to meet her at the boathouse, so he made his way down to the dock. He found her on the upper deck behind the bar, preparing drinks for the two of them. "Come on up," she called down over the railing.

Against his better judgment, he did, but she didn't seem to be aware of his reluctance. She smiled warmly in welcome and gestured with a long-fingered hand at a glass-topped table and chairs. "Sit, please."

Ward turned down the mojito she offered him, but gladly accepted an icy carbonated water with a squeeze of lime, instead. Being nervous made him thirsty, and Lysha Austin was making him nervous.

Before he could ask about it, Lysha cocked her head and lifted her glass toward him. "My boat, by the way, seems to have fixed itself. Whatever that noise was, it stopped right after I called you."

If there was nothing wrong with her boat, why had she not called and cancelled the repair? Ward wasn't quite sure how to respond to that, so he waited for her to continue.

"It's that way every time, I tell you," Lysha said with a sardonic shake of her head. "You take your car—or your boat, in this case—to the mechanic because it's making a terrible noise, but the moment you get there, it stops doing it. And no matter how much you insist that it's happening, the mechanic can't fix a problem that suddenly isn't there anymore, can he?" She chuckled, but he didn't hear much humor in the sound. "And then, of course, he just thinks you're a stupid woman."

"Sounds like you need a new mechanic," Ward mused, beginning to think she might be speaking the truth. He'd had a coworker at a marina where he'd once worked who made a point to put women in their places when taking them out on the water. The guy had ended up offending the wrong person. The woman in question had called him on the carpet for talking down to her, and Todd had found himself out of a job by the end of the day. Ward had gained a new respect for his boss that week.

"Well, thank you, Ward St. James. I appreciate your perspective."

Ward nodded slowly. "Would you like me to take a look at it, anyway?"

"No, no." She waved away his suggestion. "If it starts up again, I know who to call." She winked at him. "I know where you live, after all." She looked past him out over the lake, and Ward turned to follow her line of sight, already knowing what he'd find. Directly across the water, Hazel's place sat on a small rise that drifted down toward the little inlet—his mother had named it Misty Cove because of the way the lake fog collected there in the mornings as summer turned to fall. Still visible through a grouping of trees whose summer foliage was still filling out, was his parents' house, around the curve of the bay.

Lysha slid a manila envelope across the glass-top table toward him, drawing his attention to her again. "I have an offer for you. Before you say anything, please, hear me out, okay? I'd appreciate it if you'd take this home and read through it."

Ward leaned back in his chair, unwilling to touch the envelope. He'd seen legal papers served in such a fashion before, and although that scenario seemed rather unlikely coming from Lysha Austin, he was going to play it safe. "What's going on?"

It was a job offer.

A really good job offer that came with a jaw-dropping salary and a whole slew of benefits. The Carpe Diem Resort wanted to hire him as a fulltime Marine Mechanic Supervisor, a position in which he'd be responsible for the fleet of staff boats, as well as the rentals they made available to customers, and he would manage the staff and crew under him.

His first inclination was to shove the packet back across the table without even opening it. For one thing, Ward had no intention of staying in Autumn Lake any longer than he had to. He was here to float his folks through the rough waters they were currently in, then he was heading back across the country to California to pick up where he'd left off. He had a successful boat business of his own to keep afloat, and even though it might be operating just fine without him for now, he needed to get back to make sure it continued to do so.

Besides, there was the matter of Rochelle Trebler to see to. He wasn't comfortable with how their three-year relationship had ended. If it was truly over, he wanted to finish things right, with no regrets between them. They'd been friends, too, after all. Right now, he felt like he'd abandoned her, and that didn't sit well with him. He didn't just walk away.

Which was why he was here now. His parents had sent him off to find his own path with their blessing all those years ago, but they needed him now. He wasn't looking for another job.

But then Lysha dropped a bomb that Ward hadn't seen coming.

"I spoke with your father when he was here working on my boat." All business, Lysha wasn't smiling anymore.

An uncomfortable sensation started low in his gut. Ward sat a little straighter.

"He gave me cause to believe that you might not be interested in taking over his business when he retires. Is that correct?"

Ward tried to keep his expression neutral. He didn't want her to see his surprise at the question. Of course, she would have done her research on him before offering him this position, and his partnership in Blue Waters was no secret. Yet, she hadn't asked him about Blue Waters. She'd been poking around in his personal life by getting information out of his dad. Where was she going with this?

"That's a subject my father and I have yet to hammer out," he said, choosing his words carefully. Truth be told, he wasn't interested in taking over his dad's company, but it wasn't because of the work, itself. Ward loved everything about boats, whether at the helm as captain or repairing an engine in the hull, but he'd worked hard to make a name and reputation for his own company, one that had nothing to do with his father's, and he took great pride in what he'd accomplished. As an only child, and an only son at that, especially in such a small community, there'd never been any question that he'd take over the family business one day. But from a very young age, he'd been determined to strike out on his own and show the world that he was his own man, not just his father's son. His folks, good parents that they were, had understood his need for independence.

Pushing thirty, it didn't seem quite as big of a personal mission anymore, but that didn't change the fact that he now had his own life to live. Granted, maybe it was an easier pill to swallow *because* he'd found success out from under his father's shadow.

There was also the issue of money, though. His father's business was good. Solid. At least, it had been up until recently. Ted had managed to support his little family in Autumn Lake on the income he brought in from doing boat repairs and other boat-related jobs around the lake. They'd never had any excess, but they'd always had enough. Ward, however, had gotten comfortable with the income Blue Waters brought in, and St. James Mobile Boat Repair didn't—probably couldn't ever—compare.

He and his parents hadn't spoken about the future of the company in a long time. Ted was too young to retire; he wouldn't even qualify for Social Security for at least a couple more years. With Ward's business doing so well across the country, it just hadn't seemed to be a pressing concern.

Now, however, having spent the last several months at home, Ward was starting to wonder if perhaps the discussion was long overdue. Especially if his father was talking about the matter with other people. With North Shore people, no less.

"I understand," Lysha said, her tone conciliatory. "But I wanted to be transparent with you about why I felt confident in offering you this position. I didn't want to put it out there if you were in line to take over the family business. You wouldn't be able to do both. A conflict of interest, as I'm sure you're aware."

"In the name of transparency, Mrs. Austin, you should have asked me instead of my father," Ward said without hesitation. "Besides, as I'm sure you already know, I have a company of my own out in California."

"I'm aware. It's doing quite well, from what I hear. Blue Waters, is that right?" She leaned forward and tapped the envelope, not waiting for his confirmation. "This offer, however, includes a salary that's significantly higher than the revenue your charter boat company brings in, and it would allow you to remain here in Autumn Lake to care for your parents." She paused, gave him a gentle, empathetic—but suspiciously false—smile, and added, "Your father told me about his concerns for your mother's health. For their future, and how he'll manage."

Ward shouldn't have been surprised that she'd not only done her research on him, but on his business, too. What shook him was how seamlessly she went from talking about the objective details of the job to using his personal circumstances to pressure him into taking it.

The conversation had him feeling off-balance, and he didn't, for one moment, wonder if that was what she'd intended.

"How is Mama doing, by the way?" And there it was. Confirmation. That not-so-subtle poke at the vulnerable spot in his underbelly.

"Why, exactly, are you pursuing me for this position?" Ward asked when he could make his voice work around the knot in his gut.

"Because you're Autumn Lake royalty, Mr. St. James," she declared. "Everyone knows and respects the St. James name; your father's family has been a part of Autumn Lake for generations. We at Carpe Diem don't want to be thought of as interlopers; we'd like to see that change. You saying 'yes' to this offer will go a long way to bringing the two sides of this lake together." She paused for effect, then finished with, "People around here trust you, Ward."

"People trust my father," Ward countered.

Lysha gave him a rather placating smile, one that didn't find its way to her eyes. "They used to trust your father. Now they trust you." She took a sip of her cocktail—it was still more than half full—then nodded at his empty glass. "Would you like another San Pellegrino? Or something stronger?"

Ward hesitated briefly. He wanted to say yes to a cold drink; the turn the conversation had taken was making him a little hot under the collar. But more than that, he wanted to get off this woman's deck and back onto the solid footing of his own life. "Thank you, but no." He rose and politely pushed his chair back under the table. "If your boat is working fine, then I'll be going."

Lysha stood, too, her lips still curved up at the corners, but with a calculating gleam in her eyes. She glanced at the untouched packet on the table, but she didn't address it. "Thank you for coming. I know your time is valuable. I'll be expecting an invoice for this visit in my email." She held out a hand for him to shake, and this time, he had no excuse not to touch her.

Her hand was soft and cool against his working-man's calloused palm, and the diamond bracelet at her wrist sparkled in the afternoon sunshine against her smooth, dark skin. When she didn't let go, Ward met her eyes with a question in his.

"I'd like this to not end on a 'no'," she said. "You have my contact information. Please don't hesitate to reach out if you reconsider."

Ward waited to speak until she let go of his hand. Holding her gaze, he said, "It's a no, Mrs. Austin. But thank you for considering me for the position, anyway." Why he was thanking her, he wasn't sure. The more he thought about it, the more insulted he felt. Sure, it was a great offer, he couldn't deny that. But it wasn't one for a man who already had a successful business of his own. She apparently thought that his company was as expendable as his father's.

Mrs. Austin was a WOOT through and through, and Ward just wanted to get off her dock and back over to the South Shore where he could let down his guard.

He wouldn't be invoicing her. He wanted nothing more than to forget about this visit altogether.

BY THE TIME HE made it back around the lake and was pulling into the driveway, Ward had come to grips with the knowledge that he needed to sit down and talk with his parents about their expectations for him. He didn't like hearing it from other people, especially not from someone who obviously had ulterior motives.

He still couldn't quite figure out why Carpe Diem wanted him so badly. Sure, he ran a tight ship—literally—at Blue Waters, and he had more than proved his mettle by bringing his dad's business back from the brink in just a few months, but surely, that wasn't enough to even put him on their radar. Lysha had made it sound so simple, so noble. Bring the two sides of the lake together. Could it really be that straightforward?

Ward was tired of thinking about it, tired of conjecturing. He didn't want the job, so none of it mattered, anyway. He climbed out of the van and headed up the narrow sidewalk to the front porch. He paused on the top step and turned to glance across the little cove toward Hazel's place.

In the waning afternoon light, he could see that the front porch was empty.

Ward sighed, his shoulders drooping. There was another situation that didn't sit right with him. He had to figure out what to do about Penny Anderson. He couldn't just avoid her the rest of the summer, not in a town the size of Autumn Lake.

He pushed open the front door and called out, "I'm home," then he bent to unlace his work boots. There was no answer, so instead of taking off his shoes, he headed back outside and made his way around to the side of the house.

He found his mother sitting on the compact seat-on-wheels cart he'd given her for Mother's Day, weeding between two rows of tomato plants. "Hey, Ma. How you doing?"

"Ward! I'm fine, sweetie." Rachel got to her feet and stretched, arching her back. "Ooh, that feels good." She gave him a quick hug, then handed him her trowel. "Here. Will you put this stuff away for me? The cart, too. I think I'm done for the day." She peeled off her gloves and tucked them into a pocket on her apron.

Ward stashed her things in the little shed at the other end of the garden, then joined her as she made her way to the back door. "By the way, it's just you and me for supper tonight. Your father is out with the guys at the Old Mill."

Fried Catfish Night. Ward had forgotten about it. His father had invited him to join him and the old codgers who converged there every Tuesday night, but in the chaos of the day, it had slipped his mind, and now he was too late.

"I forgot," he said, grimacing as he held the door open for her. His mother pinched his chin as she passed by.

"You're busy. Adding Hazel's work to your schedule is a lot, and your father knows that." She hung her gardening apron on a hook in the little mudroom, then headed into the kitchen. "I've got barbecue in the slow cooker. Should be nice and juicy by now."

"Sounds great," he said with as much enthusiasm as he could muster. Talking things over with his folks would have to wait. His father wouldn't be home for at least a couple more hours, and by then, his parents would start winding down for the night.

7
Penny

THE STACCATO HAMMERING THAT woke her sounded like it was coming from right above her head. Penny groaned and pulled one of the soft pillows over her head in a futile attempt to muffle the sound. It stopped, but just as Penny started lifting the pillow, it started up again.

She'd been ensconced in Hazel's bed-and-breakfast for four days already, and had done little more than eat, read, and sleep. "Three of my favorite things to do," she told Hazel after dinner the night before when they were sitting out on the front porch watching the deluge of a sudden summer storm sweep across the lake.

She would have included gardening on that list, but she'd left it off so as not to upset her hostess.

Hazel's garden, to Penny's dismay, had changed dramatically since the summer before, and she'd been so disheartened by the weed-choked beds and unpruned fruit trees that she hadn't yet been able to bring herself to head out there and get her hands dirty. She wanted to remember it the way it once was: lush and verdant, bountiful. It was still eerily beautiful the way a child gone feral might be, but like with any wild creature, Penny wasn't quite sure how to approach it.

The hammering started up again, and Penny gave up trying to fall back to sleep. Not only was the pillow not really blocking out the jarring sounds, but she was also finding it a little difficult to breathe with it over her head, and claustrophobia was threatening to set in.

With a harrumph, she tossed the pillow aside and reached for her phone on her nightstand. Her bleary eyes widened when she saw that it was almost eleven o'clock. She couldn't remember the last time she'd slept in so late.

She could hardly be upset at whoever was swinging the hammer, could she? Not when it was practically the middle of the day, already.

Was it Ward St. James? She'd not seen hide nor hair of him since her first day in town, and Hazel hadn't said anything about him coming back to do more work on the property. Surely, she would have mentioned it, especially knowing how Penny felt about the guy.

She sat up in bed and rubbed her eyes, still bleary from her rude awakening. She'd been up until well after three in the morning, unable to put down the latest Destiny Baudelaire book she was reading, so it was no wonder she'd slept so late. She'd gone right back to The Cracked Spine after finishing *Lace it Up*, and had left the place with the remaining three volumes of the four-book series. She couldn't get enough of the author's storytelling.

Penny had arranged to meet up with a group of women she'd formed relationships with over the years she'd been summering at Autumn Lake. They were gathering at Juniper's Coffee Bar at two that afternoon, and the anticipation made her a little giddy. "I can't wait to see them all, can you?" she asked aloud, pulling the bed linens back and swinging her legs over the side of her bed. Over the last few years, she'd formed a habit of speaking to herself, and when she caught herself doing it, it made her cringe. It hadn't started out that way. When her mother had moved in with her, it had been normal conversation between them. But as Mom's attention waned, as she became more and more lost in her own little world, the conversations had become more and more one-sided. Now it was Penny who did all the talking, and if Mom responded at all, it was in nonsensical sounds and syllables, and even then, Penny wasn't sure if her mother was trying to engage or not.

She went to the window and drew back the curtain so she could look out at the glorious beauty of the lake. It was a ritual she performed every morning, almost as if she had to remind herself that she was actually here. The view out over the water always brought a smile to her lips, and today was no different. The rain that had finally lulled her to sleep had dissipated sometime in the early morning hours, leaving everything revitalized and glistening clean.

Across the narrow inlet, the pretty blue house where Ward and his parents lived drew her attention. It sat nestled up against a small copse of trees, the backyard almost nonexistent. But the front of the property stretched out in a well-maintained lawn that sloped gently toward the water and a small dock with a two-door boathouse. It was really more of a boat shed, Penny thought, with its lattice paneled sides and the tin roof, but she supposed it did the job of keeping the rigs out of the worst of the elements. Hazel had mentioned that Ted St. James kept a beautiful older model Chris-Craft in the boathouse. "I haven't seen him out on the water in that thing for a couple of years, now," she'd said with a sad shake of her head. "He just pulls it out and starts it up periodically, tinkers with it a little, then parks it back inside."

Penny had never been out on the lake on anything other than Hazel's old johnboat with its trolling motor. There'd been a time when it had been kept tied up at the dock, free for her guests to use, but this summer, the dock sat empty, and Penny had been a little afraid to ask about it, especially after seeing the garden. The top speed on the thing was about one or two miles per hour, and although it was fun tooling around in it, Penny hadn't been confident enough to go very far. She'd often watched with a twinge of envy as folks on their jet skis and their boats with big outboard motors skimmed across the water at what seemed like lightning speed. Just once, she wanted to feel the unbridled rush of the wind in her hair, the spray of water on her skin, the rumble of the engine shaking the framework under her feet.

With a deep, lung-expanding breath, Penny stretched languidly, working out the slight kink in her neck that she always got when she slept hard and long. She tied back the drapes to let the sunshine in, made up her bed with its old-fashioned white eyelet duvet and matching pillow covers, then gathered up her clothes for the day and headed into the Jack and Jill bathroom between her room and the next. Hazel no longer rented out both rooms at the same time, unless it was to family members who didn't mind sharing a bathroom. Gone were the days of such a thing, with raised awareness about hygiene, communicable diseases, and of course, convenience, making private ensuite bathrooms an important commodity in guesthouses like this one.

She double-checked the lock on the door that led into the other bedroom anyway, just in case some curious guest might happen to wander into the empty room next door.

Except that there weren't any other guests. She'd been here for several days now, and it was still just her and Hazel and the dogs wandering around the spacious place.

An hour later, showered, dressed, fully awake and ready for the rest of her day—and ravenous—Penny headed out of her room and down the hall to the stairwell. On the landing, a large window gave her a framed view of the backyard, and she had to force herself to look out at the forlorn gardens.

There was still a small vegetable plot close to the back kitchen door, and she knew Hazel planned their meals around whatever she brought in from the garden each day. Sautéed early zucchini and yellow summer squash, fried green tomatoes that hadn't yet had time to ripen on the vine, fresh coleslaw, roasted baby beets, and a variety of greens served tossed in salads or stewed in bone broth vegetable soup.

The chicken coop sat empty, too, another devastating discovery that Hazel hadn't warned her about. Hazel had assured her that the hens were all hale and happy under the care of a woman named Kimber Tate who lived in a cottage a little farther down the road. "She's taking good care of them now, so I don't have to, and I get as many eggs as I need for free. They just got to be too much for me over the winter. Even though their egg production declines radically during the cold months, I couldn't possibly go through that many eggs myself, and I live just far enough from town that folks don't want to make the trip out to pick them up." Hazel had patted Penny's hand and added, "Don't you worry about those birds. They've got a wonderful life with Kimber, and she can use every single egg they lay. Other than the ones she sends my way, of course. She bakes." She'd pressed a hand to her chest and closed her eyes at the thought. "My goodness, does she ever bake. She says the fresh eggs make all the difference in the world. Juniper sells some of her pastries at the Coffee Bar, in fact. You'll have to ask about them next time you're there."

Penny planned to do just that this afternoon when she met up with Juno, Claire from The Cracked Spine, Addison Wedgewood, and Lizette

Needham. Liz had said she was bringing her sister, too, who'd just moved back to town, and Penny was looking forward to meeting her. It still made her flush with gratitude that the amazing group of women had drawn her into their circle, and she didn't take for granted their friendship.

Downstairs in the kitchen, Penny found Hazel sitting at the counter, several messy piles of paperwork spread out around her. "Good morning," she said, then apologized quickly when the older woman startled. Penny hadn't made any attempt to approach quietly; her hostess must have been lost in deep concentration.

Hazel waved off her apology and began gathering everything into one haphazard pile. "It's hardly morning anymore, Sweet Pea," she chided, but her warm smile took any bite right out of her words. She turned the legal pad she'd been writing on upside down on top of the pile. Evidently, she didn't want Penny to catch a glimpse of what she'd been working on. "You must have needed to catch up on some sleep. I planned to give you until lunchtime and then check on you myself."

Penny nodded slowly, not missing the distracted concern lingering in Hazel's eyes. She tried not to look at the pile of paperwork that Hazel was now trying to scoop into a basket, but if she wasn't mistaken, a good portion of the stack was made up of invoices. Were they all bills? Was Hazel having financial troubles? That might explain the state of things around here. Her heart squeezed with worry, but was it her place to ask? "Um, yeah. I stayed up too late reading," she explained, hoping she didn't sound as worried as she felt. "I just discovered a new author."

"Ah. Well, I can't think of a better reason to sleep in until noon." Hazel tucked the basket into a cupboard under the breakfast bar. "Would you like some coffee? Maybe a sandwich? Breakfast for lunch?"

In a sudden flash of revelation, Penny's mind replayed the meals she'd shared with Hazel over the last few days. Eggs and pan-fried vegetables from the garden. Pancakes or crepes served with homegrown raspberry or plum preserves. Biscuits and gravy, tuna or egg salad sandwiches on homemade bread. Chili and soup... in the summer.

It wasn't just simple fare. It was very inexpensive fare. And Hazel was feeding Penny three meals a day for no extra charge.

"I'd love a cup of coffee right now," she said, not wanting to offend Hazel by refusing her offering altogether. "But I'm meeting the girls at Juno's this afternoon, so I think I'm going to save my appetite for that. Especially since I'll definitely be trying something Kimber baked using your eggs," she added with a bright smile.

Hazel cocked her head and studied her for a moment. Could she see the quandary Penny was in? "Well, I made my famous cinnamon coffee cake this morning. How about you have a small piece of that with your coffee, just to tide you over?"

Penny didn't even hesitate. "That sounds perfect." Her stomach gurgled in agreement, and Hazel chuckled and went about getting the coffee started.

❥ • ❥ • ❤ • ❥ • ❥

THE SUN WAS OUT in full force, and after the heavy soaking the night before, the cloying humidity enveloped her like an invisible wet blanket. Penny berated herself for being a chicken, for opting to ride Hazel's bicycle into town. But the St. James Mobile Boat Repair van had been parked behind her car, and although she could have gotten around the vehicle without any trouble, she didn't want to risk running into the man himself. Assuming it had been Ward up on the roof hammering away, and not Ted, of course.

By the time she reached the corner of Dahlia Drive and Camellia Court, she was sweating, her cheeks flushed, and her heart racing. "It's good for you, Pen," she muttered under her breath as she paused outside The Cracked Spine. She'd planned to stop in the bookstore before heading over to the coffee shop, but right now, she just wanted something cold to drink and an air-conditioning vent to sit in front of. Both of which could be had at Juniper's.

She clumsily dismounted, surprised at how wobbly her legs felt. Was she that out of shape? She ran around after second graders all day, for goodness' sake. She should be able to handle a leisurely fifteen-minute bike ride, shouldn't she? Because, yes, it had taken her fifteen minutes to ride the two miles from Hazel's place. *Not* a time she was anxious to brag about.

About a mile in, she'd had to take a break to catch her breath, and now, the thought of having to ride the bicycle back the way she'd come? Well, she certainly wasn't looking forward to that.

She'd imagined it to be so different when she'd pulled the beach cruiser out of the shed and filled the tires with the manual pump Hazel kept on hand. She'd pictured the breeze sweeping her hair back from her face, the hem of her sundress fluttering out behind her, songbirds accompanying her as she meandered along the country road. And coming back had included a spectacular sunset on the lake, fireflies dancing all around her, a perfect, magical end to her day out.

There'd been no breeze. Her hair clung to her face and neck in sweaty tendrils, and she'd been going so slow that her skirt had just hung limply down behind her, and then had gotten caught in the bike chain. Fortunately, she'd been able to work it free without any damage—she'd been pedaling so laboriously that she'd been able to stop quickly. And the birds? Well, they'd just mocked her with their silence. The whole way.

It was only a little after one, and the other ladies wouldn't be there for another hour. She could sit in the corner and cool down. She'd brought a book in her purse, which was strapped to the rack behind the bike seat.

Making up her mind, Penny shoved her front tire into the rack outside the coffee shop, snapped on the bike lock, and slung her purse over her shoulder. She stepped into the shade of the shop awning, swiped at her brow with the back of her hand, and then pushed open the front door.

She all but swooned as she stepped into the cool air, and for a moment, she just stood there, letting her heart rate settle and her breathing slow.

"Hey, girl," Juno called in greeting. "You're early, aren't you?"

Penny waved, took a deep, cleansing breath, then headed to the long counter with its vintage, mismatched barstools. The lunch rush was still winding down, but she found an open spot at the end and settled into the seat. Grateful she'd worn a mid-calf length dress, she tucked the fluttery fabric under her legs so she wouldn't stick to the leather cushion. "Remind me never to ride a bicycle into town again. Got anything fruity and cold to drink?"

"Not your usual coffee, then?"

"No, thank you. It was coffee that made me do it," Penny grouched, grabbing the napkin Juno placed in front of her and pressing it to the back of her neck. She'd cut her pale blonde hair into a chin-length bob a few years ago, and although it required her to visit the salon more often, it sure made her life easier the rest of the time. She was fortunate enough to be able to wash and wear the style—her hair was naturally straight, it didn't tangle easily, and even when she fell asleep with it wet, within an hour of waking up, her bedhead unwound itself and fell neatly back into place. "I drank two cups of Hazel's home brew and decided it would be a good idea to start training for Olympic cycling."

"Yikes." Juno chuckled sympathetically and held up a tall, chilled glass of crushed ice. "How about a cranberry hibiscus tea with mango chunks?"

"Oooh. That sounds delicious. And so fruity! And refreshing," Penny gushed. "Maybe if I have one of your yummy coffees right before I leave, I'll find the courage to get back on that stupid bicycle out there."

"Or maybe someone will steal it, and you won't have to."

Penny nodded slowly, as if seriously contemplating the possibility. Then she leaned forward, brought a hand up to her mouth, and spoke out of the side of it. "Do you think you could arrange for that? I mean, do your people know people who do that kind of thing?"

Juno shrugged noncommittally. "I have my connections."

Penny sighed and slouched on her stool, her forearms resting on the counter in front of her. "Would that I could be so lucky," Penny said. "But then I'd have to walk home, and I don't know if my legs would manage that any better. At least on a bicycle, I can coast on the downward slopes. And there must be more downhills going home, because I swear it was all uphill coming into town."

"You could always leave the bike here. I can stash it in the back office, and you can bum a ride off someone," Juno suggested, shooting a welcoming smile past Penny at another customer.

"You know, that's not such a bad idea," Penny mused, although the thought of admitting that she was too much of a wimp to ride her bike home made her grimace. But it wouldn't hurt to ask one of the girls, would it? And if Liz had her truck, she could just toss the bike in the back and not have to worry about coming back for it in her own car.

Juno pointed at something—or someone, apparently—just behind Penny. "Hey, you busy later this afternoon? Penny here needs a favor."

Penny spun around, a huge smile on her face, ready to greet one of her girlfriends that she hadn't seen in so long.

She just about fell off her stool.

"What's up? What can I do for you?" Ward St. James. His voice felt like someone had just run a feather down the middle of her back, and it was all Penny could do not to shiver in response.

Before she could come up with anything that wasn't completely nonsensical, a middle-aged man on the stool beside her greeted Ward with a hand thrust out for a handshake. "Hey, St. James. How're your folks?"

Ward's gaze darted back and forth between Penny and the man for a moment, then he said, "Uh, they're good, Bob. Mom's tomatoes are just starting to show some pink, so she's happy."

Penny averted her gaze and made a questioning face at Juno. Talk about nonsensical. Tomatoes?

"Sure, sure. That would do it," Bob replied with a chuckle, as though what Ward had said was a perfectly logical response to his query. "Well, you tell them Bob says hi. Looking forward to the festival."

"Will do."

Did Autumn Lake have some kind of a tomato festival? Clearly, they were talking about something she wasn't privy to, and although she knew she shouldn't be offended, Penny felt the exclusion personally.

"And here. Take my seat," Bob said, pushing to his feet. "I'm heading back to the office." He patted the countertop and said, "Thanks, Juno. Terrific lunch, as usual."

Penny froze, waiting to see what Ward would do. Surely, he wasn't going to sit down beside her and start shooting the breeze with her, would he? And hadn't he just been at Hazel's hammering away on her roof?

8
Ward

IF PENNY'S EXPRESSION WAS any indication, Ward would be wise to turn and follow Bob Runyard right out the door. But he would not be deterred this time. He wasn't accustomed to making enemies, especially female enemies—his dad had taught him by example how a man was supposed to treat a woman—but that's how things felt with the spiky Ms. Anderson.

It was really starting to bother him.

What had he done to put her off so badly? She was the one who'd tromped through his work zone like an oblivious child. Yes, she'd apologized, but she'd acted like his reaction was completely out of line, like it was all his fault for being there in the first place.

He knew he hadn't been as gracious as he could have been. His father, had he been present at the scene, would *not* have been proud, he had no doubt. Ms. Hazel Poleman had not been proud, either, and she'd made it very clear to him that he needed to make things right.

Well, he'd apologized, too, for being such a bear to her.

Hadn't he?

He'd even bought her a coffee when he'd caught up with her that first day.

Granted, she'd thought it was from Juno. But he'd brought it to her with every intention of making peace with her.

"Mind if I join you?" he asked, pretending not to see the pleading look she shot Juno's way. He didn't wait for her response, but just slid onto the empty stool beside her and began studying the menu as if he had no clue what he wanted.

Ward ordered the same thing every time he came in, and he wasn't fooling Juno one bit. "Are you suddenly having a hankering for something other than my pork green chili sandwich? Feeling adventurous today?"

The teasing note in her voice chafed, and he hoped Penny didn't pick up on it. He was really bad at playing it cool, apparently. When had that happened?

Ward had been kind of a big deal out in the coastal towns of southern California. As captain and commander of his own fleet, his own crew, and his own life, he'd worn that casual air of self-confidence that often came with being a little too young to feel so in control. He had seen and tasted the oft-times elusive fruit of his hard work, though, and he'd quicky acclimated to it.

Now, however, with his future feeling more and more up in the air, he found his confidence slipping away from him, too.

No, he wanted to tell Juno, he was not feeling adventurous today, and he obviously wasn't doing a very good job of pretending that he was. "Nah. I'll take the usual."

"Good man," Juno said, setting a napkin in front of him and placing a glass of icy water on it.

He cleared his throat and added, "And I've got the lady's drink, too."

"Excuse me?" Penny swiveled around so aggressively, that she had to grab the edge of the counter to keep from slipping off her stool. For the second time… and both near-tumbles were in response to him trying to be friendly. Was that a good thing? "Um, no, I've got my own drink, thank you very much."

So it was a bad thing.

Ward cocked his head and gave her as gentlemanly a smile as he could manage. Man, she looked pretty today. She had on another one of those flowy sundresses she seemed to favor, and her cheeks were pink from the sunshine. It was probably offense that made her big green eyes shoot off sparks that way, but there was something else in her glare that made him think she wasn't quite so immune to him as she'd like him to believe. Maybe he was going about this the wrong way.

"I'm sorry," he said. "That was presumptuous of me. And rude," he added for good measure.

He'd caught her off guard, it seemed, as she opened her mouth to say something, then closed it again, apparently at a loss for a good comeback. Which surprised him. He'd assumed she would be only too happy to agree with him.

"In fact," he continued before she could come up with something to say. "It's not the first time, either. Me being rude, I mean. I'd like to start over. I'd like *us* to start over," he clarified. He held out his hand toward her. "Hi. I'm Ward St. James. I'm your neighbor—Hazel Poleman's neighbor—out on Shoreline Drive. Welcome to Autumn Lake."

Penny must have been raised right, because although he could see that she was warring with herself, she smiled politely and—hesitantly, to be sure—put her hand in his. "Um, hi."

He waited for her to say more, but when she didn't, he nodded and shook her hand gently. "Okay. Hi. I think I can work with that." Then before he could stop himself, he said it again. "Hi." *Urgh.*

From the other side of the counter, Juno made a sound that might have been a laugh, but Ward kept his eyes on Penny. Was it his imagination, or had her cheeks reddened a little more?

"So, how long are you in town?" His jaw was starting to cramp from the effort to keep smiling.

Penny tugged her hand free before he realized he was still shaking it.

He made a self-deprecating grimace. "Oh. Right. That went on a little too long, didn't it? Sorry." He needed to stop apologizing now. He picked up his glass and took a swig of his water before returning his attention to her. "So..." Ward dragged the word out, hoping it would prompt her into sharing something about herself. *Come on*, he silently pleaded. *I'm really trying, here.*

"Here. Try this," Juno said, setting a bright red drink, complete with a skewer of mango and strawberry pieces and a yellow paper umbrella, in front of Penny. "Maybe it'll loosen your tongue a little."

Penny's eyes widened, then she muttered under her breath, but not so quietly that she couldn't be heard, "Wow. Really? Whose side are you on?"

Ward frowned. There were sides?

Juno planted her hands on her hips and glared at them both. "What is it with you two?" she asked. "If you're going to sit at my bar, you need to kiss and make up. Or take it outside."

Suddenly, all around them, conversation quieted as people at the crowded counter started to take notice of what was quickly becoming potential fodder for gossip.

"I'm sorry." Not caring that he was apologizing again, Ward shot Juno a look that he hoped translated to "chill out."

"It's okay," Penny said quickly, quietly, but he could practically feel the mortification radiating off her. "Juno's right. I'm sorry, too." She lifted her chin, even though her cheeks were now blazing red, and said, "I'm here for the summer. For the next two months. Nice to officially meet you, Ward."

"Thank you." Juno was nothing if not direct. "You two need to figure out how to be friends. I think you'd like each other, and that's a whole lot better than whatever this is. Was." To Penny, she said, "And girlie, I'm letting him buy you that drink. He owes you for booting you off Miss Hazel's property."

Ward balked. "I did not boot her off the property."

Penny once again swiveled on her stool with a challenge in her eyes. "Um... yes, Ward St. James, you did. You said I wasn't supposed to be there, you told me to leave, and then you picked up my bags and loaded them in my car because I wasn't moving fast enough."

Ward closed his eyes briefly and shook his head, hating the way it sounded coming out of her mouth. That wasn't exactly how it had all gone down, but close enough; he'd give her that.

"Hoo-boy," Juno exclaimed under her breath, shaking her head sympathetically. "You've got your work cut out for you, Mr. St. James, if you're going to make up for that blunder. Our Penny here is one of Miss Hazel's favorite people."

"So I've been told," Ward acknowledged. To Penny, he said, "But then, I'm one of her favorite people, too, so that's something we have in common, at least."

"Can't argue there," Juno quipped.

"Um, don't you have customers to tend to?" Ward asked her wryly. From the corner of his eye, he saw a smile tug at Penny's lips.

Juno completely ignored the hint to get lost. "I know how you can start making it up to Miss Penelope, here, Ward," she said, as she refilled his water glass for him. "What time do you wrap things up this afternoon? You going to be around these parts?"

Penny stiffened beside him and started frantically waving both hands in the air in front of her. "No, Juno. It's okay. Don't—"

"Is this the favor you mentioned?" Ward's gaze moved back and forth between Juno and Penny, who was once again turning bright pink, a color that he was beginning to really like.

"It's fine, sugar. It's a small town. We look out for each other."

"What's up?" Ward asked, now more curious than ever.

Juno raised her eyebrows at Penny, indicating that she should answer for herself. Then she moved down the bar toward the other end and started chatting with another customer.

Ward was never so glad to see his friend's back as he was at that moment. Penny remained silent; her gaze fixed on the contents of the glass in front of her. She dipped the skewer of fruit in and out of the iced tea, obviously feeling ill at ease. "Look," he said. "I didn't mean to cause all of this..." He broke off, not sure how to describe what had just happened.

"She's right, though, isn't she?" Penny said quietly. "I don't know about you, but this—" She broke off long enough to wave the fruit skewer back and forth between them. "I'm not usually petty or mean. Forgive me."

"There's nothing to forgive," he began, then stopped when she narrowed her eyes at him.

"Don't patronize me, Ward. I know I've been out of line. I was embarrassed when I messed up your tent—"

Taken aback, Ward interrupted her with a guffaw. "My tent?"

She rolled her eyes. "Sorry. Whatever you call your plastic curtain thing. I was embarrassed for ripping it down, and when I tried to apologize, you were mean to me, so I was mean back. I should have taken the higher ground."

Ward's brows shot up. "The higher ground? After you destroyed my—"

Penny giggled. "Gotcha."

"Oof," he declared, clutching his heart dramatically. "Too soon. Too soon." It occurred to him that he might just enjoy getting to know this woman. Alex was right. Ball of fire, yes, indeed.

She took a sip of her drink, not quite meeting his eyes now, almost like she was feeling a little shy after playing him like that. She opened her mouth to speak, shut it, then took another drink and tried again. "Look, I'm cooking dinner tonight for Hazel. We're eating a little later than usual—around seven—because I'm getting together with friends here in a bit, and I won't be home until after five. Would you maybe like to join us? Your parents, too, of course."

Ward's eyes widened in surprise. "Really?"

"I mean, if you're busy, it's fine. I know it's super short notice. It—it was just a thought," she stammered, clearly trying to backpedal in the face of what must seem to her like his reticence.

"Hmm." He eyed her contemplatively, taking advantage of the opportunity to tease her right back. "What's on the menu?"

"Really?" she asked, echoing him, but with a whole lot more snark in her tone, and an exaggerated eye roll. "I take back the invite. Hazel and I will dine like queens tonight. Alone."

Ward burst out laughing and leaned sideways to nudge her shoulder with his. "You're too quick for me."

"I have to be quick," she retorted, but she was grinning back at him. "I teach second graders and let me tell you something. Seven- and eight-year-olds are devious little manipulators. They're just young enough to make you believe they're too cute to be naughty, and just old enough to know how to use that cuteness to get away with all kinds of diabolical deeds."

Ward cocked his head. "Like what?"

"What diabolical deeds?" Penny pondered a moment. "Okay. So one day, we were getting ready for our daily dance party—"

"Daily dance party?" He had to ask.

"Yes," she said slowly, as though he needed extra time to understand. "Dancing is a great way to get the wigglies out of your system, Mr. St. James. It encourages bonding, even when everyone is doing their own dance moves, it reduces stress and improves self-esteem because it triggers a release of feel-good endorphins, and it gets everyone, teachers included, off their backsides. And it's fun."

Ward held up a hand. "You're the expert. I was just asking."

"Don't you forget it, either." Penny jabbed her fruit skewer at him. A piece of strawberry slipped off the end of it and landed on the counter, just barely missing his arm. "Oops!" she snorted, then used her napkin to scoop up the piece of fruit.

"I leave you two alone for two minutes, and now you're throwing things at each other?" Juno was back, carrying a plate with Ward's sandwich. His mouth started watering at the sight of it; he'd been enjoying himself so much that he'd forgotten how hungry he was.

"My fault," Ward insisted. "I questioned her daily dance parties."

Juno gave them both a blank stare, but then smiled. "Well, I'm glad to see you two getting along. Did she ask you for a ride yet?"

"Juno!" Penny glared daggers at her. "I don't need a ride."

"A ride?" Ward asked, ignoring her objection. "Where to?"

Juno set his plate in front of him and handed him a bottle of his favorite hot sauce. "Are you going to ask him, or shall I do it for you? He's your neighbor, Penelope Eva Anderson. It's not like he'd have to go way out of his way, or anything."

"Yeah," Ward chimed in. "Especially since we're having supper together."

"You're what?" Juno's eyes went wide with surprise, but he saw the satisfied glint in them.

Penny covered her face with both hands and shook her head. "Fine." She lifted her head to shoot lasers through Juno, then turned to him. "Ward, I made the mistake of riding my bike into town. I almost died. I am afraid that if I ride my bike back to Hazel's, I will definitely die, and then no one will get to eat my famous chicken curry tonight."

"I see," he said with exaggerated solemnity. "Wow. A near-death experience."

"Yes. Very serious stuff." She took a deep breath and pointed at Juno, who stood on the other side of the counter, her arms crossed, grinning like the Cheshire cat. "Juno here wants me to ask you if you'll give me and my bike—Hazel's bike—a ride home this afternoon so that I don't die. She'd miss me too much."

Ward couldn't think of anything he'd like more. Except maybe to make the distance back to The Garden Gate Guesthouse about a hundred times longer.

Then again, the sooner he got her home, the sooner he could go round up his parents and head back over to spend the rest of the evening with her. And Hazel, of course.

"If you'll tell me more about your daily dance parties, I'll not only give you a ride home, Miss Penelope Anderson." He paused momentarily, relishing in the sound of her name as it rolled off his tongue. "I'll also come over for supper tonight. I'll even bring my parents, too."

9

Penny

THE SIX WOMEN WERE crowded around a four-person table, the surface of which was barely visible through a myriad of half-drunk cups and empty plates that once held some of Kimber Tate's divine pastries. Hazel had been right about the woman; she could bake.

Liz had brought her sister, Candy, with her as promised, and Penny had found her to be absolutely charming. She wasn't much taller than Penny, but she made up for it in personality. A general contractor with a design background, Candy had landed a dream job on the crew of a house-flipping show on the DIY channel. Although the show had been canceled after only three years, Candy had come away from it with lots of experience and a plan to launch her own business specializing in renovating and remodeling. "I'm not that interested in building from the ground up," she told them. "I love the process of taking something old and outdated, something other people may think is too far gone, and bringing it back to life, or giving it a whole new life altogether."

It was that declaration that gave Penny the courage to speak up.

"So, I have something that I want to talk to all of you about." Penny took a deep breath, still not sure that she was doing the right thing, but desperate to talk to someone about what was going on.

"What's on your mind, girlie?" Juno asked. She hadn't stopped grinning every time she looked Penny's way, and of course, everyone had wanted to know why.

Penny had given the group a very abbreviated version of things, with Juno filling in a few details that were highly subjective. In particular, things like, "Ward St. James is in trouble, ladies. Penny's feeding him tonight, and you know what they say about the way to a man's heart and all."

"I'm not trying to find my way to his heart. Or any man's heart," Penny insisted. "Food is a language everyone understands, that's all. And when middle ground is hard to find, a shared meal is a perfect place to start."

"Oh, I like that," Addison Wedgewood murmured from her corner of the table. She was the quietest of all of them, and although she was a year-rounder, she, too, wasn't technically a local. Addison had moved to Autumn Lake about five years ago and had fallen in love with everything about the small lake town. She worked at a regional airport about half an hour's drive away, and even though her job came with as many free flights as she wanted, she insisted that she had no desire to ever leave her new little hometown again.

"It's probably a good thing you're not aiming for his heart," Claire said with a shake of her head. "He still says he's not staying past tourist season. It's been what? Nine or ten months now?"

"Yeah," Juno agreed. "But his mom is doing better, and from what he says, his dad is taking on more of the workload, too, now that Ward has set things with the business back on course. I have a feeling we may be saying goodbye to him before too long." She reached over and patted Penny's hand. "But you know what? It's kinda perfect, Penny. No strings attached—you're both leaving in a few months. Have a summer fling. I think you'd be good for each other." She sat back, a smug expression on her face.

"Ha. No. Stop trying to set me up with anyone, you guys. I'm not—"

"We know you're not interested," Claire said, cutting her off. "We've heard you say so a gazillion times."

"And yet, here we are, you all still setting me up and me still standing my ground." Penny gestured at Juno. "I mean, seriously. A summer fling? Do I look like a no-strings-attached-summer-fling kind of girl to you?" She looked around the table at her friends.

Every single one of them nodded, even Candy. "Oh, definitely summer fling material," she teased with a giggle.

Penny snorted. "Et tu, Brute?"

Juno lifted her hand to Candy, who high-fived her.

"What was it you were going to tell us about a minute ago?" Liz asked, bringing the conversation back around to Penny's request. Liz was a down-to-earth, git-er-done kind of woman. A plumber by trade, she'd landed her dream job working for the county doing water line construction and inspection right around the time that the resort started going up across the lake, which meant job security for her for many, many years to come. As a woman in a predominately male line of work, she was rightfully proud of what she'd accomplished, and even though it had taken some effort to convince her team members that she wasn't afraid of hard work, they now treated her like one of the guys.

Which didn't sound so awesome to Penny, who liked her sundresses and sandals, and who, unlike Liz, didn't own a single pair of shoes with steel toes. To each his own, though. Penny admired Liz all the more for their differences.

"You sounded kinda serious," Liz added. "Is everything okay?"

They'd all taken turns updating each other on their lives, and although the rest of them lived in the same town, it was remarkable how easy it was to go months at a time without getting personal, even when they saw each other in passing on a regular basis. It always made Penny feel less like an outsider when she wasn't the only one who needed catching up on what was going on with everyone.

She'd already told them about her mother's rapid decline over the last year, and how she worried that her summers in Autumn Lake were coming to an end. It was easy to talk to these women about her struggles with her mother, probably because of the degree of separation between her vacation life in Autumn Lake and her normal life back home.

But talking to them about Hazel was a different story altogether. She felt intrusive, like maybe she was crossing a line. But she couldn't stand by and pretend she wasn't concerned, especially if Hazel was indeed in trouble.

Penny chose her words carefully. "I'm not exactly sure, and I really hope I'm not overstepping here." She grimaced at the concern on every face in their little circle. "I think maybe Hazel isn't doing so well."

She told them about the stack of bills, about the forlorn, neglected garden. "And you guys, I'm her only guest. When I asked her when I'd have to start sharing her company with others, she simply said she hadn't booked anyone else for the next few weeks. That she needed to get a few things done around the place first."

"Is Ward still stopping by to help out?" Juno asked, tracing circles in the condensation on her glass. "What about Alex?"

"I haven't seen Alex since the first day I got here, but Ward was there fixing a leak this morning. I guess last night's rain was a doozy." According to Ward, the storm had blown a few shingles loose and had caused a minor leak in the attic.

Juno nodded. "He's so good to her."

"He really is," Claire agreed. "It's not like he's got extra time on his hands, what with taking care of his parents, running his dad's company, and keeping his own business going back on the west coast."

Penny glanced between the two of them. "Am I understanding you right? Is he doing all of that work for her for free?"

"It's called being neighborly, Penny," Liz said with a good-natured chuckle. "It's the way we do things around these parts."

That seemed to be the prevailing sentiment around Autumn Lake, Penny thought. Hazel, then Juno, and now Liz had all said variations of the same thing to her.

Their surprisingly pleasant chat while he ate his sandwich had her acknowledging that her first impression of Ward St. James might not have been quite as accurate as she'd assumed. And now hearing how highly all her friends thought of him had her feeling like a real toad for the terrible thoughts she'd had about him. Well, tonight at supper, she was going to have to make up for it with the best batch of chicken curry she'd ever put together.

She took a deep breath and set thoughts of Ward aside. "Well, here's the thing. Ward said he's doing mostly just cosmetic stuff, easy repairs, you know? Nothing that would prevent her from having guests. I'm afraid that there might be something a little less obvious going on." She hesitated, hating to put her next thought into words. "Like maybe she's got financial troubles?"

After a moment, Juno nodded. "I've been wondering the same thing myself. I was pretty surprised when Kimber told me Hazel had given her all her chickens. She loved those clucky birds." She pointed at the bud vase in the center of the table. In it was a slightly bedraggled posy of carnations and daisies. "I used to buy my fresh summer flowers for the tables from her. She'd handpick little bouquets and have them sitting in water ready for me to pick up every other day. Then back in April, she told me she was giving her garden an off year, whatever that means, but that's when I got worried. I mean, The Garden Gate without a garden?"

"Yeah, that's a big deal," Claire said in agreement, frowning down at her coffee cup. She looked as lovely as ever today in a pale blue dress with a wide Peter Pan collar. She reminded Penny of Alice in Wonderland, her blonde curls held back from her face with a black velvet headband. She looked around the table, her gaze landing on Penny. "So, what can we do to help? Can we help without offending her?"

Leave it to Claire to move quickly toward resolution. She always had a plan for everything. That was one of the things that made her such a great businesswoman. She didn't wait around for someone else to do the things that she could do herself, and if she had an idea that she thought was good, she acted on it with the confidence of a warrior. Penny wanted to be her when she grew up.

"Does she have a website?" Candy asked, reaching for her phone from the basket in the middle of the table. She paused, her hand hovering over the pile of phones in their varied and colorful cases. "May I? Or will I have to pay the bill if I get my phone? Is that how this works?" It was tradition; phones went on silent mode and got put in the pot, and they only responded to phone calls. Even then, the call had to be from someone they knew, and it had to be answered on speaker. Claire's boyfriend—ex-boyfriend now—had braved calling her once during one of their 'counseling sessions', as they all called these get-togethers. They'd answered the phone as a group, Juno had asked the disconcerted Damon what the emergency was, and when he'd said he was just wondering when Claire would be finished so he could see her, they'd collectively explained to him how much his impatient demands on Claire's time was *not* an emergency. Claire and Damon had broken up only a few weeks later, and although she'd insisted it had nothing to do with that phone call, Penny secretly wondered if they hadn't scared him just a little.

"Go ahead," Juno told Candy. "And no one pays the bill. This is all on the house." The woman was generous to a fault, but there was no arguing with her.

"Actually, she doesn't have one," Penny said in response to Candy's question. "I've asked her about getting one several times over the last few years, but she insists she doesn't need one. Says her phone works just fine, and that's how people have always booked rooms from her before."

"If it's not broke, don't fix it." Juno rolled her eyes. "How many times have I heard that woman use that phrase? Only a bajillion times, ladies."

"Except it sounds like it *is* broken," Addison said, frowning. "Believe me, people don't want to make calls anymore. They don't want to talk to real people." She pointed at the basket. "They go to websites. They text. They email, if necessary. And they call only if—and I mean, last resort—they absolutely have to."

Candy was nodding along with every word Addison said. "Exactly. They'll move on to the next place if they can't find what they're looking for online. Businesses can't afford not to have websites these days, Penny. She needs one, like, yesterday."

"Like, last decade," Liz interjected. "I didn't realize she was so behind the times. That woman is a force to be reckoned with. I'd never have imagined she'd be so stuck in her 'old-timer' ways." She sounded genuinely bemused by the notion.

"I could easily put together a website for her. I could even do a mockup first, so she can see what it looks like. I kinda need a project right now, just to keep me distracted." Candy leaned forward, her eyes alight with anticipation.

"Distracted from what?" Liz asked, turning in her seat to eye her sister. "Don't tell me you've already got a boyfriend. You just moved back here less than a month ago."

Candy elbowed her in the side. "No, Lizzy. I don't have a boyfriend. I'm waiting to hear back from my contract attorney to make sure I can go into business on my own without any issues from the television show. My contract with them included a non-compete clause, and I'm freaked out that I may have to wait to start my own renovation business. So yeah, I need a distraction. A project would be nice."

"Wow. Can they do that?" Claire asked. "Keep you tied to them even when the show is dead?"

"I don't know," Candy said with a shrug. "Which is why I'm letting the attorney handle it for me."

"Well, I think a website is a great place to start," Penny said to Candy. "But how much will it cost her? I don't know how bad things are—I honestly don't know for sure that they *are* bad—but I'd wager money is going to be an issue."

"Right. Sure. Totally understand. So maybe let me take care of it. At least for the first year. Then, if she wants to keep it—and I'm sure she will—she can pick up the tab at that point. It's not that expensive to maintain a website these days. The expense comes when you have to pay someone to create it for you."

"But you should be paid for your time," Penny protested. Juno and Claire both nodded in agreement.

"No, it's fine. I like doing techy stuff; it'll be fun for me."

Liz put an arm around Candy's shoulders. "If it sets your minds at ease, my little sister came away from that show of hers with a nice little settlement. They had a five-year contract, and they pulled it after three. Her attorney, the one who's looking over things for her now? He got her a sweet settlement for the remaining two years of her contract." To Candy, she said, "You can talk freely here, sissy. We have no secrets in this circle."

Candy nodded, her concerned expression turning to one of relief. "It wasn't my show, but yes, he made sure my whole crew got sweet settlements. This is why I can afford to go into business for myself now. It's not going to happen overnight, I know that, but the settlement bought me the time I need to do it right."

"Time she's spending with me," Liz declared, squeezing Candy's shoulders again before releasing her. "She's been a bum, lounging around my house all day. Please give her something to do."

"If you can help me with some of the pertinent information, Penny," Candy continued, not even acknowledging her sister's jab. "Like room rates, hours, meals, anything you can think of, I can put something together in just a few days."

"Absolutely," Penny agreed, reaching across the table to squeeze Candy's hand. "That's awesome of you to take that on."

"What about the rest of us?" Claire asked, not to be deterred. "Any ideas?"

Penny nodded, her bottom lip between her teeth as she quickly put together a plan that had been brewing in her head since Liz had made her comment about being neighborly. "What if we did this—" She swirled her hand in a circle around the table, indicating all of them. "Over at Hazel's? What would you all think of putting in some time in the garden this summer? I mean, I can be out there every day, of course. You all have jobs, but is there a time like this when we could just schedule... I don't know. Community work hours, or whatever we want to call it, over there? I know Hazel might balk if we act like we're doing it out of pity, but what if we started a club, or an organization of some kind, and asked her if we could have our meetings in her garden?"

"We could offer to pay her to let us meet there," Claire began, but Juno shook her head.

"Oh, girl. You know that won't happen. She'll flat out refuse any money from us."

"I know that," Claire shot back. "But then we can do the whole 'If you won't take our money, then at least let us pitch in a little around the place' reverse psychology thing. She can't say 'no' to that, can she?"

Addison nodded. "I think you're on to something, Claire. That would let her keep her dignity."

Penny felt the tingle of tears at the bridge of her nose. "You guys. You're the best." She pressed her lips together as she fought not to cry. "How am I going survive if I can't come back next year?"

"Hey. None of that," Juniper commanded, reaching over to grab Penny's hand. She squeezed tightly. "Leave tomorrow's troubles alone, okay? We have Hazel's troubles to deal with right now."

Penny nodded and sniffled, pulling herself together. "Okay. So what are we going to call our club?" she asked, needing to focus on something positive. "I mean, it has to be better than the "Save The Garden Gate Club.""

Addison's eyes sparkled with excitement. "Definitely. Hmm. Something less specific, I think. I mean, what if we find this is something we can do for more people than just Hazel? Maybe there are other businesses—or just people—in town who could also use a little neighborly help?" Her mind was clearly spinning with ideas.

"If we aren't going to name it something to do with the project, then maybe we can name it something to do with us," Liz suggested.

"Yes," Candy agreed. "Good idea. What are some things we all have in common?"

"Well, aren't we all single right now?" Juno asked.

"Yes, but we can't call it a singles club," Liz countered with a chuckle. "That's a whole different vibe than what we're going for, isn't it?"

"Besides, I don't want to be single my whole life." Candy made a face.

They all heartily agreed with that sentiment.

Over the next half an hour, they tossed around ideas and finally landed on something that worked for everyone. Not only that, but the word 'garden' was in the name, an homage to their first community project in Hazel's garden.

"It's official, then," Penny said, lifting her glass in a toast. The others lifted theirs, too, clinking them together in celebration. "Welcome to the first meeting of The Garden Variety Lovers Club, ladies."

10
Ward

WHEN HE RETURNED TO Juniper's, the ladies were all still gathered in a tight circle around a table near the back of the room, talking quite animatedly. He was terribly curious to know what they were discussing, but he knew better than to approach the hive without an invitation. Instead, he settled his backside onto the same stool he'd sat on earlier that day when he and Penny had formed their truce. He'd wait for her there.

"Can I get you something, Ward?" Poppy called down the counter from where she stood at the sink washing her hands. She'd just finished making a whipped, frothy drink, and had spilled some in the process. Ward didn't mind grease or dirt or even lake slime, but the idea of having sticky hands from cream and sugar made him grimace.

"Just a glass of water would be nice," he said, glancing back over his shoulder at the table where Penny sat with the others.

She looked up at that exact moment, and their eyes met. Her smile came quick and easy, and he grinned back at her.

All five of the other women seemed to notice her reaction at the same time, and five pairs of eyes homed in on him.

"Hey, Ward St. James," Juno called out.

He lifted his fingers to his forehead in a salute. "Hey, ladies."

It felt a lot like being back in high school again as the six of them turned back toward each other, heads bent together, then let out a chorus of laughter while tossing not-so-subtle looks at him over their shoulders.

Ward turned back around, not bothered at all by the tittering coming from the back of the shop. For one thing, they weren't in high school anymore, so he didn't have to worry about messages being passed back and forth or secret codes or any of the stuff that had driven him crazy in his youth. If he really wanted to know what was going on over there, he could just walk right up and ask.

He was a man, after all. He thumped his chest with his fist and let out an ape-like "Hoo-hoo," under his breath.

"Feeling vulnerable, are we?" Alex Frampton slid onto the stool beside him, chuckling at Ward's pitiful alpha male display. He glanced back at the table of women, but only briefly. "How's it going, big guy?"

Ward took the ribbing in stride. "All's well."

"Thought any more about Carpe Diem?"

When he'd told Alex about the offer from Lysha Austin, his friend had suggested he consider it. "You don't miss this place?" he'd asked, the conversation getting serious. "What about your parents? They're not getting any younger, and you're going to have to face that at some point. I'm still not a hundred percent sure what you're doing out on the west coast, dude." He'd said 'dude' with an exaggerated California beach bum drawl. "That's not you, and you know it. We all know it."

They'd been friends since childhood, and if anyone knew him, it was Alex. But that didn't make him right about this. "If—and I mean, *if*, Alex—I were to one day—and I mean *one day*, Alex," Ward had said, holding up a finger to emphasize his point. "If I were to one day come back to the lake to stay, there's no way I could *not* take over my dad's company. You know that. You all know that," he'd said, mimicking his friend's words. "Especially to take a job across the lake. That would be a betrayal of the worst kind to my father. Carpe Diem has taken a lot of work from us locals, and that woman made it pretty clear that even operating his business on the side wouldn't be an option. She called it a conflict of interest. I'd essentially be owned by them."

Carpe Diem Incorporated had opened its all-inclusive resort on the north shore only a few years ago. It sat there, like a displaced, entitled monarch, peering across the water at the oddity that was the Autumn Lake town center. The company had made a lot of persuasive promises to get permission and support from the town to carve out that side of the lake, but they had made good on just enough of them to forge a love-hate relationship with the year-round residents. They'd promised jobs, but only offered low-level positions to locals, such as housekeeping and grounds and maintenance.

That, of course, caused an uproar, but they assuaged the townsfolk when they brought in a big-name housing developer, Astor & Co., to put up a bunch of fancy new homes on the outskirts of the resort property. Astor and Co, at least, made a point to use local resources whenever possible, including bringing on J&J Contractors, the only construction company in town, as part of their crew. North Shore Cottages, the subdivision was called, but the smallest one had no fewer than six bedrooms. Touted as custom homes, they all looked a lot like mini versions of the resort. There were already more than two dozen houses—still mostly summer homes for the absurdly rich—that stood in a sentinel half-circle around the resort and spilled down the length of the shoreline. With folks beginning to take up residency year-round now, however, a very small percentage of that North Shore wealth was finally beginning to trickle down into the hands of the townspeople who primarily lived on the south shore.

But the line had been drawn in the sand, and although locals worked their North Shore jobs, and the wealthy came around to the "darling little Autumn Lake town center" to spend their money on the boardwalk, at the end of the day, everyone went back to their respective sides of the lake.

The Townies and the WOOTs.

It had been that way even before the resort went up—the townies and the WOOTs—but the unspoken us-versus-them attitude grew proportionally with the expansion across the water and the ballooning number of people and their watercraft in the water each summer.

People who didn't need lodgings like the ones Hazel Poleman and Katy Lawrence offered.

People whose watercraft was taken to Carpe Diem's marine mechanic rather than using the services of the likes of St. James Mobile Boat Repair.

Ward had been mildly curious why George had called them to get his pontoon worked on instead of using the Carpe Diem mechanic, but he hadn't thought enough about it to ask. When Lysha did the same, it was a whole different story, but he didn't have to ask why. Clearly, they were having trouble keeping that position filled if she was looking to hire him.

That was another red flag in his book. With the salary and perks Carpe Diem was offering, he couldn't figure out why they couldn't get someone from out of town to stick around. He'd done his homework—on the sly, of course—and they'd had three different guys in that position over the last four years. That kind of turnaround didn't bode well.

"Not gonna happen," Ward said to his friend. To his relief, Poppy approached to take Alex's order, giving him a reprieve.

"How's the lovely Miss Poppy today?" Alex flashed his ridiculous smile blushed crimson under his attention. "I like your hair like that."

Poppy's hair was long and curly, and she often wore it piled in a loose, messy bun on top of her head while at work. Today, she had it in a braid that hung down her back. Ward had a feeling that she'd be braiding her hair more often after today.

By the time Alex had finished making Poppy feel like the only woman in the room, the group at the back of the shop was breaking up. And of course, they were all heading his way. Their way, he decided, noticing that at least half of them had eyes on Alex.

Ward couldn't blame them. His friend was big and brawny, unfairly good-looking, and he knew how to make a woman smile. Alex was also hard to catch, which, apparently, made him all that more alluring to the masses.

Claire sidled up next to Alex and bumped him with her shoulder. "Hey, guys. Haven't seen either of you in my world for a while. You know, they say reading is sexy."

Alex grinned and pressed a hand to his chest. "I don't know if you all could handle me being any sexier than this, Miss Claire."

Juno, making her way around the end of the counter, narrowed her eyes at him and let out a derisive snort. "You keep telling yourself that, Alex."

Ward shot a curious look in her direction. He was pretty sure she meant it in jest, but if he wasn't mistaken, there was a hint of something ugly in her tone. Alex was a known lady's man; surely, she wasn't offended by his casual vanity. Reputation or not, Alex didn't flaunt his conquests. In fact, in all the time Ward had been back at the lake, he hadn't personally seen Alex spend time with any one woman in particular. He flirted outrageously with everyone: single, married—although, that might just be a rumor—young and old, but he didn't seem to seriously date anyone.

Liz Needham approached the counter beside him and put in an order to go for her and her sister, Candy, who had moved back to town earlier that spring. She greeted him with a quick hello, but she didn't say much else. Ward liked her; she was straightforward and matter-of-fact, and he never had to try to second-guess what she was thinking. One of the guys, he thought to himself, and then wondered if that was such a good thing. Liz did work with predominantly men, so maybe she'd gotten good at acting like them, but that didn't mean she was any less a woman. "Something to think about," he said under his breath.

"What was that?" Liz asked, shooting him a sidelong glance.

"Nothing." He shook his head. "How is it having your sister with you?"

"I love it. She cooks a whole lot better than I do, which isn't saying much, and she cleans up after herself. She's entertaining, too. She's got lots of ideas of ways I should remodel my house." She chuckled dryly. "Who needs television when you have a kid sister, right?"

Addison and Penny were approaching slowly, arms linked as they talked, and on Penny's other side, Candy had her phone out and was showing them something on her screen. "Sharing some of her ideas?" Ward asked, nodding his head toward them.

Liz turned to watch the trio, too, but the smile she wore was one of affection. "She's got lots of ideas, period. Ninety-nine percent of them are totally worth considering. She's a good egg, that sister of mine."

The look on her face made something inside Ward's chest squeeze. He'd felt a variation of that kind of camaraderie with friends, he supposed, but as an only child, he'd had to go looking for it. There was nothing like family, though, and even the best of friends drifted apart, or lost contact altogether. Family, unless it was broken, was different.

As a child, Ward would have given anything to have a brother. Even a sister. His parents had each other. He was always the outsider in his own home. The extra. Oh, they'd never intentionally made him feel that way. In fact, they'd gone to extremes to make sure he knew he was loved, wanted. But facts were facts, and they couldn't be refuted. When they put him to bed at night, they'd go snuggle on the couch together without him. When they sat down for meals, Ted and Rachel opposite each other, there was always an empty seat on the other side of the table from Ward. When they got in the car, the two of them held hands over the console in the front seat, and Ward sat behind them, wondering if he'd ever belong to someone the way they did to each other.

"She's got plans, that girl," Liz continued, apparently not noticing Ward's distracted silence. "I'm just lucky to get to be her biggest fan."

"And she's lucky to have you."

Liz grinned and propped one boot on the foot rail that ran the length of the counter. "Well, I'm not going to argue with you, there."

Penny came up behind Liz and circled her arms around her in a tight hug. "Thank you for bringing your sister today, Liz. I just love you both so much!"

Addison hung back, but Candy squeezed between Ward and Alex and greeted them both with her bubbly personality. "Hello, you two handsome stud muffins. How were your days?"

And suddenly, he and Alex were surrounded by half a dozen lovely women. "This is every man's dream," Alex declared, spreading his arms wide as though trying to embrace them all at once.

Across the counter, Juno rolled her eyes.

Penny laughed, a little shyly, Ward thought, but raised her hands to get everyone's attention. "You're all awesome, and I'm sorry I have to kiss and run, but I've got to go. I'll confirm with Hazel tonight, but barring any unforeseen catastrophe, I'll see all of you out there on Wednesday morning, right?"

They all agreed, and Ward, taking that as his cue to leave, stood and offered his stool to Candy.

"Hope you enjoy your exotic meal tonight, Ward St. James," Claire cooed, peering around Alex at him.

"And the sunset drive home," Candy added with a wink.

So Penny had told them about having him over for supper. Or Juno had. He wondered if she'd also told them about the not-so-great way they'd hit it off.

Penny blushed, her cheeks going that pretty pink color, but she gave as good as she got. "I'm trusting you all, ladies. Friends don't let friends ride home with creeps, right?"

Alex guffawed and smacked Ward on the back. "She's got your number, bro."

11
Penny

WARD WAS THE PERFECT gentleman, standing aside to let her go out ahead of him, then holding her door open for her as she scrambled into the passenger seat of the van.

"It's not the classiest ride you've ever had, I'm sure," he said before closing the door for her. "But it'll get us there. Your bike, too." He'd already slid her bicycle into the back of the van, wedging it between the rack of tools on one side and the bank of cabinets on the other. "It's our shop on wheels," he explained once he was strapped into the driver's seat. "Dad gave up the shop downtown years ago, since most of his jobs were easier if he could go to them."

"That makes perfect sense to me," Penny said, fastening her own seatbelt. The interior of the van smelled interesting, but not bad. There was a hint of lake water, maybe road food—tacos? —and something uniquely male. "Do you like working with your dad?"

Ward paused, as if pondering the question, although it seemed like a pretty basic one to Penny. Did he *not*, and was hesitant to admit it? It wasn't a bad or even embarrassing thing to not like working with one's father, though. Or any family member, for that matter. She'd heard many married couples say as much about their spouses.

"I met him a couple of years ago," she said, quick to fill the awkward space his silence created. "He seems like a really nice man."

"He is," Ward agreed. She glanced over at him and found him smiling warmly. Talk about mixed messages. "And I do like working with him. He's not just a great guy; he's a great boss, too. He taught me just about everything I know about boats."

"It's nice to hear you talk about him that way. From the rumor mill, it sounds like you're only here temporarily, and I'm glad to know it isn't because of stuff between you and your dad." Penny closed her eyes and turned her face toward the window. What on earth had prompted her to say such an assumptive, insensitive thing?

Ward chuckled, surprising her. "Wow. That was direct. But I agree. You can rest at ease; Dad and I get along great, so there won't be any awkward tension at the supper table tonight."

"I'm sorry," Penny said. "That was totally out of line, wasn't it? I think being around the girls shook loose a few of my filters. They have a tendency to do that to me."

"I get along with my mom, too, just in case you were wondering," he teased.

"Okay. I deserved that." She grabbed the handle above her window and held on as they hit a rut in the road. The cargo van was not a luxury sedan, that was for sure, and even though the seats were comfortable enough, there was no avoiding the fact that the vehicle was built with efficiency in mind.

"Forgot about that pothole," Ward said, grimacing at her. "You alright?"

"I'm good. Hopefully, that shook those filters right back into place. Thank you."

"My pleasure. So what about you? Do you get along with your folks?"

Penny should have known that this was where the conversation would lead. Her parents weren't a topic she avoided—she wasn't embarrassed or uncomfortable talking about them. But her circumstances often made other people uncomfortable. Especially people with picture-perfect families like Ward St. James and his parents. She'd learned, however, that avoiding the question often only prolonged the inevitable, particularly with people she expected to be in her life for more than the moment. Ward might not be staying in Autumn Lake any longer than she was, but she assumed they'd be crossing paths on a regular basis over the next couple of months, especially now that they'd decided they were going to be friends.

"I don't know my father," she began, her voice steady and her expression as gentle as she could make it. She felt no malice toward the man who'd abandoned them. Her mother had harbored more than enough bitterness for both of them over the course of her life, and Penny believed that refusal to forgive the man had contributed to her mother's current condition. She'd seen it eat away at her mother her whole life, and Penny had been determined to walk a different path. "He left when I was not quite a year old, and I have no memories of him."

"I'm sorry to hear that." Ward's words were kind, without judgment, so she continued.

"It's been Mom and me ever since. She's sick now, though, and I take care of her. Early onset Alzheimer's."

"I'm... wow. I'm sorry to hear that, too. That's... that sounds like it's a lot for you." He lifted his hand from the wheel, and for a moment, Penny thought he might reach over and touch her. Instead, he rubbed at the back of his neck the way he had that first day she'd come upon him in his plastic work bubble. She averted her eyes so she wouldn't stare, but not before she'd noticed how flexy his biceps were.

Flexy. She had to bite her lip to keep from giggling. Great. Now she was on the verge of giggling. And they'd been talking about such serious matters. He was going to think *she* was the creep. She took a steadying breath. "I won't lie to you. It's not easy. I lose a little more of Mom every day, it seems. It started out slow. Little things, you know? Getting confused easily, not following basic instructions. Trouble with reading, bad depth perception, things like that. But things have been progressing a lot faster these days. She doesn't sleep well. She's not safe at all, so she can't be left alone for any amount of time. She gets combative much more than she used to, and she's a lot harder to calm down. I used to be able to turn on Gardener's World just so I could get stuff done, but she's not really even aware that the TV is on anymore."

"I don't know what is too personal, but how do you work? Or have you quit teaching now? Are you her full-time... what do they call it these days? Caretaker? Sitter?" His questions moved her, and she had to swallow the knot of emotion that formed in her throat. He was being so kind. Where most people would find a way to change the subject, he seemed interested in what her life was like.

"I'm a teacher, yes." Penny smiled just thinking about the kids she'd spent the last school year with. She liked her job; she did. But there were days she'd come home utterly exhausted and wonder how on earth she would manage her mother, who had become as much of a handful as all twenty-one of her second graders collectively. "Mom goes to adult daycare while I'm at work. I was fortunate enough to find one just minutes away from my job. I can dash over there if there are any problems, or just to have lunch with her when I'm not on cafeteria duty."

They were nearing Hazel's house now, and Penny felt bad that the conversation was ending on such a serious note. "I'm lucky," she told him. "I have never doubted my mother's love for me, and that makes taking care of her now in the state she's in a whole lot easier. I've heard stories that are so much harder than mine. And she worked most of her adult life, so although things are tight, her basic needs are met by her retirement and social security. Sure, it would be nice if we could afford for me to be her full-time caretaker, but my job is necessary, at least for now. Things may change as she gets worse; I know that. Right now, she's mostly combative only with me. But if she causes trouble at the daycare, she won't be allowed to attend, and that will bring a new set of challenges." She toyed with the hem of her skirt, then added, "But she's my mother, Ward. And we'll face each challenge as it comes. That's what family does, right?"

Ward nodded slowly, his brows furrowed in contemplation as he processed all that she'd told him. When he didn't say anything, she smiled and reached over to poke him in the shoulder.

"My mom is the one who makes me come here every summer. She knew what was coming, and before she pretty much forgot who I am, she had my aunt help her set these summers up so that I would have this time to find my footing again. And do you know why she did that?"

"Why?" he asked, one side of his mouth quirking up, almost like he knew she was trying to lighten the mood.

"Because she loves me. Because I'm so doggone loveable, Ward St. James." She bobbed her head sassily. "I mean, come on. Look at this face. What's not to love?"

When he glanced her way, she crossed her eyes, wrinkled her nose, and bared her teeth at him.

Ward reached over and took her hand, holding it gently in his, like it was something fragile. Penny's face went slack, and a tingle of sensation shot up her arm straight to her heart. "What's not to love, indeed?" Then he let go and turned into Hazel's driveway. He didn't shut off the van, but instead, sat there looking at her for a long moment before he finally spoke. "Hazel said you were something else. She was right."

How was she supposed to respond to that? Her go-to reaction was to make light of it, but when she opened her mouth to do so, he spoke first.

"You're my hero, Penelope Anderson."

She felt the flush rush up her body from the tips of her toes to the roots of her hair. "I'm no hero," she contradicted. "I'm—"

"Just say 'thank you, Ward'" he said, touching the back of her hand where it rested on her thigh. "You're not going to change my opinion of you now, no matter what you say."

Penny shrugged one shoulder. "I changed your opinion of me once already today. Who's to say I can't do it again? You didn't like me, remember?"

Ward grunted and shook his head. "No. You didn't like me. And I couldn't figure out why. I mean, look at this face. What's not to love?" He made an equally goofy expression at her, and that giggle she'd been keeping at bay broke free.

"What's not to love, indeed?" she chortled, echoing him. "And now, I've got to get inside and get cooking. There's nothing that ruins a chicken curry faster than raw chicken." She reached for her door.

"Hold up. Let me get it." Ward turned off the engine and climbed out of the van. He was around to her side by the time she had her seatbelt off. He opened her door, and after helping her clamber to the ground, he walked with her up to the front porch. They'd made it up to the top step before either of them noticed Hazel sitting on the swing with Murtagh.

"Hello, you two," she greeted them warmly, her eyes sparkling with mischief. "And how was your day?"

12
Ward

By the time Ward returned to the guesthouse, having showered, shaved, and with his exuberant parents in tow, the aroma that wafted out the front door to greet them had all three of them smiling with anticipation.

"My goodness, that smells wonderful," his mother murmured as Ward held the door open for both her and his father. He'd knocked, and Hazel had hollered for them to come in.

"We're in the kitchen." Penny poked her head into the parlor as they came through and beckoned for them to follow her. "We were hoping to eat out on the porch, but the bugs are out in force tonight, and it's a little too warm outside for this meal. I hope you like a little spice in your life." She pointed at Ward. "I know you do."

He cocked his head at her, ignoring the enormous grin on his mother's face as she looked from Ward to Penny and then back again. "And how do you know that?"

She turned to head back the way she'd come, but over her shoulder, she said, "I saw you douse your sandwich with that stuff today, Mr. St. James. Your nose hairs were practically on fire."

His father guffawed, and they dutifully followed her into the dining room, where the table was already set and waiting for them. "We all like a little zip in our food, don't we, love," Ted said, ushering his wife into the room ahead of him.

"Yes, indeed," Rachel said. "And Penny, since you wouldn't let us contribute to the meal, I brought this for you." She handed Penny a bottle of sparkling Italian lemonade. "This is one of Ward's favorites. He thought you might like it, too."

Penny hugged Rachel and then the bottle. "Ward, you have great taste. This is one of my favorites, too."

"Really? Isn't that lovely!" Rachel cooed. "Well, it's best served chilled already and poured over ice. Maybe add a fresh basil or mint sprig to each glass."

"I told you, Sweet Pea," Hazel said, coming in from the kitchen. "One more thing you two have in common."

"You should put it in the fridge now," Rachel suggested. "Then maybe later this evening when it's cooled off a bit, and after all us oldies tuck in for the night, you two can share a glass out under the stars. They're supposed to be beautiful tonight, right, love?"

Ward looked from his mother to Hazel and then at Penny. "Well, that escalated quickly," he said, not bothering to pretend he didn't see what was going on. "Prepare yourself for an arranged marriage, Penny. Apparently, that lemonade was the bride price."

The food was delicious, the flavors a complex blend of savory and sweet, the chicken pieces so tender, they practically fell off the fork. The conversation was just as engaging. Ward sat back in his chair and watched as his parents conversed with Penny and Hazel. Even with the odd number of people around the table, Ward didn't feel that nagging sense of not belonging. Hazel was good at making everyone feel welcome; that was why she'd been such a great hostess over the years. Why the same people, like Penny, came back time and time again.

But Ward knew that there was another reason he felt so at ease, one he didn't want to put into words. It didn't make it any less true, though. Even as he tried to push the thought away, he could see this same gathering of people sitting around this table again and again, sharing meal and meal. And he didn't, even for a moment, have the disquieting desire to flee.

He'd shared many a meal with his parents and Hazel before. The only difference tonight was the presence of Miss Penelope Anderson.

Sweet Pea, as Hazel called her.

It suited her, he thought. She was like a delicate, colorful flower, all dainty and fluttery. She'd changed into a pair of skinny black jeans and a tomato red shirt with a wide ruffle around the top that kept slipping off one shoulder. She wore no shoes, and he'd noticed that her toenails matched her shirt. It made him smile every time he thought about it.

But sweet peas were stronger than they looked, his mother had once told him, pointing at a trellis of them growing up the side of the house. Tenacious. Clinging to life, climbing, stretching, reaching skyward just to feel the sunlight on their faces. If a sweet pea's needs were well tended, they'd bloom from spring to fall.

Ward had a feeling that Penny's summers here in Autumn Lake were her mother's way of tending to her daughter's needs.

It hadn't escaped his awareness, either, that she sat across the table from him, the seat opposite him not empty tonight. And because she did, he could watch her without being rude.

She was such a tiny thing. He studied the way her hands moved, the lift of her pale shoulder as she tugged her shirt back into place. How did she manage to care for a combative adult? Maybe her mother was just as petite as Penny, but that didn't make it any less of a concern. How did she manage on her own? It sounded like she had some support from her aunt—was there an uncle? He couldn't remember her saying.

It forced him to take a look at his own life through new lenses, and he wasn't so sure he liked what he saw in himself. Sure, he'd had his parents' blessing when he left Autumn Lake to seek his fortunes, but he'd run from something good, hoping to find something even better, and now, he'd spent the better part of a year feeling sorry for himself because he was inconvenienced by his mother and father's temporary need of his help. An inconvenience. In the grand scheme of things, that's all it was.

Penny lived a truly inconvenienced life. And she thought she was lucky.

She turned from the exchange she'd been having with his mother and caught him staring at her. So much for not being rude. She smiled tentatively, tucked one side of her shiny blonde hair behind her ear, then dropped her gaze to the empty plate in front of her.

He hadn't meant to embarrass her, and in an attempt to make things less awkward, he said, "This was amazing, Penny."

"Thank you." She still seemed to have trouble meeting his gaze again, but her smile was genuine as she pushed back her chair and rose. "What about dessert?" She began gathering dishes, and when the rest of them started to join her, she raised both hands and commanded, "Sit. Please," she added, her tone softening. "I insist."

Hazel looked like she wanted to argue, so Ward braved Penny's wrath by insisting on joining her. "I've been raised right, Miss Penny. I'll help with the dishes, and the two of us can make quick work of this." He winked at Hazel, who nodded and winked back, her expression a little smug and a whole lot satisfied.

In the kitchen, Penny rinsed dishes while Ward stacked them in the dishwasher. "I can remember back when Hazel didn't have a dishwasher," he told her. "I knew that because she often had us over for meals—and vice versa—and we all just pitched in on cleanup as if it were an extension of the meal."

Penny nodded thoughtfully. "I've always liked the cleanup part; after supper, particularly," she acknowledged. "I suppose it's a cathartic way to end an evening, especially when things get hard at mealtime. With Mom," she added. "Sometimes they do."

"I can imagine."

"But even before the wretched disease, it was just something we did together. We cooked, we enjoyed the food we'd made, then we readied our kitchen for the next time. It wasn't just cleaning, you know? It was preparation for another yummy meal. At least, that's how I see it."

"Well, you've got good eyesight then, Miss Anderson." *This woman.* Her perspective on life was remarkably untainted for someone who dealt with so much on a regular basis. He could hear his parents and Hazel conversing quietly in the other room, but the tone of their banter was lighthearted and happy. It was the same way the women at Juno's had sounded after their get-together that afternoon. Penny seemed to have that effect on everyone she came in contact with.

"Well, let's see about your eyesight, shall we?" She opened the fridge and pulled out what Ward hoped was one of Hazel's homemade lemon meringue pies. The white, fluffy topping had golden tips, and he had to fight the urge to reach over and stick his finger in it. "Take a look at this divine work of art."

His jaw muscles clenched in anticipation of the sweet-tart filling, and he held out his hands to take it from her. "Wow. I'm drooling."

"Right? Hazel made it this afternoon while I was gone, so it's had the perfect amount of time to chill. My mouth is watering so hard right now." She smacked her lips together and placed the chilled glass pie dish in his hands, but she paused before letting go of it, looking up at him, her face aglow with what he thought might be happiness. Had he put that light in her eyes? Or did she always sparkle?

She stood so close he could smell the perfume she wore. His fingers brushed hers, and for a moment, he let his gaze fall to her shapely lips. Dangerous. Very dangerous.

"Don't drop that," she warned. "It's more precious than gold."

"I wouldn't dare." His voice came out lower than he'd expected, a little husky, and she must have caught the change in it, too. She stepped back, brushed her hands together, and turned to gather up the stack of dessert plates and forks.

"I'll come back for the coffee," she said as she bustled out ahead of him.

They didn't sit out under the stars at the end of the night, after all. Ward had noticed his mother was flagging by the time they'd finished their pie, and his father's attention was growing more and more focused on her, too.

He'd considered taking them home, and then coming back, but it was already after nine, and he didn't want to jinx the direction things were moving in with Penny. *Best to call it a night while things are good,* he'd told himself.

So he loaded his parents into the little golf cart he'd brought them over in. Then, while Rachel and Ted gushed with Hazel over how lovely the night had been, Ward moved back to stand beside Penny, because he wasn't about to just let things end with tonight, not now that they had ventured into a new beginning. "Tomorrow's Saturday," he stated. "Do you have plans?"

"I have books. Therefore, I have plans."

"Mmm. Sexy," he said, wiggling his eyebrows. She made a perplexed, sorta scandalized face that told him she didn't understand the reference. "What Claire said. Reading is sexy, remember?" He grinned and shoved his hands in his pockets so he wouldn't be tempted to touch her, then he nudged her arm with his elbow. "I'm not hitting on you in front of my parents."

Except that he was, wasn't he?

"Ha. You're a little late to the party to be hitting on me. Remember? We're practically married now." She crossed her arms and bumped him right back.

"That's right. How could I have forgotten? So does that mean you'll have some time for your fiancé tomorrow?"

When she hesitated, he chuckled softly. "You can say 'no', Penny. I won't take it personally; I promise." Then he took a step back and gave her a teasing side-eye. "Or should I take it personally?"

"Of course not," she hurried to respond. "I—I'd like to spend time with you. I just had to—" She waved a hand around in the air, then tucked it back against her side again. "I'm not good with spontaneous. Even when I'm on vacation. I mean, I know I kinda spontaneously invited you all to dinner tonight, but I was already planning on cooking. And honestly," she added, one side of her mouth hitching up in a sheepish expression. "That was a big deal to me. For me to be so spontaneous, I mean. Not the cooking. I liked that. I don't get to cook like that very often. You know, since it's just Mom and me, and she likes super basic stuff like grilled cheese and Campbell's—oh, geez. I'm rambling." She dropped her gaze, causing her hair to fall forward, almost like she was intentionally ducking behind it.

Ward was glad his hands were still in his pockets. Otherwise, he might have done something stupid, like tuck her hair back so he could see her face. He really wanted to see her face. "I kinda like your rambling," he said instead.

"Well, that's good, because it happens more often than I'd like." She peeked up at him, her nose scrunched in embarrassment, and then asked, "Would you like to join us here for brunch? Hazel and I were going to have French toast and scrambled eggs and bacon. Around ten?"

He nodded slowly. That wasn't exactly what he'd been hoping for, but if that's what she was offering, he'd take it. "Sure. What can I bring?"

"Did I hear you right? You're coming for breakfast?" Hazel asked as she sidled up to Penny's other side, obviously having overheard that much. His dad was fussing over his mother in the backseat of the golf cart, but she was watching their exchange with curious eyes. There would be questions tonight; he was certain.

Hazel looped her arm into Penny's, and to Ward, she said, "If you can weasel some out of her, some of your mother's blackberry syrup would be just the thing for our fancy French toast."

"I'll weasel away," Ward promised. He said his goodbyes and got behind the wheel of the cart.

"What a precious girl," his mother said from the backseat, her hand resting lightly on his shoulder. They hadn't even made it to the end of Hazel's driveway. "How did you two meet again?"

An hour later, Ward slipped outside to the front porch, where he spent most of his evenings after his parents had gone to bed. Across the inlet, Hazel's outside light was on, but no one, human or canine, occupied any of the seats.

He pulled his phone from his back pocket. It was two hours earlier in Southern California, and with it not quite ten o'clock in Autumn Lake, it wasn't too late to put in a call to Johnny.

"Ward! My man!" Johnny's gregarious greeting rang down the line, but Ward was prepared for it. He'd learned the hard way never to have a phone pressed to his ear when calling Johnny, and he already had him on speaker with the volume turned down so as not to disturb his parents. "How's life in the Midwest treating you?"

Johnny was a charmer. A sweet talker, but in the best of ways. He was open and friendly with everyone, and he made folks feel completely at ease within moments of meeting him. Something Ward, on the other hand, struggled with. It was why they made such a good team.

They talked for several minutes about how things were going for Blue Waters. Johnny assured him that all was well, the crew was keeping busy, the charter schedule was packed, and the finances were sitting pretty. Ward had access to it all online, but it made him feel a little more involved when they spoke in person. Johnny seemed to understand that, and Ward appreciated his friend all the more for it.

"Have you heard from Rochelle lately?" Johnny asked when the conversation turned to shooting the breeze about more personal things. "She came by here asking about you. When you'd be back, that kind of thing."

Ward frowned. He hadn't heard from Rochelle since the night she'd apparently broken up with him. That was almost three months ago now. "I haven't heard from Ro. Pretty sure she's seeing someone else." Might as well get straight to the point. He didn't need her showing up at Blue Waters and disrupting their workday by bugging Johnny or the other crew members about personal stuff.

Johnny hesitated on the other of the line. "Did she tell you that?" he finally asked.

Ward's brows drew together even more. "In so many words, yes. She has my number, Johnny. You tell her to call me if she has questions about me."

"I'm not going to chase the woman off," Johnny said, his voice quiet, concerned. "I kinda got the feeling she was here looking for a little hope. Maybe you should call her. Check in on her."

Ward sighed long and loud. Why now? Had this been a couple of months ago, he would have ended this call and gotten on the line with her in a heartbeat. But it had been three months. Three months since they'd communicated anything to each other. Oh, he'd emailed her shortly after their conversation, apologizing for not making her a priority, and she'd responded to it with a gentle, one-sentence reply, thanking him for taking the time to write. He'd even texted her a few times in the weeks after, and the most he got in return was a smiley face or a thumbs-up emoji. Not even a heart. She'd all but cut him off.

Oh, he'd planned to look her up when he got back to Laguna, but not to try to salvage things. She'd made it clear that they were over. No, he just felt the responsibility of letting things slip away, and he wanted to do right by her and apologize to her face. He wanted to see for himself that she was okay, even though part of him already knew that she was doing just fine out there in her beach town where everyone loved her.

"I'll give her a call tomorrow, Johnny. You shouldn't have to deal with this."

"It's all good," Johnny insisted. "It was nice to see her pretty face around here again. We all miss you both, man."

Ward hung up with Johnny and sank back into the Adirondack chair he always sat in when he was out there. The stars were beautiful tonight, just as his mother had predicted, and he wholeheartedly wished he was sitting across the inlet on Hazel's porch right now, listening to the sparkly Miss Penny talk about her life.

"Her hard life," he muttered, wishing he could do something—anything—to make things easier for her.

He groaned softly and closed his eyes. He'd been looking forward to the morning when he'd get to see Penny again, but now, he'd have the phone call to Rochelle hanging over his head all day. If he didn't reach out to her tonight, he'd have to wait until he was finished with Penny to call her. He couldn't do it before brunch; the time difference would make it far too early for Rochelle to even be coherent.

"Get it over with," he told himself, and he picked up his phone. Rochelle was still #2 on his speed dial, right after his mom. He needed to change that.

Across the inlet, the upstairs bedroom light in Hazel's guesthouse came on. He knew it was Penny; Hazel's quarters were on the main floor on the other side of the house. He couldn't help feeling a little uncomfortable sitting in the dark, staring up at her bedroom window, especially while talking to his ex-girlfriend, so he stood and headed down the porch steps toward the dock that stretched out over the water. There were two more Adirondacks out at the end of it, and he dropped into one, only to find himself staring at all the lights of the Carpe Diem resort on the other side of the lake.

Rochelle didn't answer her phone, and although a big part of him was admittedly relieved, the sound of her voice disconcerted him. She'd changed her greeting, and she sounded... different somehow. Harder. Edgier.

He made a derisive sound in the back of his throat. "Really, Ward? You can tell that by her voicemail greeting?" He shoved his phone in his back pocket and glowered at the lights of the resort across the lake. The monstrosity was mirrored in the lake, making it feel twice as overbearing. But his attention didn't linger there.

In fact, he was having a hard time focusing on Rochelle Trebler, as well. A certain petite blonde kept intruding on his thoughts.

He turned away from the grandeur of the North Shore and headed back up the short pier toward the house. His gaze drifted back to Hazel's place, but the light on the second floor had gone out. "Sleep well, Miss Penny," he murmured.

Maybe it wasn't Rochelle who was different. Maybe it was him. Could it be that he was learning to see and hear differently, and that he was only now able to pick up on things he'd been missing—or ignoring? There must have been signs of his ex-girlfriend's discontent, signs he'd have noticed if he'd been paying attention.

"Maybe you need to start paying more attention to what's going on around you," he said aloud as he slowly mounted the steps to his childhood home.

He glanced over his shoulder one last time just as Hazel's front door opened, and she and the three dogs bustled outside. The little quartet made their way to Hazel's favorite porch swing and the woman dropped into it, setting the thing into motion. It took a few moments of comedic jockeying for position, but all three dogs managed to scramble up onto the swing with her.

Ward opened his front door, reached around to hit the light switch, and flipped it on and off three times. Hazel lifted a hand in acknowledgment.

13
Penny

PENNY LAY IN BED reliving the day in her mind. It had certainly ended so much better than it had started. She and the girls—The Garden Variety Lovers Club—had a plan of action. Hazel had given her blessing on them meeting in the back garden after Penny insisted that she'd clear a spot for them, and that Hazel wasn't to lift a finger to help. She and Ward hadn't just formed a truce, they'd broken through walls and were now well on their way to being friends. Dinner with his family had been delightful.

Then, she'd finished the third Destiny Baudelaire downstairs, curled up in an armchair in the parlor, with Hazel dozing on the sofa nearby, her dogs tucked in around her.

The icing on the cake was that Ward had asked if they could spend time together tomorrow.

She'd wanted to say 'yes' before the words were completely out of his mouth, but the sudden rush of emotions at his request had scared her. She wasn't looking for a relationship, not right now. Not with Mom so out of control. So much could change on a dime in her world, and she simply didn't have the wherewithal to invest in a romantic relationship, especially since she was so out of practice where men were concerned.

The last guy she'd dated semi-seriously hadn't lasted long after she'd finally brought him home to meet her mother. Evidently, Lance Crandall hadn't been too keen on the two-for-one package she was a part of. It hadn't helped that Judy had not been in a very good mood and had paced the room, muttering under breath, the whole time he was there. When he'd left that night, her mother had yelled at him through her bedroom window, and although it hadn't made a whole lot of sense, her message had been clear. Judy hadn't liked Lance any more than Lance had liked Judy.

The doctors had explained that early onset Alzheimer's typically progressed much faster than late onset, but that Judy could live for many years, depending on how the disease progressed. It was coming on a decade since she'd gotten her official diagnosis, and as far as Penny could tell, her mother still had a lot of life left in her.

Penny couldn't put that kind of burden on anyone else.

She couldn't put the burden of a third person in their little world on her mother, either.

But if Ward was interested in being her friend, someone she could spend time with, someone she actually enjoyed spending time with, then she'd be happy to have him in her life. Now she just had to make sure he understood that.

"It shouldn't be a problem," she whispered to herself. "He's not staying, either. Neither one of us can afford to get involved."

Penny had been so relieved when he'd agreed to come to brunch in the morning, that he hadn't been put off by her invitation to spend time with both her and Hazel. She'd have to set some boundaries up front, at least for her sake, but having Hazel at the table with them felt very casual and non-pressuring.

She'd refused to allow herself to start the last book in Destiny's series because she wanted to get a good night's sleep. She knew if she started it, she'd be up to the wee hours. But the events of the day had worn her out, and she found she was actually sleepy and more than ready to call it a day. She opened the curtains after turning off her light so she could see the diamond-studded velvet sky out her window. "I wonder if he's looking at the stars tonight, too?"

Then she sighed and shook her head at her far too romantic musings for someone who wasn't interested in romance. "Go to sleep, you ooey gooey butter bar."

Just as she started to back away from the window, Ward's porch light flickered on and off three times. Penny lifted her hand in acknowledgment, even though she knew he couldn't see her.

Saturday morning, Penny awoke with a bubble of excitement in her chest. Her eyes sprang open just after eight, the morning sunlight streaming through her open window. She didn't mind one bit. Technically, eight o'clock was still sleeping in for her, and besides, today was stacking up to be one full of possibilities.

Last night, after the St. James family had gone home, she and Hazel had settled into the front parlor for a second—tiny, of course—slice of lemon meringue pie and a little end of the day reading. Hazel had finally picked up the latest Reese Witherspoon's Book Club book and was devouring it as fast as Penny was plowing through her Destiny Baudelaire novel. But before diving into their respective reads, Hazel had casually mentioned that she'd be busy all afternoon, and Penny should find a way to keep herself busy. "I might not even be back in time for supper, so maybe you and that lovely St. James boy can grab a meal together somewhere. Or here, if you'd rather. My kitchen is your kitchen; you know that, dear."

Penny had just rolled her eyes. "You are relentless, Hazel Poleman."

"I've been told it's one of my finest attributes," the older woman had shot back. "Now, not to be rude, but I've been dying to get back to this delicious novel. There's all the good stuff in this one—mischief, mayhem, and murrrrrderrrrrr." She drew out the last word in a creepy, scratchy, old-lady voice that had Penny chortling in delight.

She decided to simply let the day play out the way it would. If, after brunch, Ward wanted to spend even more time with her, she'd be open to it. If not, she had plenty to keep her busy in the gardens, now that she had new motivation and the support of her friends. And of course, she could read, although she wasn't sure she was ready to jump into the last book in the series so soon. It would mean the end of the end, and even though she had no doubt it would culminate in the happiest of happy endings, just the thought of saying that final goodbye to Ewan Hunter and Wendy Brandt and all their friends had her almost tearing up.

Penny found Hazel already downstairs in the kitchen, sitting in the little breakfast nook that looked out over the backyard. It had once been such a lovely scene with the colorful gardens, but the expression on Hazel's face as she studied the bedraggled state of things validated Penny's determination to do what she could to set things right out there. It might not take care of things long-term, but maybe part of their plan could be downsizing the gardens instead of just abandoning them.

"Good morning, Hazel," Penny said, not wanting to startle the woman, who seemed lost in thought, her hands clasped around a steaming cup of coffee on the table in front of her.

"Oh, Sweet Pea, come." She lifted a hand and gestured toward the bench opposite her. "Grab yourself a cup of coffee and come sit with me. It's a bit of a mess out there, but the birds and squirrels don't seem to mind, and they're quite entertaining this morning."

Penny did as she was told, and sure enough, the garden was alive with activity. Only a few yards beyond the window, hanging from the trunk of a sprawling redbud tree, was a little wooden birdhouse painted to match the guesthouse. A wren was darting in and out of it with scraggly bits and pieces of nesting material.

"That's her second nest this year," Hazel told her, pointing at the busy bird. "And if I'm not mistaken, this is her third, maybe fourth year using that little birdhouse. I clean it out every fall so it's ready for her return in the spring."

The coffee was strong and dark this morning, and Penny had doctored it up with plenty of heavy cream and maple syrup. She took a slow, careful sip as she studied the woman across from her. Hazel looked well-rested today, she thought, but Penny still sensed an underlying worry in the way she sat, her shoulders a little hunched, her hands toying nonstop with the handle of her mug.

Now seemed the perfect opportunity to speak, and before she lost her courage, Penny reached across the table and rested her hand on Hazel's forearm. "I don't mean to be nosy, but is everything all right with you, Hazel?"

Hazel turned a warm smile on her. "I'm fine, dear. I'm just feeling my age; that's all. I'm sorry if I've worried you." She jutted her chin toward the garden and directed Penny's gaze back outside. "I was just thinking about how God can take even the most discouraging aspects of our lives—our weaknesses, our shortcomings, even our failures—and turn them into places where life can thrive. I may not have planted squirrels and rabbits," she said with a soft chuckle. "But they're loving it out there, all safe in the cover of the overgrowth. I also know that beneath those weeds and brambles, the things I did plant are just waiting for me to clear the way for them to return to their full glory. The hydrangeas are beautiful this year." She pointed toward several groupings of the plants with their heart-shaped leaves that were, indeed, loaded with raspberry pink, dusky blue, and even some pure white puff balls of lacy blossoms. "I can see it the way it should be, Sweet Pea," Hazel said rather wistfully. "It's lovely in my mind's eye."

Penny took a sip of her coffee and swallowed the lump that had formed in the back of her throat as she listened to Hazel. She was hesitant to say anything, though, not wanting to sound placating or insensitive.

"By the way, I have guests scheduled to arrive the first week in August." The change in subject caught Penny off guard, but she straightened in her seat and set her mug down.

"That's wonderful. Is there anything I can do to help you get ready for them?" It was still almost three weeks away, but Penny thought it might be the perfect excuse for the Garden Variety Lovers Club to step in and help, too. She pointed out the window. "Can I tackle the garden?"

"Tackle is right, honey. I'm not so sure that's on my list of things to do right now. I won't stop you from going out there, but I don't want you to feel obligated to take on putting things to right for me."

Penny nodded. "I understand. But you know me. I'm a doer. The only time I can sit still is when I've got a book in my hands."

Ward showed up half an hour early. "I'm early. I know. But I came bearing gifts." He held out a basket from his mother like a peace offering. In it was not one, but two stoppered bottles of blackberry syrup, a half-dozen fluffy, flakey breakfast biscuits, and a pint jar of jam a color that Penny had never seen before.

"You are welcome any time of the day if you come bearing gifts like these, young man," Hazel exclaimed, taking the basket from him. She held up the jar of jam toward Penny. "Do you know what this is, Sweet Pea?"

Penny sent Ward a questioning look, but he only grinned back at her, leaving her guessing.

"This, my darling girl, is Rachel St. James' award-winning, world famous, sweet tomato jam. You have never tasted anything quite like it, and once you do, you will hold all other jams to a new standard."

"My goodness," Penny exclaimed, brows lifted. "World famous?"

"Not quite *world* famous," Ward said. "But Autumn Lake famous, for sure."

"And since this town *is* our world," Hazel insisted. "Then world famous, this jam most certainly is. You must try some immediately." She unwrapped the biscuits, plopped one on a plate, slathered it with the jam, and handed the dish to Penny. "The biscuits are still warm, too."

Tomato jam? Could it really be that amazing? Penny liked tomatoes well enough, but as a savory treat, preferably with bacon and lettuce on crusty peasant bread. But Hazel and Ward both stared at her, waiting for her to taste the goods.

She smiled bravely, lifted the biscuit to her nose and sniffed it, still not sure about it.

"Don't be a chicken," Hazel prodded. "Take a big bite. Taste the tomato." She waved her hands at Penny like she was trying to put her into a trance. "You'll never be the same again."

"She's right," Ward said, his eyes never leaving Penny's face. "I know many an Autumn Laker who would wrestle you to the ground for what you have in your hand right now." His grin turned a little flirty, making Penny's cheeks grow warm as the image of wrestling with Ward popped into her head.

She blinked rapidly to clear her mind and took a huge bite of the biscuit.

The bread, itself, was to die for. A golden flakey outer layer, a soft chewy cloud on the inside, and when the jam hit her tastebuds, Penny closed her eyes and let out a moan that sounded borderline inappropriate.

"It's good, isn't it?"

Hazel's enthusiasm wasn't unwarranted. It was really, *really* good. The acidic tartness of vine-ripened tomatoes sweetened by a hint of caramel—did she use brown sugar instead of white? It wasn't syrupy sweet the way other jams were. Penny wouldn't stir it into ice cream or spread it on her waffles, although she imagined some people would be just fine doing so. But the robust flavor of it spread over her tongue, lingering in her mouth, even after she swallowed, leaving in its wake a craving to taste it again.

"You could put this on a grilled cheese or a BLT, couldn't you?" she asked between bites. "Or on crepes with cream cheese… mmmm." She was gushing, she knew, but this was a brand-new experience for her, and Penny wanted to savor it. "I mean, it's delicious by itself like this, too."

"I eat it by the spoonful when no one is looking," Hazel quipped. She shook a finger at Penny. "But don't be getting any ideas. I'll be monitoring this jar now that I know that you know that it's here."

Ward joined in with putting together the rest of their brunch. The biscuits and jam had only served to whet their appetites, and by the time they sat down to their meal, they were more than ready to dig in. They'd opted to eat outside that morning, the sprawling branches of a hedge maple cast extra hours of shade over the northeast corner of the house, which included that end of the porch.

With the lazy dogs lounging close by, just in case little treats happened to fall like manna from heaven, the conversation around the table meandered comfortably from one topic to another. But Penny could tell they were all being very intentional about the things they weren't discussing. Such as Ward's eminent return to California, Penny's looming August departure, and the fact that Hazel's guesthouse remained empty, even though the summer was almost half over.

Finally, Hazel patted the tabletop with both hands. "Well, children. What a lovely way to spend a Saturday morning; with two of my most favorite people in the world. But I have a full afternoon ahead of me, so I'd best be getting on with things."

"Of course," Penny said, pushing to her feet and holding out a hand toward her hostess. "Please, Hazel. We can clean up. You go do what you need to do."

Ward got up, too, and hurried around the table to pull Hazel's wrought iron chair back for her, making Penny smile appreciatively at him. He was such a gentleman. If she ever got the chance when it wouldn't be awkward, she'd have to thank Rachel and Ted for teaching him such respect. It wasn't a lost art; Penny knew many men who were deferential toward women. But Ward was proving her first impression of him wrong every time she was around him, and it didn't feel disingenuous. It seemed to her that perhaps, indeed, he'd been having a rough day the first time they'd run into each other.

Penny didn't miss the gleam in Hazel's eye as she readily agreed to leave them on their own to take care of the aftermath of their feast. "There are two slices of lemon pie left in the fridge, just in case you need a little sustenance this afternoon. Not sure what you two have planned, but if you're around the guesthouse, you're welcome to it. To anything you can find, for that matter."

"We got it, Hazel." Penny gave her the stink eye, but the woman ignored the look and headed inside, Murtagh and Delilah following close on her heels, Jimbo following close on Delilah's heels.

She and Ward made quick work of the cleanup, and when the last of the dishes was dried and put away, the counters wiped down, and the jars of goodness from Rachel tucked carefully into a shelf of the refrigerator door, Penny was fully prepared for Ward to say his goodbyes.

Instead, he leaned against the counter, bracing his hands on either side of his hips, and cocked his head at her. "So? What's next on the agenda? Feel like getting out on the water?"

Penny's eyebrows shot up as a surge of unexpected excitement coursed through her. "Out on the water? What does that mean?"

Ward eyed her suspiciously. "Don't tell me you're afraid of the water, Miss Penelope Anderson."

"No!" she declared, a little more vehemently than she'd intended. "Not at all. I love it. I just wanted clarification. Hazel still has her old John boat out in the barn. We can probably use that." She broke off, wondering if she wasn't completely off base. For one, there might be a good reason the boat wasn't out on the water: a leak, a broken motor, or just Hazel not wanting to hassle with it. For two, if anyone had a boat fit for the water, surely it was a boat repairman's son. And for three, maybe Ward hadn't meant 'on' the water in a literal sense at all. Maybe he was asking if she wanted to go for a swim.

"I had something else in mind," Ward said, with a grin that had Penny planting her hands on her hips.

"You're scaring me." She gave him the same stink eye she'd given Hazel earlier. "And I don't scare easy."

"Good to know," Ward said, nodding slowly. "How about you meet me at the end of Hazel's dock in half an hour?"

"Hmmm." He couldn't be planning anything too crazy right out there in the open, right? "Do I need to change?" She wore a pair of cutoff jeans shorts and a cap-sleeved t-shirt the color of apricots, and she hoped he wasn't going to suggest a bathing suit. She wasn't quite ready to break out the shiny teal one-piece she'd bought to wear to the YMCA pool when Mom was still able to exercise. It was identical to the one her mother wore, matching intentionally so Judy could keep track of her in the water. She was sure Ward would understand the matronly suit, but that didn't change the fact that it was just plain unflattering on anyone, including Judy. "I have quick-dry water shoes, too." She'd been a convert her first summer at the lake when her regular sneakers never seemed to get completely dry after their first soaking.

"Perfect. If you don't mind a little water, what you're wearing is fine. Just add sunscreen. You'll thank me." Well, that didn't clarify much, but it didn't sound like they were going swimming. At least not intentionally. Ward straightened the dishtowel he'd been using where it hung on the oven door. "We good here? Half an hour."

"Half an hour," she repeated, still a little uncertain. But she reminded herself that she'd planned to let the day take her where it would, and she was on for the ride.

And ride, she did.

Twenty-eight minutes later, Penny heard the hum of a motor kick on not too far away, and she turned to see Ward easing a jet ski out of the boat house at the end of the St. James' dock. By the time he pulled up in front of her, she was practically giddy with delight, bouncing up and down on her heels. She actually clapped when he held out a life vest toward her.

"Put this thing on and climb aboard," he said, grinning up at her. She couldn't see his eyes clearly behind the sunglasses he'd put on, but at the edges of the frames, she saw laugh lines.

When she'd buckled the straps and tightened them to fit snugly around her petite frame, she took his proffered hand and stepped carefully off the dock and onto the back of his watercraft. The seat was already a little damp, but in her excitement, she hardly noticed, and she certainly didn't care.

"All set?" Ward asked over his shoulder.

"All set."

"You're going to want to hold on," he said, giving her a flirty, crooked smile. "There's a handrail behind your seat that you can grab, or, since we're practically married, you can just put your arms around me. I won't bite. I promise."

"Right. Yes." The words came out a little breathless. She reached back for the handrail and quickly decided that wasn't going to work for her. She slid her arms around his waist, careful not to cling too tightly.

"Ever done this before?" When she shook her head, he said, "Lean with me, not against me, okay? I may rise up off the seat a little on a turn, but I won't stand up completely, so you should be able to keep holding onto me. Or you can grab the handrail, too. I'll take it easy at first, but do you like speed?"

Penny pressed her lips together and nodded, afraid if she opened her mouth to speak, she'd squeal like a little girl. Was this really happening? She'd dreamed of this every summer she'd come to Autumn Lake, to fly over the water on a jet ski, to have her hair whipping around her face as the wind stole her breath, the rumble of the motor blocking out all other sounds except for her shrieks of exhilaration.

And now, here she was, settling onto the back of Ward St. James' watercraft, preparing to do just that. No wonder she couldn't find her voice.

"Then let's do this," Ward said, revving the motor a few times. He let the jet ski idle until they were several feet out into the water, then they started picking up speed.

The first of many sounds came flying out of her mouth, and Penny stopped caring what Ward might think of her.

14
Ward

WARD COULDN'T REMEMBER THE last time he'd had such a great Saturday. Or such a great day, period. His father had insisted on taking any repair calls that came in, so Ward had turned off his ringer for the first time in months.

He and Penny spent more than an hour out on the water, returning to shore wet and windblown, but almost euphoric. Had he known the woman had yearned for years to ride on a jet ski, he might have tried making amends with the offer of a ride, instead of buying her a cup of coffee, one that she still didn't know was from him. One day, he might tell her.

Penny had opted not to learn to drive the thing herself. "I just want to relax and enjoy this," she told him. "I don't want to be responsible in any way for what goes on out on the water, other than keeping myself from falling off."

He'd been happy to oblige her, and he'd gotten a jolt of endorphins every time she let out an exhilarated shriek behind him. He didn't even mind when she let them out a little too close to his ear; he knew the day would come when the thrill of the first ride would wear off, and he wanted her to remember this day, to remember that she'd experienced this with him.

He wanted her to remember him, no matter what the future held.

As he walked her up the path to the guesthouse, Ward started second-guessing himself. She'd already told him that she had a few things to do that afternoon, and the way she'd said it made it seem like they were things she wanted to do on her own. Did that mean she was ready for the day to end, altogether, though?

There was only one way to find out; he had to ask.

"So." Penny spoke before he did. She unlocked the front door but didn't open it. Instead, she turned around and leaned against it so she could look up at him. "I know I said I was busy this afternoon, and I am." She said it like she was trying to convince both of them that it was true. "But I was wondering if you'd like to come over for supper again tonight." She lifted her shoulders, reminding him of a little turtle on the verge of tucking her head inside her shell. "Of course, your parents are welcome to join us, too."

Ward nudged the tip of her shoe with his own. "Would you be upset if it was only me?"

"No." She was blushing. He could tell, even though her cheeks already glowed from the sun and wind. "If they can't come, that's fine. It's short notice. Again. I seem to do that to you a lot, don't I?"

"Well, what's on the menu?" he asked, teasing her the way he had last time, too.

She rolled her eyes. "Whatever *you* decide to bring, Big Man. Maybe this Little Lady here is too tired to cook."

"Oh, I see how it is." Ward crossed his arms over his chest and narrowed his eyes at her. "How about this? What if neither of us cooks? I could take you out to dinner somewhere."

Penny stiffened ever so slightly, but it was enough for him to notice. "Um, I don't know," she began. There went those shoulders again.

"You can say no, Penny. Remember?" He dipped his head so he could look her in the eye. "I don't want to do something that's going to make you feel uncomfortable."

"Right. Of course. I—I know that." Once again, she sounded like she didn't quite believe the words coming out of her mouth. "I'm kind of a homebody, Ward. I like people well enough, but this whole thing that I do each summer? It's..." She broke off and pursed her lips as if worried he might not understand. Finally, she said, "This is my Psalm 23 time. It's about being by still waters." She gestured one arm in a wide circle. "About restoring my soul. My spirit. Does that make sense?"

Ward was nodding before she asked. "And Saturday night out on the town—even one the size of Autumn Lake—doesn't quite fit the bill."

Penny let out a short, dry laugh. "Even the size of Autumn Lake."

Ward thought there might be a little more to it than that, but he didn't want to press her for details that she might not be ready to share with him. "I understand. Really, I do. So here's another option, one I think will work for both of us. What if I pick us up pizza? I'll make sure to bring plenty for Hazel, too, even if she doesn't show until later."

Penny's delighted smile made his pulse pick up, and he stepped back, almost like he'd been pushed. Gently, of course, but pushed, nonetheless. He lifted a hand to his chest and pressed the heel of his palm over his heart. When he saw her watching the gesture, he acted like there was something on his shirt, and he swept his hand over his shoulder, his fingers brushing against his sleeve. He hoped she hadn't seen right through the ruse.

"I can't think of anything better," Penny declared. "Although, I am going to go inside right now and make myself a piece of toast with tomato jam. Would you—would you like some, too?" She reached for the doorknob.

But Ward could tell the invitation hadn't come easy, so he put out a hand to stay her. "I'm wet. I'm going to head home, shower, and change my clothes, then I need to make a few phone calls." He grimaced reflexively. Just saying the words out loud was like summoning a dark cloud. But his conversation with Johnny the night before had revealed to him that in his prolonged absence, he'd let more than just his relationship with Rochelle get sidelined. He knew if he didn't take the bull by the horns and draw some lines in the sand, there was a possibility that he might be looking at a mutiny of sorts. From what he could tell, Blue Waters seemed to be operating just fine without him, and Johnny's casual goodbye had made it sound like Ward's delayed return wasn't a concern at all. "You go and enjoy your tomato jam sandwich. I'll tell Mom you're a fan. Maybe she'll throw another jar in with your bride price. You know, along with the lemonade from last night."

"The lemonade!" Penny exclaimed, reaching out to rest a hand on his forearm. "I totally forgot about that. We'll have it with our pizza tonight, okay?"

"Works for me."

When he climbed back on the jet ski, Ward paused, a little off balance, before he realized that he missed the feel of her on the seat behind him, the pressure of her arms around his waist, the length of her body against his back. "Go home, man. Take a cold shower," he muttered, then started up the engine and swung the craft wide as he motored across the inlet to his own dock.

Inside the house, his mother was resting, and he found his father working on a jigsaw puzzle in front of the television. The thousand-piece barnyard scene was almost complete. "Hey, Dad. What are you watching?"

"Oh, you know. One of those Hallmark movies your mom loves so much." He glanced up at Ward with an unabashed expression, then over at the television just as the attractive woman on the screen sat down on a park bench and began to weep quietly. Ted pointed at her. "The man she's falling for left on tour with his band, and she just saw a picture on some social media site of him with his arms around another girl."

"Really? Doesn't sound like someone worth crying over," Ward said, trying not to smile. His dad was kinda into it, from what he could tell.

"Oh, it's all a misunderstanding. It always is. The girl in the picture is going to turn out to be his cousin, or maybe his long-lost sister. But she won't believe him because she's been hurt before by a boyfriend who cheated on her, or her dad cheated on her mom, and then the hero will have to do some grand gesture to convince her that he loves her. He's a musician, so he'll probably find some public setting and play the song her wrote for her in front of all the people who are important to her." He cocked his head and studied the scene playing out. "In fact, see that little bandstand in the park behind her? I'll bet it happens right there. Probably during a strawberry festival or a summer music festival, or something like that."

Ward's brows rose; he couldn't help it. "Huh. Are you sure you're not watching this because you like it, too? Not just Mom?"

"Oh, I love these movies. I'm not ashamed to say so, either. They're predictable, sure, but they're comfortable that way. I always know that things are going to be okay, even when things feel hopeless." He paused, cleared his throat, and said, "Your mother and I started watching them together last year while she was sick."

Ward nodded, a band of emotion squeezing his chest.

"You should watch one with me," his father suggested. "They're all about people making mistakes and then fixing those mistakes. I learn a lot from them, Ward. Particularly about women."

"Hopefully, one woman in particular," Ward teased, flipping the words around.

His father picked up a puzzle piece and held it out to Ward. "Here. Find where this goes."

Ward stepped closer to take it. It was a corner piece, and there was only one still missing. "You're giving me the hard ones," he said with a curious smile. Was his father trying to make a point?

"It's not the piece that's easy or hard. It's finding where it goes that can be tough. But when you stop focusing on just the individual pieces and look at the bigger picture, it's a whole lot easier to see where things fit. And where they don't," he added.

Well. If there wasn't a deeper meaning in that, Ward would eat his shirt. But was his father referring to Ward's situation or his own?

Ted waited until Ward had pressed the piece into its spot before he spoke again. "If there's one thing I've learned above all else from these shows, it's that people need to communicate better." He chuckled and patted his heart. "But that's the condition of the human heart, isn't it? If we're not acting out of love, we're acting out of fear. Fear that we're not good enough to be loved. Fear that we're not 'the one' in another person's life." He made air quotes around the words, 'the one'. "Fear of rejection. Of embarrassment. Of being found out."

"You learned all of that from the Hallmark Channel, Dad?" Ward teased, trying to lighten the mood. Things were getting heavy, and Ward wasn't sure he wanted to go there right now.

"You may mock me, son, but let me tell you something. No man—or woman, for that matter—should ever stop learning about love. I'll take the Hallmark Channel over laser guns and torpedoes, any day."

"Even over football?" Ward asked, frowning in feigned shock.

Ted chuckled. "That's a tossup, I admit." He pointed at the empty chair across the card table from him. Mom must have been helping him with the puzzle earlier. "Sit. Enjoy the life lesson with me. Or we can turn it off, and you can tell me how your time with that lovely Miss Penny went today."

Ward shook his head. "Sorry, Dad. I'm soaked through. Besides, I've got a phone call or two to make back ho—" He broke off, the word 'home' catching on the way out. "To California," he amended, grimacing over the unsettled sensation in his gut that had started up last night when he couldn't reach Rochelle. He needed to deal with whatever was going on with the woman. He didn't like that she continued to be a presence at Blue Waters, even while he was away. Especially while he was away. It wasn't sitting well with him, and now with the afternoon free ahead of him, he couldn't just let it go unaddressed.

His father studied him for a moment, then nodded. "Sounds like a plan. We're having chili for supper tonight. Making it an earlier night so we can be up in plenty of time for church in the morning."

Ted left the statement there, but Ward heard the unasked question. *Will you be joining us?* He also knew his father was asking about both supper *and* church.

"Don't wait dinner for me. I'm having pizza with Penny... and Hazel over there tonight." Why he'd added Hazel's name like that, he couldn't quite understand. Maybe it was because of the way his father's face lit up when he said Penny's name. Ward didn't quite understand that, either. Why would his parents—or Hazel, for that matter—be so keen on him dating Penny? They all knew that he no longer called Autumn Lake home. And Penny never had.

Maybe that was why it bothered him so much. His parents knew he wasn't planning to stay, that he had his own life somewhere else. They knew he had a business that he'd built from the ground up, something he was immensely proud of. And yet, they all acted like it was expendable. Hazel included. Even his friends here in town, now that he thought about it. They all seemed to think he could just walk away from it all, move back home to the lake, and pick up where his good old dad left off.

At least Lysha Austin had offered him a real job with a real future.

"It'll probably be a late night, too, so don't count on me for church in the morning, either." It was the most brutal thing he could think of to say in that moment. His words hit their mark, too, as his father's shoulders drooped, almost like he'd gotten a puncture wound and all the air was slowly leaking out.

He worried the back of his neck, wishing he could take the flippant words back. Not just because of the effect they'd had on his father, either. If he knew Hazel, and he did, she'd be at church sitting only a few rows behind his parents. If he knew Penny, and he thought he was starting to, she'd be sitting right next to Hazel.

And he'd be home alone with his principles, stewing in regret.

THE PIZZA PLACE WAS packed when Ward pushed his way inside to place his order. He hadn't bothered calling it in, not on a Saturday night. He'd be lucky if they even picked up the phone during the dinner hour.

"Yo, Ward!" Alex sat against the wall near the pool tables, watching a match between a couple guys Ward had seen around town. He didn't remember their names, but then again, other than trips back for the holidays, he'd been gone for more than a decade. Just because he was local by birth didn't mean he knew everyone in Autumn Lake. Not anymore.

Ward hesitated for just a moment, then added a drink to his order and headed over to join Alex while he waited for his pizza.

"What's up?" Alex said, lifting his bottle to clink it against Ward's glass of tea.

"Picking up an order to go."

"Oh yeah? Heard you spent some time out on the lake with that shiny Penny today. Pizza for two?" Alex wiggled his brows at him, then took another long pull off his bottle. Ward was relieved to see that it was an off-brand soda and not alcohol.

"For three," he corrected, even though as far as he knew, Hazel wasn't home yet. He hadn't seen her car parked behind the house when he drove by on his way here. But he felt compelled to protect Penny, or maybe to protect himself, from the hazards of small town gossip, and by keeping Hazel in the mix, folks would have less fodder to chew on. "Six, if you count Hazel's dogs," he added, trying to make light of his defensive tone.

"Dude. You should see your face. You've been hit, man." Alex set his bottle aside and leaned forward over the small table, resting his weight on his forearms. "So what's keeping you from going for it with Miss Penny?"

"Going for it?" Ward scoffed, evading the real question his friend was asking. "How old are we, again, Alex?"

"Get your mind out of the gutter, bro. You gonna have yourself a summer romance, or what?" Alex amended with a capricious grin. "I saw the way you two were eyeing each other. Maybe she'll give you a reason to come back to the lake more often."

"You, too?" Ward asked dryly. "I'm not here for romance, okay? I'm here to help my parents, and then I'm going home. Back to California," he clarified, more for his benefit, it seemed, than for Alex's. Why was it starting to feel odd calling California home? He'd been here too long.

"I know, I know. You keep saying so." Alex held up his hands as if to deflect Ward's response. "Hey, I'm heading up a crew for Founder's Day. You in? I'm in charge of putting together the stage on the boardwalk."

Every October, Autumn Lake held its annual Founder's Day Festival, and although preparation for the event didn't start in earnest until September, Labor Day essentially kicked off the holiday spirit that would carry the town through until after the New Year. The Labor Day celebration was a bit like a teaser to the Founder's Day parade, but the townies never turned down an opportunity to gather as a community.

"When do you start the build?" Ward was certain he'd be back in California long before Founder's Day, but he'd be happy to pitch in on the prep while he was in town.

"We start pulling stuff out of storage the weekend after Labor Day. Once everything's on site, it usually goes up pretty quickly if we have enough hands on deck. Usually takes us about two weeks."

The stage was set up every year at the beach end of the boardwalk. Although several of the downtown streets were blocked off with vendors and food trucks, the stage stayed busy all day with school plays, variety shows, cutest baby competitions, and more. The Founder's Day celebration culminated on the beach with live music on stage and fireworks out over the lake.

"If I'm still here, you can count on me."

Alex nodded confidently. "You'll be here, dude."

15
Penny

"WANT TO SEE WHAT I did this afternoon?" Penny asked after directing Ward to set the two pizza boxes on the counter. She was proud of what she'd accomplished in only a few hours.

She'd first changed out of her wet things and into another outfit she didn't mind getting grubby. She made herself a sandwich with cream cheese and tomato jam topped with a handful of the alfalfa sprouts Hazel always had growing in a Mason jar on the windowsill over the kitchen sink. Then she headed out into the garden with it and a large glass of water.

She swept the debris off a little table just off the back stoop and sat down to enjoy her mini meal while she came up with a plan of attack.

That had been her intention, anyway. However, she spent most of her mid-afternoon snack break thinking about Ward and the exhilarating lake time she'd just shared with him. At first, his body had felt foreign in the circle of her arms. It had been a long time since she'd really hugged anyone for more than a few moments, and even then, it was the tense, boxy frame of her mother, or an affectionate, squirmy second grader. There were others, too, of course. Aunt Jean and Uncle Rob, coworkers who were also friends, and parent volunteers she formed sweet, but temporary, relationships with, because they rarely visited her classroom again after their children moved on, something she never took personally.

Technically, it wasn't hugging. She knew that. But still, she'd had her arms around Ward St. James for over an hour that afternoon. Whether she'd ever admit it out loud to anyone, she'd enjoyed it a little too much, as far as she was concerned. Especially for someone who wasn't looking for a summer fling.

Determined to set her mind to the task at hand, she'd tugged on a pair of work gloves she'd found in Hazel's little barn and started by pulling weeds.

"Come," she told Ward now. "I'll show you." She led him out the kitchen side door around to the back, but just stood quietly to see if he would notice.

Ward gazed out over the garden and nodded slowly. It was still rather sad and one woman with a couple of hours could hardly be expected to make much of a dent, but Penny could see a measurable difference in the area where she'd been most aggressive. "Wow," he said, drawing the word out. "Impressive, Miss Anderson. You've been busy."

"Yes, I have." She practically preened under his praise. "And I have bramble scratches and bug bites to show for it." She held out her arms for his inspection.

"Battle scars," he declared, taking both her hands in his and turning her arms this way and that. "They look good on you," he added with a half-smile. "But then, pretty much anything looks good on you, Penny."

She'd stepped out of the shower only minutes before Ward had said he'd be there. Without much time to primp, she'd taken a blow dryer to her hair just long enough for it to not be dripping wet, slipped into a simple, emerald tank dress, and spent the last few minutes applying a little makeup. He'd already seen her without it in the aftermath of their water play, but the dress made her feel pretty, and the smoky eyeliner and hint of plum shadow highlighted her green eyes.

The compliment made her blush, but she met his gaze, anyway, and thanked him politely. The same could be said for him, she wanted to say, but she couldn't seem to get her voice to cooperate.

"Are you hungry?" he asked. "Maybe you can tell me about your gardening adventure over pizza and lemonade."

"I take it you're hungry?"

"I've been carting those pizzas around for the last ten minutes, and the smell is driving me crazy. I'm hungry, yes. That's why there are two larges in there." He pointed at the kitchen door they'd left standing ajar. He offered his arm. "Shall we?"

She slid her hand into the crook of his elbow, her palm resting against the curve of his forearm. The soft rasp of hair on his arm felt oddly intimate, and she resisted the impulse to brush her fingertips against it.

Oh my, she heard her own voice utter inside her head. Yikes, did he smell good, but should she say so? What if it was just his deodorant? *Wow, your pits smell great!* Yeah, no. That would just be awkward for everyone.

The pizza was still hot inside the boxes, and Penny discovered that she, too, was ravenous. She loaded up her plate with three large pieces and gave Ward a warning glare when he eyed her plate with one raised brow. "I'm not going to pretend I don't like my 'zah," she explained, ending the word with a breathy 'h' sound. "I know people claim that leftover pizza is the bomb, but I prefer it fresh and hot, and with the cheese still stretchy. Even if it means I get to—I mean *have to*—eat a whole one by myself." She lifted the lid on the box she'd just taken a slice from and made a big to-do about counting the remaining slices. "Hazel can share her piece with the dogs, you think?"

They sat at the breakfast nook where they could look out over the garden. It was still going to be light for another hour, so they had plenty of time before they had to move out to the front porch so they could watch the sunset over the lake. Ward waited for her to sit before he slid in opposite her, then he popped the stopper on the fizzy lemonade Penny had pulled from the fridge and filled their glasses as full as the foam top would allow.

"I don't think I need to keep any of this a secret from you," Penny began after they'd both pounded down their first two slices of pizza. "But this does not get back to Hazel, you hear?"

"My lips are sealed," Ward said around a mouthful of food.

"Ew. Not that sealed, they're not."

Ward guffawed, but he at least put a hand up to cover his mouth. When he'd swallowed, he apologized. "I'll just say 'mmhmm' from now on."

"To everything I say?"

"My mother taught me that women are always right, and my father taught me to always agree with the woman."

"You know, I like Ted and Rachel more and more every day. I deal with a lot of parents, both good and not so good. Here's to your awesome parents." Penny lifted her slice of pizza in a toast. "Don't take them for granted, Ward St. James."

A dark cloud passed through his eyes, but he recovered quickly and raised his own slice in the air between them. "Hear, hear. Now tell me this not-so-secret secret of yours."

Penny hesitated, curious about his reaction, then decided against asking him. If he wanted to talk to her about it, he would, wouldn't he? Besides, it really wasn't any of her business. They'd only been on speaking terms for a little more than twenty-four hours.

Huh. It sure felt like a lot longer than that.

She first explained to him about The Garden Variety Lovers Club. "You know everyone in our little club, right?"

"Mmhmm," he said, even though he didn't have food in his mouth.

"So you probably also know that we're all single." She felt her cheeks grow warm at the admission, and she hoped she wasn't overstepping any girlfriend rules.

"Now I do," he said. "But there's nothing wrong with being single, right?"

"Exactly," Penny shot back. "I mean, have you seen the options this town has to offer? Is it any wonder?"

"Mmmmmmmhmmmmm." He dragged the sound out and narrowed his eyes at her.

"Oh, I don't mean you, Mr. Stud Muffin. But you're not sticking around, so you don't count."

He propped an elbow on the table and struck a pose with his chin resting on one fist. "I'll have you know; I like to read, too."

"Of course, you do." She reached over and pressed her thumb to the middle of his forehead. "Here's a gold star for you. Now let me finish my story."

Ward waved his hand in a 'go ahead' gesture and went back to his pizza.

"Well, we may all be single, but we all also don't necessarily want to stay that way." She paused and considered how her words made them sound. "Not that any of us are desperate," she clarified. "But we all consider ourselves to be lovers of love."

"I doubt you're the only ones," Ward said solemnly, but the glint in his eyes told her he was doing his best not to tease her.

"And we're all very different, but not in a weird way." She pointed at him and shook her head. "Don't you dare. We're not weird, got it?"

"Mmmmmhmmmm."

Penny cracked a smile. "You're not funny. But anyway, we're all unique, but also fairly normal. And we're going to be holding our meetings—counseling sessions, as we fondly call them—here in Hazel's garden. The term 'garden variety' is a poetic way of saying that something is common or normal, right? So it's a play on words. We are normal girls meeting in a garden. Garden variety lovers."

"That's pretty clever," Ward concurred, nodding in affirmation.

"Thank you. That's us. Normal *and* clever." Penny paused in her explanation to start in on her third piece of pizza.

"So what exactly does this club of yours do?" Ward pulled one of the boxes closer and loaded up his plate again.

When she could talk again, she gave him a quick overview of the plan for Hazel's guesthouse and gardens that The Garden Variety Lovers Club had come up with.

"And why is this a secret from Hazel?" he asked.

Penny sighed, once again wondering if she was sharing stuff that was too personal. Stuff Hazel wouldn't want a bunch of people to know.

"You don't have to—"

"I know," she said, cutting him off. "I don't have to tell you. You say that a lot to me."

He pretended to zip his lips shut.

"I think Hazel's in some financial trouble. She says she's not sick. Yes, I asked her. But she has no guests—actually, someone is coming at the beginning of August—but usually, this place is hopping, if not exactly packed the whole time I'm here."

Ward set down the uneaten portion of his slice and wiped his hands on a napkin. He was not smiling anymore. In fact, he looked concerned. Well, good. They were all concerned.

"And then there's the garden." She gestured out the window. "Hazel—or The Garden Gate Guesthouse, for that matter—without a garden?"

"I see."

That wasn't exactly the response she'd expected, but maybe she wasn't making things clear. "So, we are going to start having our club meetings here, and since Hazel won't let us pay to use the space, we are going to work in the garden as a tradeoff. Between the six of us, we should have this place looking well on its way back to its former glory in a few weeks, don't you think?"

"Huh."

Penny barreled on, beginning to feel defensive. "Candy is putting together a website for the guesthouse, too, one that will allow people to make reservations online, instead of just by phone. Hazel doesn't have one, can you believe it? She says the learning curve is too much for her to manage at her age, but she won't have to manage it. One of us will do it for her. And once it's up and running, the reservations should start picking up again. This place is charming and unique. There's no reason it shouldn't be full."

There was a long pause, and then Ward said quietly, "Unless Hazel doesn't want it full."

Penny dropped her gaze to her glass where she drew circles in the condensation with her thumb. She'd thought about that, of course. But Hazel had told her she had guests coming in August.

"Don't take me wrong, Penny. I think it's a great idea." But his voice was laced with censure. "If you're sure she'd think so, too."

She was as sure as she could be without coming right out and asking. In so many words, though, hadn't she? Hazel just said she was feeling her age, not that she was making plans to retire. Or close the guesthouse. "I—we're helping her get back on track, Ward. Just like you're doing with your parents." She sounded as defensive as she felt.

Ward cocked his head and frowned at her. "My parents asked me to come."

"Did they? Because Hazel told me that she asked you to come. That your parents weren't going to." Yikes. That came out sounding way too much like a challenge. A line drawn in the sand. Weren't they supposed to be on the same team now? Part of Penny wanted to spool the words back in, but another part of her wanted him to see her vision, to back her up on this, and she felt like he was taking her out at the knees, instead.

Ward visibly stiffened. "Really." It wasn't a question, but there was a whole lot of meaning in that single word.

"You tell me, Ward. Is that true? Or at least, is that the way you remember it?" She'd learned with her students how true the old 'perception is 99% of the truth' adage was.

"My parents *were* sick, though, Penny. My mom almost died. My dad needed help because he was too busy helping her. I don't think you can compare the two scenarios." He'd gone completely still as he spoke, and Penny felt a horrible sinking sensation in her stomach.

Or maybe that was the third piece of pizza; they were enormous slices.

But Ward was right. Her comparison wasn't fair. She wasn't Hazel's daughter, or any kind of relative, for that matter. They'd become friends over the course of the summers she'd been coming, but technically, she was Hazel's paying guest. A lodger.

"I'm sorry," she said, almost too quietly to hear. "You're right. It's not the same. I was out of line."

Ward didn't speak for far too long, and Penny closed her eyes, letting her shoulders droop. But when she opened her mouth to say more, Ward finally said, "Look. I think you all are doing a good thing. *You're* doing a good thing here, Penny. You're trying to help. You *are* helping. I see how your presence alone has lifted Hazel's spirits, just since you got here."

"You don't have to placate me, Ward," she said, beginning to second-guess everything.

"I'm not placating you." He paused, and when she kept her eyes down, he said. "I wish you would look at me. I want you to see that I mean what I'm saying."

She glanced up at him, but she couldn't hold his gaze. He continued, anyway.

"I believe you're right about there being something else going on. She asked me to help shore things up around here. Not fix them. Shore them up. Those were her words."

"She said the same thing to me the other day," Penny acknowledged grudgingly. She hated the way this conversation was playing out. Loathed it. They'd been having so much fun, and now she felt like she was being chastised. It felt demoralizing; she could think of no better word, even though she also felt certain that was not Ward's intent. In fact, he seemed to genuinely be looking out for the best interests of everyone involved. Including hers.

But could she bear having him tell her she was wrong? No one liked to be told such things, did they?

"She has always called Pete Johnson to help her with repairs in the past. J&J Contractors. It seemed out of character that she would ask me to do the work for her, especially since I'm a pretty basic handyman on a good day."

The tools he'd had the day she walked in on him led Penny to believe that he was a little more skilled than he was letting on, but she just nodded and kept her mouth shut. She'd already stuck her foot in it far enough.

"I got the impression, though, that what she really needed was the kindness of a neighbor," he said, seeming to choose his words carefully. "Not the efficiency of a contractor. Although Pete is a great guy. It's just that everything she's had me do has been cosmetic. Other than fixing that leak from the rain, it's been minor stuff. Honestly, stuff she could have done herself; stuff she *would* have done herself in the past." He sighed and rubbed the back of his neck.

"I walked in on her with a huge stack of bills." Penny straightened, finding her nerve enough to speak. "Right there at the counter. She just shoved them all in a basket when I came in and acted like I hadn't seen them."

"I don't know. I suppose it's possible that she couldn't afford Pete's services this year, but like I said, she could have done all the things I've done with one hand tied behind her back. She didn't need me to do them for her." Ward's brow furrowed in thought. Finally, he said, "What I'm saying, Penny, is that maybe the cosmetic stuff we're doing is just that. On the surface. And that the problem, whatever it is, goes much deeper."

"I asked her the other day if everything was alright. That was when she told me she wasn't sick. She just seemed... I don't know. Sad, I guess.

Things are so different this summer, Ward." After a beat, she added, "I'm worried about her. I may be going about this all wrong, but I can't just sit around enjoying my vacation if there's something wrong with our Hazel."

"I agree." Ward stretched his hand across the table. She hesitated only a moment, then put hers in it. With their palms pressed together, his fingers brushed against the tender inside of her wrist, and Penny's pulse jumped. "Maybe talk to your friends about this again. There might be things that have come to the surface with the others, too, now that you all have had a few days to process through what you want to do for Hazel."

"They'll be here Wednesday morning. Do you think I should cancel? Or maybe we should meet at Juno's again, instead."

"I would still meet here. Let them all see what they're up against," he said with a half-laugh. "I'll be here, too."

"You will?" Penny's heart skipped at the thought, partly because the thought of seeing him again made her heart do that, but also because she wasn't sure how focused she could be if he was wandering around the property looking all manly in his tool belt.

"The roof repair was just a quick fix until I could get shingles to match what she's got up there. They come in on Monday, but she called me this morning to tell me I'll have to wait until Wednesday to put them up because of a scheduling conflict. Thankfully, we don't have more rain on the forecast until the end of the week, so I was fine with that."

Why had Hazel told her there'd be nothing going on around the place on Wednesday morning, then? Had she forgotten about their meeting when she spoke to Ward that morning?

He chuckled and squeezed her hand. "I can see the wheels turning in there. You're thinking the same thing I am, aren't you? Miss Hazel is making sure our paths don't stop crossing, am I right?"

Penny shook her head. "She is so subtle."

"Between her and my mother, it's all over but the crying... Crying babies, that is."

"Hush your mouth, Ward St. James. Hazel could walk in at any moment. I wouldn't want to give her any ideas."

"What ideas don't you want to give me?" Hazel was home. And the dogs came tumbling after.

16
Ward

Ward surprised his parents by being awake and ready to not only eat breakfast with them, but also to attend church with them Sunday morning. It felt good to see the delight on his mother's face, and his father's gruff, "Good morning, son," was more than enough confirmation that he'd made the right decision.

They were invited to have Sunday dinner with a family from across town, and although Ward was hoping to spend more time with Penny that afternoon, in Autumn Lake, as in so many small towns, Sunday dinner was all about family. He couldn't just abandon his parents to go hang out with the girl next door.

Penny, it turned out, had plans anyway. She and Hazel were heading to a popular German restaurant in Evansville where they were going to meet up with a few of Hazel's friends. They got together once a month for Reuben sandwiches and potato cakes, the Sunday special.

It had been a long time since Ward had been to the Bavarian House, and if Penny came back talking about how much she liked it, he'd put that on his growing list of places to experience with her while they were both in town.

That evening, he texted her and asked if she'd like to have dinner on the dock on Monday night. It took her more than an hour to respond, and when she did, it was with a simple, three-word answer. *We'd love to.*

So Hazel would be there, too. He supposed he'd better invite his parents to join them as well. Evidently, Miss Penny hadn't picked up on his picnic-under-the-stars-just-the-two-of-us vibes.

Or had she picked up on them and was putting out you're-too-much-for-me-to-handle-right-now vibes?

He'd have to wait until tomorrow to find out. Texts were a terrible way to send nuanced messages, and as enemies becoming friends, there were a lot of nuances to potentially misread.

Now he just had to figure out what to serve her. "Them," he corrected himself.

And whether to have Hazel and Penny over at their place, or to take his folks over to Hazel's dock. What table should he use? And now with so many people attending, did he need to have better lighting? Should he set up lanterns along the dock?

How did this suddenly get so complicated? "I just wanted to sit on a blanket and eat sandwiches and complain about the lights of Carpe Diem blocking out the stars," he grumbled.

Monday ended up being far busier than he'd imagined, and at the last minute, he called home. "Hey, Mom. I'm still stuck at this job over at Jerry's Pontoons. I need a huge favor."

"Of course, honey. What can I do for you?"

An hour later, Ward pulled the van into the driveway and under the carport to get out of the light, but steady rain that had started falling about an hour ago. He should have expected this, he chided himself, since the weatherman had said there wasn't a chance of it coming before the weekend.

It had been over ninety degrees that afternoon, and he was hot and grimy, and he still had to go back the next morning to finish up. Jerry had called time on him; the man's wife had all but threatened to pack up the hot meal she'd made him and give it to the neighbors if he didn't get his patootie home to eat with her. Her word, not Jerry's, but Jerry hadn't been shy about sharing.

And now it was raining. So, no dinner on the dock. Penny would understand. Maybe they could try again tomorrow. Maybe he'd be in a better mood then, too.

Right now, all Ward wanted was a shower, a fortifying meal, and a few hours during which he didn't have to worry about being anything or anyone but himself.

He climbed out of the van and reached back in to grab his wallet and phone from the console. When he turned around, his eyes landed on

Hazel's house across the inlet, and on the two women he could make out, even through the rain, sitting on the front porch. They were both waving at him, and he couldn't help smiling.

It might have been the first genuine smile he'd put out all day.

"That's about how I feel when I come home at the end of the day." His father stood under the cover of the side porch, his eyes on Ward. He lifted a hand and circled his own face with a finger. "Your face says it all."

"Really, Dad? You, too?" Ward shook his head. He sounded like a broken record these days, but it was starting to feel like the whole town was in cahoots with the whole Ward and Penny thing these days.

"Me, too, what?" his dad asked, feigning ignorance. "I know that look, son. It's been a rough day; I get it. There's no place like home to wash away the cares of the day and put things back in their rightful places."

Maybe Ward was feeling a little too defensive. His dad had never really been the meddling type before. "Yeah, you're right. I need a shower something fierce."

Ted winked at Ward.

He *winked.*

Ted St. James never winked.

"Good plan, son. I hear Miss Hazel and Miss Penny are joining us for supper this evening."

Inside, there was no evidence that company was coming. The vintage Dutch oven burbled away on the stove with what he assumed was his mom's pot roast stew by the mouthwatering aroma that filled the house, and the table was set for three. His mother was taking her usual rest before the meal, so he headed to his own bedroom at the other end of the house to clean up, figuring he'd better be prepared for anything.

The shower he took did wonders for his body and mind. By the time he was dressed, he felt much more prepared to be sociable. "Hey, Mom," he said, coming into the kitchen where she was putting cling wrap over a plate of cookies. "It smells great in here. What can I do to help?" It was obvious the meal was just going to be the three of them; Dad must have misunderstood. Ward would call Penny later that evening to apologize for having to take a rain check—literally—and reschedule for another evening.

"Not a thing." Rachel tipped her head in the general direction of the guesthouse. "Hazel should be here any minute to join us." When she saw him eye the table, she shot a funny look at his father who was filling the three glasses with iced tea. "Your father didn't tell you, did he?"

Ward frowned. "I must not have understood." He wasn't going to throw his dad under the bus; at least, not until he knew who was driving the thing.

"Hazel is joining your father and me, and you're heading next door to have your picnic with Penny on the front porch. It's not raining anymore, but it's still wet and slippery out on the dock, so she thought it would be best. Besides, you know how inaccurate the forecast can be. It might rain again, anyway." She held out the plate of cookies for him to take. "Here you go."

He looked from her to the cookies and back again. "I think I missed something. I invited Penny to have dinner with me. Not the other way around." Had she cooked again? The whole point was to take his turn, to cook for her. Or, as was his backup plan, to have his mother cook for her.

"You're going to be late. You're already late. Get a move on."

"Mom."

Rachel leaned a hip against the counter and crossed her arms, making a long-suffering face at him. "Honey, do you know the saying, 'Pennies from heaven?'"

Ward closed his eyes so she wouldn't see them roll. Really? Pennies from heaven? Could it get any cheesier? "Of course, I do."

"Do you know what it means?"

"I do." He opened his eyes to the smug look on her face.

"Good. Then take that plate of cookies next door and be grateful for your Penny from Heaven. She's a truly unexpected gift, isn't she?"

"She's not *my* Penny." He frowned, returning her stern gaze, then he eyed his father, too. "Guys, you all need to ease off a little. Penny and I are just becoming friends. And believe me when I say that it's been kinda hard won. I would like to not lose ground."

"If she's *your* friend, Ward, then she's *your* Penny," Mom reasoned, a little irrationally. "Maybe only for this evening. Maybe only for this summer. But why wouldn't we want you to spend time with such a lovely young lady? You spend far too much time here at home at the end of the day, sitting outside on that chair, making your phone calls or staring morosely at that monstrosity across the water." She made a shooing motion with her hands. "Go. Do something fun with someone your age. You're allowed to have fun, you know, even when you're babysitting your parents."

Ward flinched at her words. "I'm not babysitting you," he retorted, trying to keep the impatience out of his voice. "I'm helping you."

"You're kind of hovering, too." Rachel reached over and took Ted's hand, tugging her husband over to stand beside her. "You learned from a master hoverer, and you both have the best motives, so I'm not complaining. But I am giving you, Ward, permission to fly free for the night. I have Teddy here. He'll take good care of me."

"And we'll have Hazel here, too," his father chimed in, apparently not taking her remarks as anything derogatory about him. "She'll take good care of both of us. That's what she does. She's a nurturer, right, hon?"

Rachel nodded and smiled expectantly at Ward. But he just stood there, cookies held in front of him, looking back and forth between his parents. Finally, he said lamely, "She wasn't supposed to cook tonight."

"She didn't cook. Now, does that make you feel better?" When he still didn't move, his mother clapped her hands, startling him a little. "Go!"

His father chuckled. "Better hoof it, boy. Your mother means business when she claps like that."

Then he winked again.

Ward spun on his heel and left the house, but not so quickly that he missed his mother's parting words, taken—not quite accurately—out of Louis Prima's 'Pennies from Heaven' song. "Turn your umbrella up, up, upside down!"

He passed Hazel coming down the lane with her three dogs in tow. She wouldn't take them into his parents' house with her, but they'd make themselves comfortable on the front porch and wait to walk home with her at the end of the evening.

"Did you leave any cookies for me?" she asked, eyeing the plate he held.

"You, Ms. Poleman, are going to have to ask your partner in crime. I have apparently become a pawn in whatever game this is."

"Crime?" Hazel chortled. "Crimes of passion, maybe."

Ward had no words. He turned and continued on, shaking his head at the outburst of laughter behind him.

It did, indeed, start raining again not even an hour later, but the temperature had dropped considerably with the condensation, so eating outside under the cover of the porch was the perfect compromise. Fortunately, he'd had the foresight to turn his parents' porch light on as he left, so they'd know when the crazy old people across the way were wrapping up their shenanigans.

Penny had, indeed, done no cooking. Between them on the table was an old-fashioned soup tureen in which was a generous portion of his mother's stew. Penny had also pulled a tray of open-faced grilled cheese sandwiches from under the broiler. "Hazel made these for us while I was in the shower. And your dad dropped off the stew right before you got home. I didn't get to cook a single thing tonight." She pointed at the plate of oatmeal chocolate chip cookies he'd brought. "Not even dessert. Oh. Don't let me forget. There's yummy salted caramel ice cream in the freezer that will go perfectly with those."

Over their meal, Ward regaled her with a wryly humorous version of the happenings of his day. By the time he wrapped it up with his father's wink, Penny was groaning and giggling simultaneously. "I think we may have to fake an engagement at this point. Otherwise, our families are going to die of broken hearts."

He grinned at her slip of the tongue. Apparently, she hadn't realized she'd called Hazel family. "What diamond cut do you prefer, Miss Penelope Anderson? I mean, you're going to need a ring if we're going to make it official."

"Hmmm." She tapped her chin with her finger, making a show of pondering her options. "I guess I don't really mind what shape it is as long as it's large and imposing." She flung her arms wide. "Like I am."

He pretended to write down her preferences on his napkin. "Big and bold. Check."

She picked up her tartine—Penny insisted on calling the cheese sandwiches that—which she had generously slathered with some of his mother's tomato jam. But instead of taking a bite, she just held it, almost like a prop. "Here's something about me that you probably don't know. It's a personal vexation."

"A personal vexation? What is that, Miss Teacher?"

"A pet peeve. A grievance. Complaint. You know."

"Ah. I see."

That's when she took a bite. And chewed. And chewed. And chewed.

When he was just about to ask if she needed a spit bucket, she swallowed, took a drink, then grinned over at him. "Sorry for keeping you waiting. I just wanted to build a little suspense since it's such a dumb thing."

"I can only imagine."

She took a deep breath in, held it, her cheeks puffed out like a blowfish, then let it out along with the words, "I'm short."

Ward stared at her, waiting for more. When none was forthcoming, when she just looked at him like she'd dropped a bomb and was waiting for his reaction, he figured he'd better say something. "You're... petite," he countered. "Not short. Dainty. Cute."

"Nooooo," Penny wailed, dropping the remainder of her sandwich on her plate in despair. "Cute? Come on! That's like a death knell for single women. Probably for single guys, too. It's almost—" She broke off, shook her finger at him, then said, "No, it is. 'Cute' is just as bad as 'nice.'" She made air quotes with her fingers. "And I can't believe you just said that about me."

Ward gave her a bemused look. "I take it being cute is your personal vexation?"

"No." She balled up her napkin and threw it at him. He caught it before it landed in his soup. "My personal vexation is being short. And something that makes me want to go jump in the lake—" She broke off and snickered. "My mom used to say that all the time to me, especially when I was a kid. 'Go jump in the lake.'" Her smile went soft and sweet, and he let her reminisce. "I was always underfoot. Kinda clingy. I'm the one who hovered in our relationship. I had to know exactly where she was, what she was doing, who she was with at all times. That's probably what stunted my growth. Worry for my mother." She made a sad little snort. "Look where that got me."

"I'm sorry, Penny."

"No, no, no." She held up both hands like she was trying to hold back the tide. "We were talking about how cute I am. Let's go back to that." She propped her elbows on the table, her chin in her cupped hands, and blinked her big green eyes at him.

Ward reached over and booped her on the nose. "Cute as a button, little lady. There's no two ways about it."

"And something that makes me want to go jump in the lake," she repeated, narrowing her eyes at him. "Is when people call me things like 'little lady' or 'pixie' or—or—I don't know. Small names."

"How about Thumbelina?" He held up one of his thumbs, closed one eye, and acted like he was gauging her size by it. Fortunately, even with one eye closed, he saw her hand coming in time to jerk his back before she smacked it out of the air. "Munchkin?"

She put both hands flat on the table and glared at him.

"Hobbit? I have a thing for hairy feet, you know."

"I'm warning you, Ward St. James." She started to push up out of her seat like she was going to launch herself at him.

Heat shot up his neck at the thought, and he did his best to quell the rush of desire in his gut. "I know. Smurf. I mean, Smurfette."

Penny plopped back into her chair. "Smurfette." She said the name as though it brought shame to Smurfs everywhere. "Now that girl has a story."

Ward chuckled. "Really? And you know it?"

"You don't?" she shot back, bobbing her head like a drama queen.

"Actually, I don't," he countered. "And I'm not ashamed to admit that, by the way."

Penny smirked. "You know, I probably would have called you 'cute' *and* 'nice' if you actually knew anything at all about the Smurfs."

"Whew." Ward swiped the back of his hand across his forehead. "Dodged that bullet. But now I'm curious. What's her story? And why do you know it? Are you a Smurf fan?" He wiggled his fingers at her in a tell-me-more gesture. "I feel like I'm getting to know some very deep and personal things about you right now."

"I'm a teacher. I know things, okay? It's our superpower."

"Do tell."

"Okay." She lifted both hands in the air in front of her as though setting the stage between them. "So there's this evil wizard who hates happiness."

"As all evil wizards do." Ward sat back, thoroughly enjoying the easy banter between them. He used to have conversations like this with Rochelle; he was sure. Except that he couldn't recall when it had ever been this... well, this easy.

"Exactly. And the Smurfs are all happy, right? They're all cute and nice guys, by the way, and they get along and work well together."

"As all cute, nice guys do." He crossed his arms over his chest and settled back into his seat to listen as she explained Smurf lore to him.

"Here's the thing that chaps my hide." She let out a little 'grrr' for emphasis.

"You're a cowboy now?"

Penny rolled her eyes. "There's a cowboy inside all of us, Ward St. James. Keep up." She waved one hand around between them like she was trying to get him to hurry along. "So the thing that chaps my cowboy hide is that when Papa Smurf changed her from bad to good, the only thing that really changed about her was her appearance. She lost her cute, choppy black hair and got those long golden waves. Her comfy white peasant bootie slipper things got traded in for high heels. Yes, high heels in the woods. Have you ever walked on the grass in high heels, Ward?"

"I can't say that I have." He shook his head slowly. She didn't expound, but he thought he could figure it out.

She started ticking things off her fingers. "Her nose got smaller. Her eyes got bigger. Her lashes got longer. Her voice got higher. And instead of standing casually like all the guys, she started standing like this." Penny got to her feet and struck a pose that looked like something straight out of a Betty Boop cartoon.

"Wow." Ward's eyebrows rose with appreciation. "Look how fired up you are over the little blue people."

"Yeah, well, this is the kind of grooming my second graders are getting, Ward." She pronounced the 'd' at the end of his name as "duh," and he bit his bottom lip to keep from busting up. He wasn't so sure she was really joking around anymore, but she was definitely, ridiculously, endearingly, sparklingly cute.

What had Alex called her? A ball of fire, indeed.

"You know, Miss Penny. I think I'm going to go grab that ice cream you mentioned. Maybe cool off a little?"

Penny, still standing, propped her hands on her hips. "Are you mocking me?"

"Oh. You mean, because I used the word 'little' just now?" He slid his chair back and stood, too, grinning like an idiot. He suddenly knew how Jimbo felt looking at Delilah. He could follow this girl around all day, he thought.

She circled the table and shook her fist up at him, her eyes twinkling playfully. "Why I oughta..."

Ward wrapped his fingers loosely around her wrist, and Penny's words trailed off, her eyes going wide. "You oughta what?"

Suddenly, all around them, the world went quiet. The rain still came down, the wind still blew across the water, and the trees still swayed, swishing their branches to and fro out under the murky sky. But Ward could hear nothing except the shallow breaths Penny took, the pounding of his pulse thudding inside his skull, and Louis Prima singing "Pennies from Heaven" somewhere in the distance. At least it wasn't his mother's voice.

Penny's fist slowly unfurled as she began to pull free of his loose hold, but instead of stepping back like he thought she would, she turned her hand and laced her fingers with his. "Ward." His name came out of her like a sweet sigh, and he swallowed hard. "I'm—this..." She squeezed his hand, hard, her fingers trembling noticeably. "We should—" She broke off again, blushing furiously. "I mean, we shouldn't."

Or maybe we should, he wanted to argue, but he held his tongue.

He did not want to scare her. He did not want to offend her. He did not want to lose her.

He very much wanted her. Period.

17
Penny

SHE'D STOOD HER GROUND. She hadn't given in to the pull of him, to the need that had nearly overpowered her. And now, because she'd been strong when it mattered, she could be weak when no one would know. Her stomach hurt from being tied up in knots all evening long, and her fingers seemed to tingle every time she thought about how they felt intertwined with his.

Penny drew her legs up and wrapped her arms around her knees as she lay on her side, gazing out at a sky washed clean of the murky clouds that had hung like a shroud around them most of the evening. The weather hadn't dampened their spirits, though, and in spite of her sticking to her side of the table—for the most part—they'd had a wonderful evening together.

It was Ward who ended the evening with an apology, explaining that he had a full schedule that was starting earlier than usual because of the pontoon repair he'd not been able to finish that afternoon. Hazel hadn't made it back by then, and she walked with Ward to his parents' house so she could escort the woman and her dogs home.

They arrived at the walkway leading up to the front porch just as Hazel stepped outside, and the poor pups who'd been waiting so patiently for her didn't know who to go to first. They just zigzagged back and forth between Penny and Hazel, who both showered them with pets and scratches and "Good dogs."

"I was going to pull the golf cart out," Ward's father said. He'd come out right behind Hazel. "Why don't you take the ladies home instead, Ward?"

So Ward had helped them into the cart, along with all three of the dogs, including Murtagh, who wasn't so sure about the whole endeavor, and wheeled them back down the lane to the guesthouse. He waited until they were inside, then headed back out into the night.

Penny hadn't stayed downstairs for very long. Hazel had seemed more tired than usual, and Penny had a few things she wanted to think about without feeling guilty. They'd said their goodnights and then headed to their respective rooms.

Ward had told her about the Tuesday Night Catfish Special at The Old Mill and that he'd be joining his dad there for dinner. "Mom looks forward to Tuesday nights all week long," he'd said wryly. "She gets the house to herself for a few hours with us guys out of the way. She can eat whatever she wants, do whatever she wants, and watch whatever she wants. Although, I think she and Dad like the same stuff these days."

"Don't tell me," Penny had teased. "He's a Hallmark Channel junkie."

The look on Ward's face had been priceless. "How did you know? Did my mom tell you?"

Penny had laughed out loud. "I was just kidding. Are you serious?"

"He just gave me a lecture on why and how much he likes them, and how he thinks I should start watching them. So I can learn something. About women. Yes, I'm serious," Ward declared.

What was it about Ward St. James that made her want to break all her rules just this once? Was it the knowledge that this might be her last time here for the foreseeable future that was making her want to push against the self-imposed restraints? And that he wasn't sticking around here, either?

A summer fling was looking better and better to her.

She sighed and stretched and rolled onto her back to stare up at the ceiling, wishing she could turn off her thoughts the way she did the light. Just flip a switch, and voilà!

But she'd see him Wednesday morning here at the guesthouse when their club met in the garden. "I'm kind of glad you all will be here," he'd told her. "Sounds like Alex might be able to get a few hours off to help me, but he may not get here until after I get started, and I don't like working on a roof without someone else around, just in case."

Penny didn't want to even think about what 'just in case' meant.

On the one hand, Wednesday could hardly come soon enough for Penny. She'd see Ward again. She'd speak with Ward again. She'd look into his eyes and imagine kissing him. Again. Yes, she'd already imagined kissing him a zillion times since that insane moment of weakness on her part. "It's not the same as actually kissing him," she murmured defensively.

Another part of her worried that the girls, Juno in particular, would take one look at her and know that she was in trouble. She could just hear Juno's clucking tongue. She could just see assumptions in Claire's twinkling gaze. She'd never pull off casual if Ward was anywhere in the vicinity.

❥ • ❥ • ❥ • ❥ • ❥

WEDNESDAY MORNING SHOWED UP drenched in summer sunshine, with temperatures skyrocketing to somewhere between ninety degrees Fahrenheit and face-melting hot by ten o'clock in the morning. So the women of The Garden Variety Lovers Club ended up holding their first meeting in Hazel's kitchen where they could still look out the breakfast nook window at the garden. Penny had spent time out there daily since the weekend, clearing handfuls of weeds one section at a time, and it looked noticeably better to her. Candy had come by on Tuesday to talk about the website, and the two of them had taken advantage of the much nicer temperatures and had cleaned up the espaliered apple and pear trees along the south wall. Thanks to Google, between the two of them, they'd also figured out how to lightly prune the trees, even though it wasn't really the right time to do it, and they'd removed the worst of the water shoots that would only use up energy the trees needed to put into the fruit that would be ready to harvest in the early fall.

Other than Candy, none of the others had seen the state of Hazel's garden before Penny started cleaning it up, and she could tell by their careful expressions that they were struggling to be impressed by the hours she'd put in. Admittedly, it still looked like a jungle out there. "See that section over there?" Penny pointed out beyond the stone wall where she'd not even had a chance to explore yet. "That's what the whole thing looked like last week."

Juno shook her head. "It's been ages since I've been out here. This is not Hazel's garden, people."

Claire shook her head solemnly, but she said nothing.

Although Addison had met Hazel on multiple occasions crossing paths in town, she'd never even been out to The Garden Gate at all. "I think it's beautiful," she said, her eyes devouring the view out the windows. "Everything about this place is beautiful."

"Well, thank you," Hazel said, sweeping into the kitchen, her dogs trailing behind her. "I'm so sorry it didn't work for you to meet outside, but it's nice and cool in here, isn't it?" She went to the fridge and pulled open the door. "Don't mind me. I'll be out of your hair in a heartbeat."

"Why don't you join us?" Juno asked, patting the empty chair beside her at the breakfast bar. Penny and the others shot her questioning looks that Juno ignored.

Hazel turned back around, a quart of cream in her hand. "Oh, I don't want to intrude."

Penny then saw what Juno must have. Hazel wanted nothing more than to be a part of what was going on in her kitchen; it was written all over her face.

"Delilah wants to stay, don't you, pretty girl?" Penny asked, leaning down to scoop up the fat little dog. They both grunted with the effort.

"Well, if you insist," Hazel said, a twinkle in her eyes. "I don't have any of your foofy coffee, Juno dear, but I can certainly brew up a nice French roast for all of you. I have cream. And a frother!" She snatched the little battery-powered whisk off the counter and held it up victoriously.

It didn't take long for Hazel to start asking questions that told Penny she might be on to them. "Why is it that you all want to meet in my garden, girls? It's a mess. There are so many better places to gather. My front porch seems a better option than that jungle out there if you're insisting on being outside, weather permitting."

After a taut moment of silence, Juno spoke up. "Penny said no one was using it. She told us she was planning on spending some time out there cleaning it up, and we thought you might consider letting us use the space for free if we pitched in and helped her."

Hazel narrowed her eyes at Penny. "Is this your way of coercing your friends into doing my dirty work around here?" She said it with a note of levity, but Penny's pulse ratcheted up at the way her hostess was studying her.

Claire must have sensed the mounting awkwardness, too. She got to her feet and grabbed the coffee carafe off the counter, then returned to the table with it. "Refills, anyone? And Penny, I keep forgetting to ask. What's going on with you and Ward these days? How did dinner go last Friday?"

That got Hazel's focus off of her for the time being as she answered in Penny's stead. "You haven't heard?" Hazel asked, a mischievous grin on her face. "Ward and Penny are engaged. His parents already paid the bride price, right, Sweet Pea?"

"Hazel!" Penny snort-laughed, caught off guard by the woman's saucy response. "This is how rumors start, you crazy woman."

"Oooh. Give us the deets, girl," Juno demanded, leaning forward at the breakfast bar, elbows on the counter, her chin resting on her hands. "How much did you get for her, Hazel?"

Penny explained the ridiculous scene that had turned into a standing joke with her and Ward. Between her and Hazel, they relayed the evening's events to the other women, who all oohed and aahed at the right moments.

"Then on Saturday," Penny began, then paused for dramatic effect, wiggling her eyebrows up and down suggestively.

"On Saturday?" Claire prompted. "What happened on Saturday?"

"She was out on the lake on the back of his jet ski," Juno supplied. "Holding on so tightly to him that people had to look twice to see that it was two people and not one. It was the four legs that gave them away."

"You guys are the worst," Penny complained, but she was chuckling right along with them.

"They had a picnic on the porch on Monday night, too," Hazel said, elbowing Penny to keep talking. "Has he kissed you yet, Sweet Pea?"

"No!" Penny knew she was blushing furiously now. "Although..." She paused for dramatic effect again.

"Although what?" Juno asked, leaning forward, her face aglow with questions.

"Although there was a moment or two when I thought the potential was there for it to happen." The words came shooting out of her mouth.

"So?" Addison turned to Penny and asked, "Does this mean you're going to think about moving to Autumn Lake permanently? Now that there's a guy in the picture?"

"What? No." Penny shook her head. "You guys. No. It's not like that, okay?" Growing serious, she said, "I would love nothing more than to move here, to call this place home. Part of me already does." She met Hazel's eyes. "It always feels like coming home when I pull into your driveway, Hazel."

"I know, Sweet Pea. I feel the same way when you show up. 'She's home!' I always say. Ask my dogs. They'll tell you it's true."

"But my mom needs me, and because she needs me, I need the job I have, and we need to be where I can get help with her. The daycare she goes to while I work is paid for by her insurance, and it's only a couple of blocks from the school. And of course, my aunt and uncle are there, too. An hour away, but accessible if I need them for an emergency. So for now, until she is in a place where I can no longer care for her, moving here is not an option."

"Does that mean that there will come a day when it *is* an option?" Liz asked the question in her usual direct approach.

Penny nodded slowly. "It's my dream."

"And speaking of dreams…" Claire said, letting the word linger. "Or shall I say 'dreamboats?' When are you seeing Ward again?"

Penny put both hands to her cheeks. She hadn't been able to stop smiling for more than a minute or two for the last several days. "Well, it's not exactly 'seeing him', but he's supposed to be here working today."

"Hey, ladies." And there he was, coming through the kitchen side door. His gaze locked on her, and his smile kicked up a notch. "Miss Penelope."

"Oh, Ward," Hazel began, gesturing toward the window. "It's hot enough to scald a lizard out there. I can't let you get up on the roof."

"I'll be fine, Hazel," Ward assured her. "Alex will be here shortly, too. We'll get it done in no time with the two of us on the job."

"Alex is coming? Here?" It was Claire who asked, but she sent a sidelong look at Juno.

"In about ten minutes," Ward clarified. To Hazel, he said, "I need your keys to the side door of the garage. I left some tools in there."

Hazel pulled a collection of keys off a row of hooks near the door, separated the requested key, and handed it to Ward. "Please take breaks," she instructed, not letting go of the key until he promised to do as she said. "Come inside to the cool air and drink lots of water. I'll be watching you." She narrowed her eyes at him. "Like a crazy old lady."

"We'll be watching you, too," Claire echoed, as he turned to leave. She raised her voice a little louder as he pushed the door open. "Especially Penny here."

"Claire Maitland!" Penny hissed, but then paused when she heard Ward's response just before the door shut behind him.

"We'll be sure and put on a good show for you all."

Juno chuckled, shaking her head. "I don't know how you're going to hold out, girl. That was some sizzling electricity sparking between you two, that's for sure."

Penny sighed and scrunched up her nose. "I know," she groaned, covering her face with her hands. "I know," she repeated. "What am I going to do?"

"Sounds like you're going to have to kiss him," Hazel quipped. "Get him out of your system. And then tell us all about it."

"Please don't." Liz shook her head. "I mean, you can kiss him. I give you my blessing there. But don't tell us about it. Or at least wait to gush about it until I take a bathroom break. It's been way too long since I had my lips on anyone else's, and although I won't begrudge you getting a little action, I don't need to hear about it. My ovaries will start aching and all that."

The conversation moved to comparing stories about past romantic escapades, and pretty soon, it was time for Juno, Claire, and Liz to head back to work. Addison had the day off, and she and Candy had a mani-pedi date, followed by an afternoon of playing tourist down on the boardwalk.

"Want to meet us there?" Addison asked, already familiar with Penny's aversion to pedicures.

"Or come with us for our mani-pedis," Candy suggested. "Both of you. You come too, Hazel."

"I don't do pedicures," Penny said. "I just can't handle anyone touching my feet. But I might do a little shopping with you later in the day. Call me when you get there?"

Hazel turned down the invitation, too, claiming she had things that needed her attention around the house.

With everyone gone, Hazel turned to Penny. "Will you do me a favor and go check on the boys out there, Sweet Pea? They should have come in for a break by now." She went to the fridge and pulled out a plastic container of cut up fruit left over from the supper they'd had last night. "Here. Take this and a couple of forks and plates. Make them eat some, you hear?"

Penny didn't even bother arguing. She headed out the side door through the garden, gasping at the wave of heat that hit her the moment she stepped out of the shade cast by the trees close to the house.

"Hey, there, little lady," Alex called to her from where he stood with his feet braced wide, holding an extension ladder steady for Ward as he climbed down from the roof.

Ward paused at Alex's greeting and looked over his shoulder at Penny. He cracked up when she scrunched up her nose in distaste.

"What?" Alex asked, glancing back and forth between them. "You two got secrets already?"

"You might want to come up with some other cute little name to call Penny," Ward suggested nonchalantly, once his feet were both on terra firma. He emphasized the words 'cute' and 'little' and sent her a mischievous grin.

"Really?" Alex asked, clearly bemused. "Does 'little lady' bother you? I'm sorry—I meant no offense, okay?"

Penny waved off his apology. "It's fine, Alex. It's just that I already know I'm way too short, you know?"

"You are not too short, Penny," Alex declared, surprising her with his adamance. "Who told you that?"

Penny shrugged. "Boys at school. Girls at school. The gym teacher who made teams pick me but never made them give me a chance to actually hold the basketball. Not that I could ever have made the shot, but still. Or just the teachers when they lined us up for every single picture or event." She made her voice higher pitched and waved a hand at Alex as if beckoning him to come closer. "Up here, Penny. The short kids down front."

"Okay." Alex drew the word out as he pondered her point. He propped one hand on the ladder and studied her. "I see what you mean. But honestly, I don't think of you as diminished in any way, just because you're shorter than I am. Your stature on the outside may not be like mine, but if I'm only looking at what you are on the outside, then that says more about me than it does about you, right?" He shrugged his very large shoulders. "I say embrace it, Penny. I like you just the way you are." He flashed her his charming, boy-next-door grin, the one that Juno had warned her about. "In fact, I think you'd look weird if you were tall."

A pleasant warmth settled in her chest, and it had nothing to do with the blazing sun. She smiled sweetly at Alex, having gained a whole new perspective on the guy. She'd made assumptions about him because of his outward appearance, that was for sure. Maybe her issue with her size truly was her own prejudices, her own assumptions about what everyone else was thinking. And maybe she was wrong.

Ward stood with his arms crossed, watching their interaction with a shuttered expression—she didn't dare read anything into it—and she handed him the bowl of fruit she'd been carrying. "Hold these, please."

He took them, still not saying a word.

Penny turned and marched over to Alex, then wrapped her arms around his waist, the top of her head not even reaching his chin. He hesitated only a moment, then draped his heavy arms loosely around her in return. Peering up at him, she said, "Alex Frampton, I love you." Then she stepped back and made a face. "Ew. You're all sweaty. And gross."

Alex laughed out loud, then reached over and patted her on the head. "I love you, too, Little Lady."

Penny acted like she was going to punch him in the chest, but with his hand on her head, she could swing all she wanted, and she'd never hit him. "You're the only one in the world who can get away with calling me that, you know." Giggling, she glanced over at Ward, only to find him frowning. Intensely.

"Ah, come on, man. She loves you, too," Alex teased, holding out a hand toward Ward for the bowl of fruit. "What did you bring us, Shiny Penny?"

"Oooh, I like that. What do you think, Ward? Do I look like a Shiny Penny?" She swayed back and forth, the skirt of her short, cinnamon-colored sundress swishing against her thighs. She didn't wait for an answer—his expression made her wary. "I brought you guys watermelon, mango, and berries. Strawberries, blueberries, and maybe some blackberries, too, I think. Hazel says I'm supposed to make you eat them. Not sure how I might do that, but I'm feeling pretty big and bold right now, so don't cross me." She took one of the forks from Ward and handed it to Alex. "If you don't want to share the bowl, I can grab some plates."

Ward dropped his gaze to the bowl he still held and cracked open the lid. Now, he wouldn't look at her.

Great. And they said girls were too emotional. If she was a betting woman, she'd bet that Ward wasn't happy about her hugging Alex, even though it was a completely and utterly justifiable hug. The man had just changed her perspective on one of her biggest personal vexations, for the love of Pete. He deserved a lot more than a hug; except she wasn't that kind of girl.

Ward could just get over himself. She'd readily hug him, too, if he wanted one. She'd certainly given him one on Monday night. When he'd said goodbye after bringing them home in the golf cart, he'd stood on the front porch and wrapped his arms around her like he was heading off to war. She'd been so sure he was going to kiss her, too, but he'd stepped away, thanked her again for the evening, and practically launched himself down the steps and out into the night.

The guys apparently had no qualms about sharing germs, and within minutes, most of the fruit had been demolished. Alex noticed her watching them, stabbed a piece of watermelon, and held it out toward her. "Want some? It's nice and juicy."

Penny leaned forward and took the bite off his fork, laughing when the juice dribbled down her chin. She lifted the hem of her skirt to wipe it away.

"Whoa!" Alex exclaimed, turning his face away.

"I'm wearing shorts, you pervert," she retorted, and beside her, Ward half-snorted, half-choked on his own bite. "I'm a teacher. I know about dresses and boys, you guys. And I'm not going to tell you to grow up, because I know it's a futile pursuit. Hence, the shorts."

"Hence?" Alex pointed his fork at her. "You talk good, Miss Teacher. I've always wondered; what exactly does 'hence' mean?"

"Hence. Therefore. Consequently. Thus." Then, because she was starting to feel a little uncomfortable about what seemed to her to be his growing ill will, she sidled up next to Ward, peered inside the bowl he still held, and pointed. "Get me that blueberry right there."

Ward hesitated only for a moment, then stabbed the poor little piece of fruit and fed it to her. He swallowed when she did; her eyes tracked his Adam's apple as it moved up and down.

Behind her, Alex chuckled softly, and she stepped away from Ward, suddenly feeling quite self-conscious. "It's kinda hot out here, wouldn't you agree?" Alex asked. "I think I'll head inside to cool off in the air conditioning." He pointed his fork at the bowl. "You going to finish that? Or do you want me to free up your hands and take it in for you?"

Penny blushed and ducked her head, but Ward dropped his fork into the bowl and handed it to Alex with a "Thanks." Then he reached for Penny's hand and added, "We'll be in shortly."

Alex just whistled a silly tune as he headed around the house, leaving them to stand there in awkward silence.

"He's right," Ward finally said. "You would look weird if you were tall."

Penny laughed out loud and turned toward him. He hadn't released her hand, and now there wasn't more than a foot of space between them. "You'd better not get any ideas, Mr. St. James. Just because I awarded a concession to Alex, doesn't mean you get to call me Smurfette. Or Gnome."

"That wasn't the idea I was having right now," he said, tugging her just a little closer.

"Oh, yeah?" The challenge came out borderline breathless, but she lifted her chin boldly.

"Oh, yeah." His eyelids lowered just the tiniest bit, then his gaze went to her mouth. "Want to have dinner with me tonight?" he asked, still staring at her lips.

"I think I'm having dinner with Candy and Addison on the boardwalk tonight," she managed to eke out. Had she a hundred percent committed to that? She suddenly couldn't remember.

"How about breakfast in the morning?" He moved a hair's breadth closer.

"Hazel is going to teach me how to make her amazing crepes." She lifted her free hand to cup around her mouth and whispered, "It's her secret recipe."

"I like crepes."

"I do, too," she said with a grin. "Why are we standing so close to each other in this heat?" She was still whispering.

"Because we like it," Ward whispered back. He was so close, in fact, that she had to crane her neck to hold eye contact. "And because you like my sweaty grossness more than you like Alex's."

Penny snorted, and started to step back, then changed her mind. She slid her arms up around his neck and leaned into him, relishing the way she seemed to fit just perfectly in his gentle embrace. She rested her cheek against his chest just long enough to hear the thump of his heart, then she drew back. He let his own arms fall away, but his flushed face told her he had enjoyed the brief interlude maybe as much as she had.

"Ew," she teased, trying to bring levity to what had quickly become a very serious moment. "So sweaty. Why did you make me hug you?"

"That was all you, Penelope Anderson. I was just standing here, and you sashayed over and took advantage of me."

Her mouth fell open in mock dismay. "I did not sashay."

He made a low, appreciative sound in the back of his throat. "But you did take advantage of me?"

"You just stood there," she countered. "What else was I supposed to do?"

The unbearable heat finally sent them inside to the coolness of the house, where Hazel stood at the sink in the kitchen, washing lettuce. "Everything all done out there?" she asked, eyeing the two of them curiously.

"Where's Alex?" Ward asked, glancing around.

"He had to take off. Said you guys were finished, and he had to get back to his other job."

"Oh. Okay. Got it." Ward fumbled over his words, then he nodded. "Yeah, we're done. He didn't tell me he was leaving."

"He got a phone call," Hazel said. "He told me to let you know."

Feeling more confident than she had in some time, thanks to Alex's casually life-affirming words, Penny reached over and hooked her pinky with Ward's. "I invited Ward to have crepes with us in the morning, Hazel. Is that okay? I won't tell him your recipe."

Hazel waved a leaf of Romaine at them. "Your mother already knows my crepe recipe, Ward. It's no secret on this stretch of the road, anyway. We'd love to have you."

Penny smiled up at him and let go of his hand. She had to cool it. They had to cool it. They had to stop flirting and toying with each other's feelings this way. But how did they spend time together without stirring this stuff up? She certainly didn't want to *stop* spending time with him. That was out of the question.

She'd just have to keep her schedule too full to be readily available. She had a feeling this wasn't going to be the last time he asked her out this summer.

18
Ward

He couldn't seem to get enough of her. Every free moment he had, he filled it with her. Sometimes it worked out that they could spend the time together, other times, they talked on the phone or just texted, and when she wasn't available to reach out to, he lost himself in his thoughts about her. It had been just over a week since they'd started spending time together, and he felt like a man without water in a desert every time he was away from her.

It was Sunday night, and he'd spent the evening with Alex and the Brewster brothers, Walter and Dustin, at Patsy's Pizza Parlor, the only place in town the locals could really call their own. Penny had gone out with some of her friends, and now, as he sat in the dark on his parents' front porch, he peered up at her dark bedroom window, wondering if she was home yet.

He had all but forgotten about trying to reach out to Rochelle, but a conversation with Johnny earlier in the afternoon had him picking up his phone and dialing her again. Rochelle, it seemed, had taken to stopping in at Blue Waters on a regular basis.

This time when he called, she answered, but in a clipped tone that made him feel like he was inconveniencing her. It only served to irritate him; hadn't she been the one who wanted to hear from him? If she didn't want to talk to him, that was fine by him.

"What is it you wanted?" she asked after a brief and awkward exchange of small talk. "I'm kind of in a rush. I'm almost to the paint store to pick up supplies for a job I start next week."

He didn't want anything from her. Not anymore. But he'd called her, not the other way around, and he wasn't going to be intentionally rude.

He wasn't going to beat around the bush, either. "I just got off the phone with Johnny. He told me I needed to call you."

Rochelle paused, then said, "Huh. I'm sorry, Ward. I'm not sure why he told you that."

"Okay." Ward wasn't going to demand that she talk to him when it was obvious that she didn't want to. He pulled the phone from his ear and glared at it a moment before bringing it back up. "Then I'll let you go. It was good to hear from you. Glad you're doing all right." *Liar.* Well, he was, in fact, glad she was doing okay. But good to hear from her? He could have gone all summer long without hearing another peep from her. And now he sounded a little too much like an ex-boyfriend with potential stalker vibes. "Say 'hi' to Johnny for me."

"Excuse me?" Rochelle's tone changed noticeably. "Why would I do that?"

Ward closed his eyes and rubbed the back of his neck, wishing he could just hang up and pretend he hadn't heard her response. "It was just a polite thing to say, Ro." And why was she so upset by it? Because it was obvious that she was. "I just meant that next time you stop by Blue Waters, say 'hi' to Johnny for me. You'll see him before I will, right?"

The phone line was silent for so long that he thought she'd hung up. "Rochelle? You still there?"

"I'm here." He knew her. Not as well as he should have after three years of dating, he realized, but he knew her well enough to recognize *that* tone. She was ticked off. At him?

"Okay." He tried to inject a little more friendliness into his tone. "Listen, I gotta go. Take care of yourself."

"He told you, didn't he?"

The hair on the back of Ward's neck stood on end. "Told me what?"

Rochelle made an impatient noise in the back of her throat. "Don't play games with me, Ward."

"I'm not playing games," he said with a dry laugh. "Look. Obviously, this is not a good time for either of us to talk. I'm just going to hang up—"

"You called me, Ward." She cut him off, her voice strident. "You called me," she repeated. "Why?"

Ward took a deep breath and let it out slowly. "Forgive me, Ro. I had no intention of upsetting you. Johnny hasn't told me anything about you except that he'd seen you recently and thought I should give you a call." He left out the part about *where* and how often Johnny had seen her. "That's it. I figured we were still friends, and if he thought I needed to reach out to you, then that's what I'd do." He stood up and moved to stand against the porch railing, eyes on the resort across the way.

"I'm fine. I don't know why he would think I needed you to call me; that's all. I'm fine," she said again.

"That's great. Then we're good?" He just wanted to end this ridiculous phone call.

"I have to go. I'm at the paint store."

"I have to go, too." She didn't exactly answer his question, but he wasn't going to poke the bear. "Bye, Ro."

She didn't say goodbye, and he shoved his phone back into his pocket. Johnny was right, Ward thought. Something was definitely wrong with her. But was it Ward's responsibility to find out what it was? To try to help her fix it? Hadn't she rejected his responsibility in her life by breaking up with him?

As he stared out over the water, he thought about the job Lysha had offered him at Carpe Diem almost two weeks ago. He'd heard nothing from her since, nor had he sent her an invoice for his visit. But he found himself thinking about it more and more these days. And he knew why, too.

He felt the pull of home in a way he'd never thought he would. When he was younger, all he'd ever wanted was to leave Autumn Lake and seek his fortune out in the great big world. Now, having spent nearly a year back in the community that had once been his, he felt a new ache for it deep in his bones.

He now saw the sacrifices his parents had made to release him into the wild the way they had. He saw it in the way his mother cared for his father, in the way his father looked after his mother. The way they, as a couple, and as individuals, tended to the needs of their community. He saw it in the way they paid attention to the parts of him he shared with them, and the longing in their eyes to know more, but to not press him for what he wasn't willing to give them.

He hadn't liked the reminder that it had been Hazel, not his parents, who'd asked him to come back. And when he'd heard the words spoken in Penny's voice, he suddenly saw it from her perspective, and he realized how little his father and mother ever asked of him.

And how much he owed them.

But there was another reason that he was thinking about the job at Carpe Diem. Another reason he was questioning where he wanted to call home.

A reason that liked fluttery dresses and reading and good food.

If he were to even consider moving back to Autumn Lake, he'd need a job. Maybe not that job in particular, but he'd need something, and there weren't a whole lot of options in a seasonal tourist town. He couldn't take over his father's business; Ted was too young to retire, and from what Ward had seen of the books, St. James Mobile Boat Repair couldn't really sustain two full-time incomes.

He'd need someplace to live—his childhood bedroom wasn't an option—and for that, again, he'd need a job.

And he'd need to figure out what to do with Blue Waters.

Ward sighed. He loved his company. He really did. But there were times when the unpredictability of the Pacific coast took a toll on him. Sure, the lake could put up a good fight, but the ocean could rage like there was an underwater battle going on, and it could last for days, weeks, and sometimes longer. As much as the townies complained about the WOOTS, the folks in Autumn Lake had it pretty good. On the beaches of Southern California, where millionaires were practically paupers, there was a whole caste system in play that put the South Shore-North Shore prejudices to shame. But the perks of being his own boss, of captaining his own boats, of managing his own crew, had been more than enough to sustain him before. So why was he beginning to question even the good things?

Johnny. He couldn't ask for a better business partner. They didn't question each other's motivation, they didn't step on each other's toes, and they both took their very different roles seriously. It was one of the reasons their company thrived when so many others like theirs didn't

His apartment. It was miniscule, to be sure, but when one had the sand and the sea in your backyard, it more than made up for the limited space indoors. The small bedroom, one bath, and the open floor kitchen, dining, and family room were more than enough for him as a single man. He'd thought, in passing, about whether it would work for a family, but since marriage and children hadn't been on his radar—Blue Waters was his California love child, after all—the size of his living space hadn't been a pressing issue.

Besides, Rochelle had said she'd never live anywhere but the sprawling beach house that had been in her family for generations, and Ward had figured they'd probably end up living there after they married. One day.

His community... Ward frowned as he thought about the faces that made up his circle of friends in Laguna. "Hmm." He hadn't heard a thing from any of them in months, now that he thought about it. Then it struck him: they were all Rochelle's friends. They'd come with her. Or rather, he'd come with her. She'd brought him into her world, and her people had accepted him with open arms. But now that he was no longer a part of her world, it seemed that maybe he was no longer a part of what had become over the years his own world, either. At least not the one in Southern California.

Yet, here in Autumn Lake, after being gone for over a decade, Ward had known without a doubt that his friends would welcome him back as if he'd never left. Which is exactly what they'd done.

He squeezed his eyes shut, the lights of the resort still twinkling against the backs of his eyelids, and he uttered a prayer of frustration heavenward. "What am I supposed to do, God? Help me know what to do, please."

19
Penny

SHE AND WARD HAD gone to Alberto's for supper that night, a lovely little Italian restaurant about half an hour away. The food had been delicious and filling, and they'd opted to take their desserts to go—tiramisu for Ward, cannoli for her, and they added a lemon ricotta cake for Hazel, who loved all things lemon.

Hazel had been tickled that they'd thought of her, but Penny had seen her eyeing each of the desserts with equal exuberance. They'd opted to split each one three ways, then took their plates of treats outside to the front porch to enjoy.

"So remind me again, Penny," Hazel said as she pressed the tines of her fork into the last remaining crumbs on her plate. "You and your girlfriends aren't coming until Saturday this week, correct?"

Penny nodded, lingering over her own desserts, savoring the flavors with each bite. "Liz has made a shift change and now has her weekends off, but that means she can't do Wednesday mornings. It's not the greatest time for Juno and Addison, but Juno has a great crew who are usually happy for the extra hours, and Addison is working on trying to switch hours with another agent. She's good for this Saturday, and starting next week, if everyone can make it happen with their schedules, we'll go to every other Saturday."

"I just think it's wonderful that you girls are making your friendships a priority this way. And that you include me in the group is just lovely. I don't even mind that we spend the majority of the time working in the gardens—collective group therapy, right? Especially since I'm reaping the benefits." To Ward, she said, "Have you seen the back yard lately, Ward?"

"I haven't," he said. "I've been too busy entertaining your houseguest." Ward shot Penny a curious look. She quickly dropped her gaze to the last few bites of her cannoli.

"Well, maybe you two can take a romantic stroll out there on your next date," Hazel suggested with a playful smile directed back and forth between them. "The paths are clear enough to walk down and so many things are blooming right now."

"We'll have to do that," Ward said.

"We're not dating, Hazel," Penny said at almost the exact same time.

"I know, Sweet Pea. But an old girl can dream, can't she?" Hazel patted Penny's arm, then said, "I'm done in, kids. I think me and the dogs are going to call it a night."

A few minutes later, after the sounds inside the house had settled, indicating that Hazel had closed herself in her own quarters, Ward turned to her. "I take it you haven't said anything to Hazel about why your club is meeting." It wasn't a question, and a stone of discomfort settled low in her stomach.

She pushed her plate toward the middle of the table, feeling a little sick after so much rich food. "I decided to wait until the garden is all cleaned up. We're almost there. My goal is for it to be finished by the time her guests arrive in August, but we're going to officially tell her about it and the website the week before."

"Huh. Okay." He took a sip of his coffee—it was probably lukewarm by now—and grimaced just the tiniest bit.

"I know you think I should tell her now, but I want it to be a surprise. I think it will mean so much to her that all these women are gathering together to support her this way. It's a good thing, Ward."

He nodded slowly as he toyed with the handle of his mug, his finger tracing the curve of the handle, up and down, up and down. "I agree that it's a good thing, Penny. And I think she'll be deeply touched by your efforts."

"But?" she prompted when he didn't continue.

He lifted his gaze to hers and smile gently, making Penny squirm. She wasn't going to like what he had to say; she just knew it. "But what if you're wrong?"

"Wrong about what?"

"Wrong about what she wants and why she's let things happen the way they have. What if she's not in financial trouble? What if she simply doesn't want to spend her summer months entertaining strangers? What if she's slowing down and she's just fine with it?"

Penny got to her feet and crossed the porch to rest her hands on the wide rail. With her back to him, she could think a little clearer. Over her shoulder, she said, "You know, what we're doing in the garden isn't hurting anyone. It's making her home a nicer place, that's all. We're not creating more work for her. We're not making her do anything at all. And the website? She can just say 'no' if she doesn't want to go that route. But what if she sees it and realizes that all her fears about it were for nothing? You should see it, Ward. It's beautiful," she said, turning back to face him. "And so simple—"

Ward was only a few feet from her, his hands in his pockets as he made his way over to stand beside her. She hadn't even heard him get up from the table.

"It's the why that bothers me. Not your why. I know why you're doing this. Because you're an amazing human being who wants to bring a little extra sunshine into everyone else's lives."

Penny had to look away from him, unable to hold his gaze. The way he looked at her as he said those words made her knees weak, and she was glad she still clutched the railing in both hands. She leaned against it, but before she could thank him for the compliment, he went on.

"It's Hazel's why that's been eating at me. I can't imagine she's let things go simply because she doesn't care."

"Of course not," Penny agreed.

"And she says she's not sick."

"We already covered that, and I haven't seen any sign of illness, Ward. Believe me, I've been watching for it, too. I don't think she'd out and out lie to me, but I do know she's holding something close to the vest."

"It doesn't make sense that it's financial, then." Ward spoke quietly beside her, but he was no longer looking at her. "If she needed money, she'd find ways to fill all the rooms. If it meant a website, she'd have gotten one ages ago. She only uses her age when she needs an excuse people can't argue with."

"Well, if its not financial, what do you think it is?" Penny asked, getting a little irritated. She didn't want to argue, and this felt a lot like it was heading in that direction.

He hesitated for a weighted moment, then said, "Has she said anything to you about selling this place?"

"What?" Penny gasped. The thought had never crossed her mind. The Garden Gate Guesthouse without Hazel? It didn't seem feasible. "No, Ward. She's never even so much as mentioned it."

"Okay." He turned around and braced his backside against the rail so he could look more directly at her. Then he reached over, took her hand in his, and lifted it to his lips to plant a kiss on her knuckles. "Let's not argue about this, okay? I trust you, Penny, because I know you. I know your heart and your intentions, and they're good."

Penny let the words wash over her, a soothing balm to her soul. He did know her. He may not know everything *about* her, but he knew her. And it felt good to be known by him. "Thank you," she said, wondering what it would feel like to have him plant a kiss on her lips instead.

As if reading her thoughts, still holding her hand, he slowly drew her closer until she was standing in front of him. The porch light behind her shined on his face, and she could see the play of intense emotions in his expression. "Penny."

"Yes?" The word came out rushed and breathless.

"I want to kiss you." He brushed the curve of her jaw with his fingertips, his thumb tracing the dip just below her bottom lip. "May I kiss you?"

Penny opened her mouth to list all the reasons why they shouldn't let whatever was happening happen, but her voice decided to suddenly and inexplicably go AWOL on her. Flapping her bottom jaw like a guppy, she shook her head, managed to get out, "Uhh," then she closed her mouth hard, her teeth clacking together.

Ward took a small step closer, and Penny knew she should take one giant step back, but apparently, her feet had gone on strike, too.

And why wasn't she breathing? She was starting to feel lightheaded. *Breathe! Take a breath! Now!*

Ward's gaze dropped to her lips, and she tried to swallow, but instead, made an odd gulping sound at the back of her throat. Her whole body flushed hotly from the cauldron of feelings swirling through her.

As though someone stood behind her, pushing her gently in the middle of her back, she leaned forward until she was so close, she could feel the heat of his body. "Ward," she whimpered.

Yes, she whimpered. *Gah*.

"Penny?" This time her name was a question, a request for permission. His voice didn't sound any stabler than hers did, and a tremor of anticipation skimmed down her spine.

He turned her hand in his and pressed it flat against his chest right over his heart. Before she could freak out over what to do with her other hand, he slid an arm loosely around her waist and drew her up against him.

That was all it took for her limbs to figure out what to do on their own. Her free hand skimmed up his arm and over the curve of his shoulder until her palm rested against the back of his neck, her fingers buried in his hair.

"I'd like that," she whispered, and then she stood up on tiptoe, pulled his head down, closed her eyes, and pressed her mouth to his.

Ward kissed her like a starving man at a banquet, cupping her face in one hand, clutching her close with his other arm now wrapped around her waist. She moaned softly against his lips, surrendering to the sensations that flooded through her.

Still up on tiptoes, her knees began to tremble, her ankles wobbling, and she wrapped both arms around his neck, stretching up into him as tall as she could go.

He must have felt her wobble, because he made a harsh sound against her lips, then scooped her up in his arms, his mouth not leaving hers for more than a moment. Effortlessly, he carried her over to one of the large patio chairs and lowered them both into it, so that he was now cradling her on his lap. Penny sighed softly and settled more comfortably into his embrace.

The pure luxury of no longer having to hold herself upright, of leaning into someone else for a change, of surrendering the tight-fisted control she clung to every day of her life washed over her like a wave. To her utter mortification, tears began to trickle from the corners of her eyes, even while her mouth moved over his.

He didn't jerk backward or say something insensitive, like, "What's going on?" in a freaked-out guy voice. No, Ward did something worse. He began pressing tender kisses along her jawline, on each cheek, the tip of her nose, her eyes—he'd probably get mascara on his lips—and then he rested his forehead against hers. He just held her, their breath mingling, hearts racing, the cocoon of emotions wrapped around them.

"Wow." The word came out of him drenched in awe. "I've been wanting to do that since—since—" He broke off like he wasn't quite sure when he'd started thinking about kissing her.

"Since I tore down your bubble tent?" she asked softly, teasing, but half serious, too. If she remembered right, he hadn't been completely unaffected by her that day. Oh, she wasn't delusional. She doubted he'd been desperate to kiss her from the moment they met. But there'd been a moment or two when the sparks between them had seemed borderline explosive.

"Well, maybe not at that exact moment," he said, lifting his head just enough so he could see her face. "But when I came charging out of the house to save you—you screamed, remember? And I saw you flirting with Alex on the front porch—"

"I wasn't flirting with Alex," she snorted, stiffening in the circle of his arms.

"Maybe not, but Alex was flirting with you, and it was at that moment that I thought maybe I'd screwed up by chasing you off."

Penny stared at him in confusion. "Then why did you act like that? I mean, you picked up my stuff and practically threw it in my trunk. You couldn't wait for me to be gone."

Ward pulled her closer, his arms tightening around her, lacing his fingers together at the back of her hip. "I couldn't wait for Alex to not have access to you," he admitted sheepishly. "I figured I'd try to make it up to you later, when his handsome mug wouldn't be around to compete with."

"Oh." She rested her head against his shoulder, glad he couldn't see her burning cheeks. "Oh. I see."

"That coffee?"

She lifted her head again. "What coffee?" she asked slowly.

"That was from me. That first day at Juno's. It really was a peace offering." Ward's smile curved up on one side, and he planted a kiss against her temple. "I knew I'd messed up with you at Hazel's, and I was hoping for a reset. But then I went and messed that attempt up, too."

"That should have set off warning bells in both our heads, you know," she murmured, breathing in the clean, crisp smell of his shaving cream or aftershave or soap or whatever it was that guys used around their faces. Having grown up without a father, she didn't have much experience with watching a guy perform his ablutions, and the variety of products—for both men and women, if she were being honest—was a little confusing to her. "You smell so good," she gushed. Then she stilled, hoping he wouldn't laugh. Not that she'd blame him if he did. "Sorry. I didn't realize I was going to say that out loud."

He did laugh then, and the gentle rumble of it vibrated through her. "Warning bells?" he asked, referring to what she'd said a moment ago.

"Yeah. You know, in romance novels or movies, when the main characters start out all scrappy and snarky with each other? They're bound to end up together. That's just the way it happens."

"Even in real life?"

Penny straightened and slipped a hand up to cup his jaw, the hint of stubble a slight rasp against her palm. She looked at him and smiled. "Apparently so." Then she kissed him, light and sweet.

The kiss didn't stay light and sweet though, and a few fathomless minutes later, when his phone rang from his back pocket, they both jumped and jerked apart as though they'd been caught doing something they shouldn't.

"I—I'm not going to get that," Ward said, breathlessly. He started to pull her close again, but she braced a hand on his chest.

"You can't just let it ring," she admonished, even though she was breathing just as heavily, and wanted just as badly to get back to the kissing. "Don't you at least need to see who it is? What if it's your parents?" A tiny tremor of fear tickled the back of her throat as she imagined the worst.

"Right. Sure." He reached back to pull it from his pocket and brought it around so he could see the screen.

She felt it. She was cradled in his arms, her body pressed against his. There was no way she couldn't have felt the way he stiffened when he saw—when they both saw—the name and contact photo on his phone screen.

Rochelle. A very, very beautiful woman named Rochelle whose contact picture was of her and Ward, arms around each other, cheeks pressed together in one of those theme park photo booths.

And it wasn't just a phone call. It was a video chat.

Ward silenced the ringer and shoved the phone back into his pocket. "Sorry. Not important."

But when he made to pick up where they'd left off, when he tried to draw her back to him, Penny resisted, gently unwinding his arms from around her. He closed his eyes and let her slide off his lap.

"I'm sorry," he muttered, looking up at her. "That's not—she's not—" he broke off completely and scrubbed his hands over his face. He leaned forward in the chair, bracing his elbows on his knees, and looked up at her. "That wasn't what it looked like," he finally said.

Penny backed up until she bumped into the edge of the swing behind her. She dropped clumsily into it, setting the thing rocking wonkily. "I'm not exactly sure what it looked like," she said, watching him. He still hadn't looked at her. "But she's obviously important to you."

"She was," he corrected, finally meeting her gaze. She read the truth in his eyes, but then why was she calling him at ten o'clock on a Monday night? "She's not anymore."

Penny took a steadying breath, but her pulse was racing so hard that it felt like her heart might burst through her ribcage at any moment. "That picture—and the fact that she's calling you this late—kind of says otherwise."

"It's two hours behind in California," he said, as if that made things so much better. He said nothing in defense of the picture.

"It's okay, Ward." This was why she needed to stick to her rules. This kind of drama was what she *didn't* need in her life right now. "I should have asked if there was anyone else—"

He cut her off. "There's no one else, Penny. She's my ex-girlfriend. It's been over for months." His eyes pleaded with her to believe him. "She decided I wasn't worth the distance between us."

She did believe him, but she wasn't going to argue her case. Because in another five and a half weeks, she was heading home to care for her sick mother, and from what Ward had told her, he planned to wrap things up in Autumn Lake by the end of the summer, too. He would be returning to California. He would be returning to her. The distance between them would no longer exist.

"She's not in my life anymore, Penny."

Penny blinked once, slowly, then said, "But she is, isn't she? She just called you. A video chat, no less. She wanted to see you. And if I hadn't been here? If you weren't in the middle of kissing me? You'd have taken her call, wouldn't you?"

Ward lurched up out of the chair and paced to the railing. He turned around and leaned against it again, but she could tell there was nothing casual or relaxed about him. "I'm not going to lie to you, Penny. I would have taken the call. We had a strange conversation the other day, and I've been a little worried about her."

Penny nodded, glad he wasn't lying, but her stomach hurt over what he'd just acknowledged. "So this isn't just some random call from her. This is an ongoing conversation."

Ward shook his head. "That's not what I meant. I haven't talked to her since early April, Penny. Months ago. Then two weeks ago, my business partner—I told you about him, right? Johnny suggested I call her; said he thought something was wrong. I did, and she pretty much shut me out. I had no plans to call her back after that, but her behavior toward me was not normal, validating Johnny's concern. So yeah, if I hadn't been with you, I probably would have answered the call."

Penny nodded again. She felt a little like one of those dashboard dolls, the way her head kept bobbing up and down.

"But that doesn't make me a bad person, Penny. It doesn't change the way I feel about you. And it shouldn't change the way you feel about me." He started toward her, but she rose, too, and held out both hands toward him, palms out in a gesture that plainly told him not to come any closer.

"It doesn't change how I feel about you," she told him, her eyes beginning to sting at how much it hurt to admit that. "It only changes what I do about those feelings."

"Please, Penny." He reached out a hand toward her, but she backed up. "If you want, I'll call her back right now and you can listen in on the conversation."

"What? Why on earth would I want to do that?" she asked, appalled at the suggestion.

"Because I'm telling you the truth. There's nothing between us. It's over." His phone beeped in his pocket. She'd left a message. A long message, apparently.

"Maybe you should check that," she said, turning to the table and starting to gather up their dessert dishes and coffee cups.

Ward practically whipped his phone out of his back pocket and swiped it open. "Yes. Of course. Listen to her message with me. You'll see."

"Ward, you sound desperate."

"I am desperate. I'm desperate for you to believe me."

"I do believe you," she insisted, but he kept tapping on his phone screen. "Stop it. I don't want to hear—"

"Hey, baby. Facetime me back as soon as you can, okay? I want to see that gorgeous—" Ward let out a low growl and ended the message.

Penny stood frozen on the spot, a plate in each hand. She wanted to throw them both at him, but thankfully, she couldn't seem to get any of her limbs to cooperate again. Which was a good thing, because the plates were delicate cut-glass and part of a large set, and they would not have survived. "I think you'd better go home, Ward."

20
Ward

He'd known the moment Rochelle's message started playing that he and Penny would hear two very different things. Why had he insisted on playing the stupid thing before listening to it himself?

"Hey, baby," Rochelle had purred, and Ward had known the call wouldn't be a good one. Not because she'd do something stupid like beg him to take her back. No. She'd probably already done something stupid and wanted him to be okay with it.

For the life of him, he couldn't figure out what it could be. He honestly didn't care what she did with her life anymore, as long as she lived it far away from him.

Which meant that she needed to stop going by Blue Waters, especially once he got back to California.

If he ever got back there. He wasn't so sure he was dead set on it anymore.

But of course, Penny would hear the sultry sounds of a woman making sweet with a guy whom her sweetness had worked on in the past. Penny would put together that voice and the picture she'd seen on his phone and come to a very different conclusion.

Why hadn't he updated his phone like a normal person? Deleted that picture she'd put on his phone as her contact picture? Why hadn't he deleted her from his phone altogether? Had he really been hoping she'd take him back? Or had he been too lazy to update it? Had he cared too much to let her go? Or too little to bother with it all?

Well, he cared now. He wanted to rip the stupid phone out of his pocket and throw the cursed thing in the lake.

"I mean it, Ward." Penny set the plates she'd been holding back down on the table and dropped into a chair, like her knees could no longer hold her upright. "I need to—to think. By myself. I need you to go."

Ward was at a loss. He couldn't insist on staying, not when she'd made it very clear that she didn't want him there. He couldn't force her to change her perception of what she'd heard; even if he explained everything, it still didn't look or sound good. And she didn't want to hear it from him, anyway.

"Can I call you in the morning?"

Penny shook her head, and the movement shook loose a tear from each eye. Ward dropped his chin to his chest and squeezed his own eyes shut. He wanted to cry, too. "Will you still have dinner with me tomorrow after work?"

"Tomorrow is Tuesday, Ward," she said, her voice calm, giving no indication that the tears were now starting to trickle down her cheeks. "You're going out to eat with your dad."

"Not if I can take you out, instead," he rushed to say. He'd forgotten everything except this terrible moment they were in.

She shook her head again. "Please don't do this," she said, her voice breaking.

"Can I call you tomorrow night, then? After I get home? I can't go like this." He stood there, arms akimbo at his sides. His feet felt like they were stuck in concrete. "I'm not going to just leave everything so messed up between us."

Penny kept her gaze averted, but she stood again and crossed her arms, hugging herself. "I'll call you when I've thought through this."

"You promise, Penny? Promise me that you'll call." He came closer anyway. He reached over and gently brushed his thumb over her cheek, wiping at the tracks her tears were making. "I need to hear you say it."

"I promise," she whispered.

Then, to his surprise, she reached up and cupped her hand around his and pressed her face into his palm. He flinched at the flare of heat—of *hope*—that tore through him, racing up his arm to land a direct hit to his heart. He moved closer and dipped his head, not to kiss her, but to look into her eyes.

He needed to see her soul.

"No," she whimpered, her voice cracking on the word. "Stop." She pushed his hands away. "Goodnight, Ward."

And with that, she turned on her heel and headed inside, leaving the aftermath of their lovely night still scattered all over the table.

He waited alone on the porch, hoping against hope that she'd have a change of heart and come back out. But when she didn't, he stacked the dishes in a neat pile for her, swept the crumbs into his hand, and tossed them out into the yard for the birds and other critters to feast on in the morning.

Several minutes later, he was sitting out at the end of his parents' dock, holding his phone to his ear. He hadn't even gone inside, not wanting to risk the chance of running into his dad or mom. He couldn't bear having to answer their eager questions about how the night had gone.

Maybe Penny would look out her dark bedroom window and see him. He wanted to wave, just in case she was there, hidden in the dark behind her curtain. But he restrained himself, and instead, focused on the phone call he was making.

"Hey, Ward," Rochelle said in a much nicer voice than the one she'd answered his call with last night. "Why aren't we Face-timing? Here, I'll switch us over for you," she said, as though he didn't have the technical savvy to do so himself.

How many times had he heard variations of those words come out of her mouth? She said stuff like that all the time. "I'll just do it for you. You'll never figure it out." That's why his phone had that picture of them as her contact photo; Rochelle had put it there. The picture made her look like a model. It made him look like a grizzled old sea captain. Or at least that's how he felt now as he looked at it. He shook his head, misery wrapping its cold, slimy arms around him.

"I don't want to video chat." He hit the 'decline' button. "I'm sitting outside in the dark. You won't be able to see anything anyway."

"Are you alone?" She said 'alone' in about four syllables.

"Yes. What was it you were wanting?" He used her words from yesterday. Apparently, he was going to be rude after all. "I'm kind of in a rush."

"Well, well, well," she cooed, even now, her velvet voice sending an unsettling shiver down his spine. "Did I disrupt something?"

Yes! He wanted to rant into the phone at her. *You are disrupting my life.*

"What do you want, Rochelle?" he asked again.

"Okay. Fine. I'll get right to it." She took a long breath and let it out on a giggle.

Rochelle wasn't a giggler. Was she nervous? Great. What had she done now?

❤ · ❤ · ❤ · ❤ · ❤

HIS BUSINESS PARTNER ANSWERED after four rings, and for a moment, Ward thought he'd gotten his voice mail. "Hey, there, partner," Johnny practically shouted into the phone. "Everything all right?"

It was a fair question. They'd talked just two days ago, and a second call this soon was unusual. Ward didn't beat around the bush. "Finally spoke to Rochelle last night." He waited, hoping Johnny would take the bait so that Ward didn't have to spell it out.

No such luck.

"You did? How is she? You guys make up?"

Ward groaned inwardly and clenched his teeth together so hard that his jaw threatened to spasm. So this was how it was going to go. "She told me that she's seeing someone," he said, forcing the words out past the tightness in his throat. "She didn't want me to hear it from anyone else." He hated this kind of cat and mouse game, but that was one of the downsides of confronting a salesperson as skilled as Johnny. He could be slippery, that was for sure.

"Ah, man. Sorry, dude. That sucks. I thought maybe you two might manage to straighten things out between you. You sure there's nothing there, still? I mean, I knew she was starting to check out the field a little, and I should have told you, but you know, I was rooting for you, man." Johnny sighed heavily on his end, and Ward could hear a fast-paced clicking sound in the background. The guy always clicked his retractable pen whenever he was working on a deal. "She's quite a—"

"She told me she's dating you, Johnny."

The sudden silence coming from the other end of the line was all the confirmation he needed that Rochelle hadn't been making it up. Not that he'd really thought she was, but part of him had thought that maybe she was fabricating the whole thing. Maybe she was hoping he'd be jealous and come racing back to California to stake his claim on her.

But Rochelle hadn't told him about her new romance in a cruel way. She hadn't waved it in his face. In fact, she'd asked him if he was okay with it, and she'd even said that if he wasn't, she'd be willing to back off until he had time to get more accustomed to the idea. "I really like him, Ward. And he's all in. With me, with this town. With this life."

Her implication was that Ward hadn't been, and that had stung. It felt like she was comparing the two, even if that wasn't her intent. She clearly wanted someone who had both feet, both hands, and a hundred percent of their heads planted firmly in her Pacific Coast beach town.

This time last year, Ward would have considered himself to be just that guy. They'd talked about marriage several times, and Ward had thought that was the direction they were moving in. But Rochelle had explained to him that she'd been hesitant to take their relationship to the next level because she hadn't believed that he was as wholly invested in the life they had together as she was.

"I never felt like I really had you all the way, Ward. Like there was always a piece of you missing, or somewhere else. Or with someone else." If that was true, then maybe she'd seen something in him that he was only now starting to discover about himself.

"There was never anyone else," he'd told her. But he hadn't denied there might have been a some*where* else. Even if he hadn't known it at the time, he could see now that Autumn Lake would always have a hold on him, even if he never called it 'home' again.

Ward knew he needed to get back to California.

He needed to get back to the helm of Blue Waters, to see for himself that the business was as he'd left it. But now, the thought of it turned his stomach. Because even if things looked great on paper, there *had* been a mutiny, hadn't there?

"Man. Ward. I'm sorry. I don't mean for things to go this way." Johnny's voice, for once, was hushed. Careful. Tentative. Words Ward had certainly never before used to describe the man. "It just happened; you know?"

"Don't pull that with me, Johnny. This stuff doesn't 'just happen'. You could have picked up the phone. You could have said something to me at any time during our weekly calls. Instead, you took the cowardly route and threw Rochelle at me."

"She wanted to be the one to tell you." Johnny's voice rose insistently. "I told her we should have talked to you sooner, but she wanted to hold off. To make sure whatever this was between us was more than just a rebound."

Ward frowned, confounded by what he was hearing. "And you were okay with that? It didn't bother you that you might be just a rebound?" He used Johnny's words but threw in a heavy dose of sarcasm.

"That's not what I meant. I knew I wasn't a rebound. She wanted to make sure you didn't accuse her of using me as a rebound. She wanted to talk to you first, to make sure you would be good with all of this. Honestly, we figured you'd take it from her better than from me." He sounded a little belligerent, Ward thought. Like he didn't appreciate what Ward was suggesting about his new girlfriend.

Except that Rochelle wasn't the kind of person to be manipulative that way, and Ward needed to remember that before he went off on Johnny again. "Listen. I'm not good with any of this. I'm not good with my ex-girlfriend dating my business partner. We were together three years, man. How am I supposed to come back and just be good with everything? Isn't it a little weird for you, too?"

"That's just it. It's not weird." Johnny insisted. He sighed, and then in a gentler voice, said, "It's not weird, Ward, because you're not around to make it weird."

The words hit him like a mule kick in the chest. He pressed his palm to his sternum; he was finding it a little difficult to breathe. "I'll be back at the end of August at the latest. Sooner, if I can swing it," he finally managed to say. "I'm beginning to wonder if you and I have very different ideas about what a partnership looks like."

"Ah, come on, man," Johnny cajoled. "Don't do that. We're adults here, Ward. Things happen that we don't plan for; there's no getting around that. It's how we react that separates us from the animals."

"You don't need to sell me anything, *man*." Ward spit the word out, but he used every ounce of willpower to rein in his temper. "I think I'm reacting appropriately. Not like an animal at all, in fact. I'll be out there in a few weeks, and when I get there, you and I can sit down and compare notes."

"She's just a woman, Ward. Don't get your panties in a bunch."

Ward froze. "Repeat that, Johnny. I'd like to record you saying that and send it to Ro. She deserves far better." His voice came out oozing disgust.

"Geez, Ward," Johnny railed over the phone at him. "I just said it to lighten things up. To get you to call off the dogs, you know? She's not *just* a woman. She's the one and only Rochelle Trebler. She's amazing, okay? But you and me, man. We go way back. Back before any woman, right? That's all I meant by that."

Slippery. That was Johnny Bolton. He could make a person believe just about anything he wanted them to. But Ward wasn't having it tonight.

"I'll see you in a few weeks. I'll let you know as soon as I book my flight."

"That's great, man. It'll be good to see you again. I mean it. We miss you around here." Something in the way he said the words made Ward shift uncomfortably in his chair. It sounded like Johnny found him expendable, too. Rochelle certainly did. She'd had no trouble casting him aside. Out of sight, out of mind.

21
Penny

"WHOA!" PENNY HELD UP both hands. She could feel her cheeks growing warm, and she hoped they wouldn't assume it was evidence of guilt. "Actually, I haven't seen him since Monday night. We—we had a disagreement," she said, avoiding meeting anyone's eyes.

"You argued after I went to bed?" Hazel asked, aghast. "You were being so sweet to each other. That's why I called it a night early." She pressed a hand to her chest.

"You two are perfect for each other," Claire chimed in. "He brings you pizza and watches Sandra Bullock movies with you, Penny. You said he even laughs at all the right places."

"We didn't argue," Penny tried to interject.

"Wait. He watches romcoms with you?" Candy pressed a hand to her chest and sighed dreamily. "If you don't want him, can I have him?"

"And you really haven't seen him since Monday, Sweet Pea?" Hazel wasn't about to let it go so easily. Her brows were drawn together in concern. "I thought you two were getting along so swimmingly. I peeked outside once more after I left you two alone on the porch, and you were snuggled up together on that chaise—"

Penny held up a hand to stop her, not surprised at all that Hazel had spied on them. "I haven't," she said with a sigh. Then she forced a bright smile on her face. "But I'm sure he's been really busy."

"What happened?" the older woman asked, seeing her expression for what it was. "Oh, dear."

"Nothing really happened," Penny insisted, picking up her mug so she could hide behind it. "At least not the way you're thinking."

"How do you know what I'm thinking?" Hazel snapped, her irritation growing, if the look on her face was any indication. "I might just have to have a talk with that young man if you don't give me a few more details. I don't like this kind of drama, and I know for a fact that you don't either." She circled a hand in front of her, indicating the women gathered around. "You're among friends, dear. We are here to help you."

"And support you, no matter what you do or don't tell us," Addison said, her voice gentle.

Penny might as well get straight to it. She'd eventually spill her guts to this group at some point, she knew, and now, while the pain was fresh, she might as well be real with them.

"He got a call from his ex-girlfriend while we were—um, snuggling on the chaise lounge."

"Oh no," Juno muttered under her breath, her eyes narrowing. "I knew that woman was going to be a problem."

"Yeah." Penny dipped her head and blinked quickly. She was not going to cry. She'd done enough of that already in the privacy of her room. But if she let the dam break now in front of them all, she might never be able to stop. "I don't think she's as much of an ex as he'd like me to believe. Maybe not as much of an ex as he'd like himself to believe, either." She set aside her mug, not sure her churning stomach could handle another drop of cooling coffee. She swallowed hard around the lump that gathered in her throat every time she even thought about Ward St. James.

"Yikes," Juno said. "He was in yesterday, but he didn't stay to eat. Just grabbed a sandwich and coffee to go. He's always a little hangry when he comes by at lunchtime, but he seemed off. I should have asked."

"No, please." Penny shook her head. "Please don't ask him anything, you guys. At least not about us, okay?" She was suddenly starting to have second thoughts about discussing the situation behind his back. She knew these women cared about him, but she certainly didn't want to be the source of any false information circulating about him. "Can we just keep this conversation between us? I'm sure he'll figure things out, and everything will be set to right with him soon."

"With him, but not with you?" Addison asked. Her face was a mask of concern. "Where does this leave you, then, Penny?"

"I'm going back home in a month, Addison." She smiled bravely, wishing they'd change the subject. "It leaves me right where I was when I got here."

A silence like a lead blanket settled around the table, every one of them drooping under the weight of it.

"I'm assuming you want us to change the subject," Liz said. It was more of a statement than a question, and Penny had never appreciated her bluntness more.

"Yes, please," she said with a half-laugh, but even to her, it sounded more like a half-sob.

She didn't just want to talk about something other than Ward; she wanted to *think* of something else besides Ward, too. She had spent far too many hours over the last four days thinking about him.

THAT EVENING, PENNY AND Hazel sat out on the porch together, listening to the quiet drizzle that had started to fall about an hour ago. The summer cloudburst would pass over soon, and tomorrow would be another hot, humid day. The lake looked moody and dark under the shrouded sky, and Penny could relate. The porch light across the inlet remained off.

"Hazel, I have to tell you something." Penny had been dreading this conversation all afternoon, but after their club meeting that morning, after everything that had happened with Ward, she just didn't feel right keeping the project a secret any longer. Hazel had asked some rather probing questions about their club, what the purpose of it was, and what would happen to it after Penny left. Well, she'd answer all those questions now if she could, and if Hazel wanted it to stop, she'd go to the girls and that would be the end of it.

"What is it, Sweet Pea?"

Penny shifted Jimbo so that he wasn't pressed right up against her. The rain had cooled the air, but the humidity made sitting close to any warm-blooded creature uncomfortable. "I told my friends that I was worried about you. About Garden Gate. And I am worried. I saw your stack of bills the other day. You have no guests. The garden—" She broke off when she saw Hazel's smile fall away. "Oh Hazel, I'm sorry. I didn't really think of it as being deceptive. Not at first. Ward said he thought I should tell you, and even then, I kinda figured that he was a guy, and he didn't understand how much we women like nice surprises. But then today, we kept having to circumvent your questions. It made me really uncomfortable that you didn't know why we were there, even though we were there with the best intentions."

Hazel nodded slowly. "I see."

Penny licked her suddenly dry lips. She was in it this deep already; she might as well jump. "Are you? In trouble, I mean?" Penny asked, her voice barely above a whisper. "I just... I just want to help if I can."

Hazel sighed deeply, then Murtagh sighed, too. She scratched his head between his ears, and he flopped his tail in appreciation. "I suppose you could call it that, although not in the way you're thinking." She let out a wry chuckle. "Not that I presume to know what you're thinking," she added, apparently recalling the similar conversation they'd had that morning.

Penny's heart lurched. "Are—are you sick?"

"No, honey. No, I'm not sick. But I'm getting old, Sweet Pea. Finally," she added with a chuckle. "I'll be eighty-four this year; did you know that?"

Penny shook her head but didn't say anything. She'd thought the woman was in her seventies at the most.

"Well, I will be. And I'm tired. You girls talked today about your dreams for the future. Business ventures. Romance. Travel and more. I've lived my dreams, Penny girl. And now I'm ready to do less, not more."

Penny nodded. "I can understand that. But what about this place? What will you do?"

"Well, now, that's the dilemma, isn't it?" Hazel made a show of covering Murtagh's ears. "I don't have children," she said sotto voce, then let go of his ears and scratched between them. "Or even other family members who might be interested in this property. So I'm going to have to sell it."

"Oh, Hazel."

"I'm not quite ready to do anything yet; don't worry. It's probably ridiculous of me, I know, but I want to handpick the new owners. I won't have anyone moving in here who will just tear this place down and put up a mini version of that monstrosity across the lake. I couldn't do that to Rachel and Ted. Or the rest of our little community. But this property is large, and with the home and the outbuildings, and it being waterfront, it's worth a lot of money. It's going to take a very specific buyer, and I need to start looking now, because it may take years to find him or her."

"What are you going to do if you find a buyer sooner than later?" Penny couldn't imagine The Garden Gate without Hazel at the helm. "Where will you go?"

Hazel let out a dry chuckle. "There's another catch. I've been looking at retirement homes in the surrounding areas. I don't want to leave Autumn Lake, but there's nothing like that here. However, I'm so discouraged by what I'm finding out there." She pointed over her shoulder toward the general direction of the kitchen. "That's what the pile of paperwork is in there. Old folks' home brochures and price sheets, contracts, and menus, the works. It's a little overwhelming trying to keep all that stuff straight—who does what and when and where and what's included in the prices and what isn't."

"I'm so sorry I assumed." Shame washed over Penny.

Hazel shook her head. "Don't be sorry. Your heart is in the right place. Anyway, I've been visiting different homes over the past few months. That's where I was the morning you arrived, in fact. I've been to two others since then. I had dinner at a place about half an hour from here Monday night while you were out with Ward; I won't even consider a place if they don't let me have a meal or two to test it out."

"Sounds reasonable to me," Penny agreed, pushing back the overwhelming desire to weep for both of them and the big changes looming ahead.

"Some of the facilities I've seen are downright gorgeous, and the apartments, although frighteningly small after living here, are quite elegant. But nothing I've looked at so far has felt like home to me."

"Home." Penny said aloud. The word seemed to be on everyone's lips these days.

"This is my home, Sweet Pea. It's the only real home I've ever known. I grew up here, and although I lived away from here for the two years of my marriage before my husband died, I came right back here so I could grieve and grow old in the sanctuary of this place. I've never wanted to live anywhere else."

"I can't blame you," Penny murmured. In Hazel's shoes, she wouldn't want to have to move, either.

"But I don't want to be one of those awful news stories you hear about." She held up her hand like she was framing a headline. "Woman who lives alone slips and falls in the shower. Her body is discovered a week later when passersby report a cloud of flies hovering over the chimney."

"Hazel!" Penny covered her mouth with one hand. "Don't say such things."

The older woman chuckled softly. "Don't worry. I'm very careful getting in and out of the shower. I even had grab bars installed several years ago, and I have a seat in there, too. One I use, just so you know. I'm quite aware of my limitations."

"Have you—have you ever considered hiring someone to help you run this place?" Penny asked, not sure that was really the solution Hazel was looking for. "Maybe even just while you're looking for the right buyer?" Oh, if only she had a million bucks.

"I have, but unless the guesthouse starts making money again, I really can't afford to pay someone in anything other than room and board. But I'm not so sure I want someone moving in with me. I'm old and set in my ways, and the idea of having someone else running what has always been my life scares me a little, I have to admit." She smiled grimly. "It's a terrible catch-22 I've gotten myself into. I'm sitting on a golden egg here, and once it sells, I can easily afford to do just about anything I could dream of... except stay here. I just waited too long to make too many changes, it seems." She tugged gently on Murtagh's ear, and the dog stuck out his long tongue to lick her wrist. "I always thought I'd live forever."

Penny could tell she wasn't even half serious, but she understood. Hazel did seem ageless, timeless, in so many ways. "I wish with all my heart that I was in a position to help you," Penny declared. "I'd move in here in a heartbeat, and together, we'd get this place up and running again in no time. You wouldn't even have to pay me. Ever."

Hazel blew her a kiss. "You're my favorite person in the whole world, Sweet Pea."

"So you're not mad at me?"

"I could never be mad at you, darling girl. Frustrated? Perhaps. I do wish you had come directly to me with your concerns. I wasn't trying to hide anything from you. I just didn't want to worry you." She snorted wryly. "And look how that turned out. So I can't be mad at you, can I? I'm the one who created the situation in the first place."

Lying in bed later that night, Penny let the tears that had been gathering all evening trickle from the corners of her eyes as she poured out her heart to God. She prayed for Hazel's difficult dilemma, for Ward as he, too, seemed caught in a tug-of-war over circumstances in his life. She prayed for her group of friends here at the lake, thanking God that He'd brought such wonderful women into her life. She prayed for her mother and aunt and uncle back home, and finally, she prayed for herself. She asked for courage to face the new challenges that were just around the corner, for wisdom in making the right decisions for her mother's future, and for peace in whatever circumstances He allowed Penny to be in.

She was just drifting off when her phone rang, the sound shockingly loud in the quiet of her cozy room.

"Penny." It was Aunt Jean. She sounded distraught.

"What is it?" Penny gasped, lurching up in bed.

"It's your mother. She got out at some point over the last two hours. We thought she was asleep in her room, but I got up to use the bathroom and checked on her, and she's gone."

"Gone? She's lost? Or is she—is she dead?" It was her worst nightmare come true; that her mother would slip away, and she wouldn't be with her. She turned on her lamp and threw back her covers, struggling to untangle her feet from the sheet in her haste.

"Oh, honey, no. Don't assume anything like that. We just haven't found her yet. The police and other emergency services are here with search teams, and several of the neighbors are out looking, too. They all know Judy; we take walks with her every evening."

"No. Oh, no, oh no." The syllables tumbled out of her mouth and ran together. "I'm coming home. I—I'll get dressed and get on the road right now. I can be there in about six hours. Maybe five."

"Penny, no. Please don't drive right now. I didn't want to wait to tell you, but I don't want you to risk racing home with this weighing on you. We are doing everything we can, and I will keep you updated."

"I can't just sit here and do nothing!" Penny practically shouted into the phone; her words made harsher by the tears that clogged her throat. She was already tugging open her closet door to find something easy to throw on. "I have to come."

There was a knock at Penny's door, and she hurried to open it. Hazel stood there, her long silver hair spilling in disarray over her shoulders. "What's happening? I heard shouting," she said, eying the phone Penny had clutched to her ear.

"Penny?" Aunt Jean was trying to get her attention. She thrust the phone at Hazel.

"Here. You talk to her. I have to get dressed."

A few minutes later, despite her trembling hands and whirling thoughts, Penny had managed to pull on a pair of yoga pants and a t-shirt and was running a brush through her hair when Hazel ended the phone call and stepped in front of her. She took Penny by the shoulders and firmly told her to sit down.

A wave of fear washed over her, and she covered her mouth with both hands. She dropped to sit on the edge of the bed, certain Hazel was going to tell her the worst.

"I'm not going to let you get behind the wheel of a car right now," Hazel said, her eyes as steely as her voice. "You want to do something to help find your mother? Then you and I are going to sit here and pray. That's what you can do. It's the most powerful action you can take right now. And I'm going to be right here with you, fighting alongside you, got it?"

"I need to get home. I need to be there. She must be so afraid." Her words came out in broken sobs, but when Hazel stepped forward and put her arms around her shoulders, Penny sagged into her. "I shouldn't have left her," she sobbed. "I knew something like this would happen. Oh, Momma, where are you?"

True to her word, Hazel sat with Penny and prayed with her. Hazel said all her words out loud, while Penny's just ran in circles inside her head, but she knew God was more than capable of deciphering them.

And also true to her word, Aunt Jean kept them apprised of what was happening.

After what seemed like an eternity, but was, in fact, little more than an hour later, Aunt Jean called to tell them that Judy had been found, that she was safe. "She walked several houses down—" She broke off and cleared her throat before continuing. "The same way we walk every evening. We should have known. She wandered into the backyard through a side gate that had been left open, where she sat down on a lawn chair and fell asleep."

"Is she okay? Is she scared?" Penny could hear a myriad of noise in the background from Aunt Jean's side of the conversation. It sounded like utter chaos to her, and she imagined the worst.

Jean let out a shaky laugh. "She doesn't seem to be any the worse for wear, honey. She's not distressed in any way that we can tell. The paramedics are checking her over right now, and I wish you could see her. She's eating up the attention from all those handsome boys in uniforms."

Penny could imagine. Her mother had always had a thing for men in uniform. "She's really okay, though?" she asked again, desperate to hear the words repeated.

And once more, Aunt Jean assured her that she was.

"I'm going to come home anyway," Penny told her. She'd already made up her mind.

"Don't cut short your time away. I'll feel so bad if you do," Aunt Jean pleaded.

"And I'll feel bad if I don't. It's not about us, Aunt Jean. It's about Mom. I need to be there with her." She straightened her shoulders, the weight of worry and guilt lifting a little as she set her course. "I'm going to try to get some sleep, then I'll head out in the morning. I'll see you tomorrow afternoon sometime. I'll keep you posted on my ETA."

Penny slept surprisingly well. She bustled out of bed in the morning and started packing her belongings, hoping Hazel would be willing to ship anything that she left behind in her haste.

A knock sounded on her door, and Hazel pushed it open and stepped inside. "Good morning, Sweet Pea. Can you take a break just for a few minutes? Here. For you." She handed her the cup of coffee she was carrying.

Penny took the coffee, not caring that it was black. She took a fortifying sip. "Thank you," she said, glancing around the room, looking for anything she might be missing.

"Please," Hazel said, drawing her attention back to her. "Will you sit? I have a proposal for you."

22
Ward

"Okay. I'm going to ask the question that, apparently, no one else is. What do you have in SoCal that you can't have here? Your girlfriend dumped you for your business partner." Alex made a disgusted face. "That's the lowest of the low, my friend."

"Thanks for pointing that out."

"No problem," Alex shot back. "I just don't think you really get how big a deal that is. Why would you want to go back to that? How are you going to hold your head up in front of your crew?"

"Back off, Alex," Ward growled at his friend. It was Friday night, and for reasons of their own, neither of them had anyone else to spend it with. They were sitting at a table at the Old Mill where they'd both ordered the fried chicken plate for dinner, and now were finishing off the meal with apple pie and coffee.

Alex didn't back off. No surprise there. "I just don't get it. There's an amazing little lady right here in Autumn Lake who looks at you like she wants to take a bite out of you."

"Nice," Ward muttered, shaking his head in disgust. But... he couldn't help remembering the way she'd looked up at him, how the expression on her face had made his knees go weak. The way she felt in his arms, how her body had curved into his. Her mouth, the sounds she made while he kissed her... before Rochelle had dropped into things like an atom bomb.

"It's true." Alex took an enormous bite of the second slice of apple pie he'd ordered.

"She's not from here, remember? She's a summer laker. A WOOT." Wow. Why? Why had he tossed that in there? How was that any better than the way Johnny had talked about Rochelle? Why did people say stupid things—hurtful things—about other people just to make themselves look or feel better? Especially since it didn't work. The look on Alex's face told him his friend was wondering something similar. "Okay. She's not a WOOT," he admitted. "But she's not a townie, either."

"She comes here every summer, Ward. She's more of a townie than you are, my friend." Alex scratched at the stubble on his jaw. "But it's not just our Shiny Penny."

It didn't escape Ward's notice that Alex had casually claimed Penny as one of their own. *Our* shiny Penny? Did that 'our' include him? Alex was right; she'd come to the lake every summer for almost a decade, according to her, for at least two months out of the year. He'd been back a few days a year, at the most.

Alex shoved his now empty pie plate toward the middle of the table. "You've got a business out there that's apparently running fine without you, right? I mean, you've been away for what? Nine months? Ten now? Are you sure they want you back?"

"Shut up, Alex."

"I'm serious, dude. Think about it. You've got two—count 'em." He held up two fingers, then pointed them at Ward. "Two great businesses here in Autumn Lake who want you. In fact, they both need you."

Ward just shook his head, wishing he'd gone home with his father.

"And your folks are here."

"Believe me, I know that. I know all of this." Ward swallowed down the rest of his coffee and grimaced. It was cold and muddy, and he regretted that he hadn't saved one last bite of his pie to wash down the nasty taste of the coffee. "But you forget that I have a life somewhere else—"

"No, bro." Alex cut him off, leaning forward even more in his vehemence. "I'm not the one who seems to be forgetting things. You may have a life out there." He made air quotes around the word 'life.' "But this place? Autumn Lake? This, my dude, is where you really live. This is home. You'll always come back." He reached across the table and thumped Ward in the chest with a fist. "This place is in here. Your folks are here." He thumped him again. "Your friends are here." And once more. "That little lady should be here."

"I got it," Ward said, shoving Alex's fist away. "Back off."

Alex guffawed. "You're just mad because you know I'm right."

❣ · ❣ · ❣ · ❣ · ❣

"THIS MAY NOT BE the right place for this," Ward began, looking back and forth between his parents at the supper table the following night. "But there are some things we need to talk about." He'd surprised them both when he told them he'd not only be home for the meal, but that he'd bring dessert. He'd stopped by Juniper's and grabbed a box of pastries on his way.

Fortunately, Juno had not been there. She knew him well enough to recognize that something was wrong; he'd seen it in the way she'd watched him from the other end of the counter when he'd come in on Thursday and ordered his meal to go. He figured Penny had probably given all her girls the scoop on things, and he didn't want to hear from the outspoken woman. Ward was sure Juno had more than a few opinions on the situation; she'd always had issues with Rochelle.

"What is it?" his mother asked, putting a hand on his arm. "You know you can talk to us anytime, anywhere."

His father cleared his throat. "Does this have anything to do with that job offer from the resort?"

Ward balked. "You know about that?"

Ted nodded slowly. He picked up his fork, then set it down again. "I do." Rachel reached for him with her free hand. She'd always been that connecting force in their home, Ward thought, looking at her sitting there with a loving hand on each of her guys.

"We do," Rachel said. "It's a small town, sweetie."

Ted picked up his fork again. This time, he wiped it clean with his napkin before setting it back down on his dirty plate. "Actually, I have something I need to talk to you about, too."

Ward sat back in his seat, subconsciously pulling away from them. His arm slipped out from under his mother's hand, but she left it there on the table. Ready, he supposed, for when he decided to come close again.

"And I think I should start. Maybe it will help you sort out what you have to say," his father added. To Rachel, he said, "Would you like to move into the living room where it's more comfortable?"

"Oh no, honey." His mother smiled and patted Ted's arm. "I'm just fine. Let's not put this off a moment longer. I think this conversation is long overdue as it is."

Ward studied her face, her posture, just like his father was doing, but she seemed fine.

"Son, I need to apologize to you. I've been meaning to for some time, but I've been struggling to figure out what to say. How to say it."

Ward waited, feeling completely in the dark. What did his parents have to apologize to him for? Wasn't it the other way around?

"I'm the reason Lysha Austin offered you that job." He cleared his throat again. "Well, you're the reason she offered you the job, but I'm the one who told her about you. I recommended you for the position."

Ward had no words. This was the last thing—the very last thing—he'd expected his father to say.

"She came to me, to us, with the proposal first," Ted said, dipping his head toward Rachel to include her. "The offer she made me isn't the same as the one she made you, but it was still good enough for me to feel compelled to consider it. She didn't want to hire me. She wanted to contract with me to do the resort's boat repair, which would have been quite a coup for us, but the contract would have made resort repairs priority over my other customers."

Rachel nodded. "That was kind of a deal-breaker for us," she said softly.

Ward was trying to keep up. "A contract, but not a job offer?"

"Yes. She rightfully guessed that I wouldn't even consider working for them if it meant giving up St. James Mobile Boat Repair." Even after all these years, Ted still spoke the name of his company with a note of pride in his voice. "But everything about that contract was solid, Ward. She wasn't trying to pull one over on us. What they were offering me was a substantial increase in my income and a retirement plan I could buy into."

"Which is something we've always worried we didn't have enough of," Rachel interjected.

"Yes. There were other perks, too, such as access to the resort and the guest-only services over there, but none of that really mattered to us."

"But in the end, it would have meant potentially sacrificing the welfare of our loyal customers for money."

"Which we weren't willing to do," Ted said, finishing the sentence for his wife.

"I had no idea," Ward finally managed to say. "And I'm at a loss. That's definitely not the job she offered me. In fact, she made it very clear that I couldn't do both. I would be employed by the resort, and I could not help out here because it would be a conflict of interest, or so she said."

His father nodded. "Right. I can see why that might be the direction she chose to go in."

"And what part did you have in all of that?" Ward was still trying to wrap his head around the idea of Lysha approaching his father about the job first. Had he misjudged her all this time? Had he really been so blinded by his own self-importance, his own vanity, to think she'd come to him because she wanted him for more than just work? Had he judged her because she was a WOOT?

"I suggested that she approach you with the job."

Ward grimaced. "I already have a job, Dad. In fact, I don't just have a job. I have a business that provides a dozen people with jobs."

"I know," Ted said. "I know that. And that's what I'm apologizing for. I should have come to you, Ward. I should have asked you if you'd be interested in even considering the position before I threw your name in the hat."

"You're not getting it, Dad. It's not about whether I'm interested in the job or not."

Ted frowned, his expression mirrored on Rachel's face. "Then what is it? I want to know, Ward. I want to do this right."

Ward shook his head in frustration. "When was the last time you came to California to check out my life? My business, Dad?"

"Well," Ted began. He turned to look at Rachel, then back at Ward.

"Exactly. Never. You two have never come to California to see what I've accomplished. In almost twelve years, Dad. I moved out there more than a decade ago, and I have always been the one to come visit you. Not the other way around. Why is that?"

His parents eyed each other again, but when neither of them spoke immediately, Ward continued.

"Do you know why I left Autumn Lake?"

"We do, Ward," his mother said, her fingers fluttering on the tabletop as though she wanted nothing more than to reach for him. "You needed to find your way out from under us. We understood that. We still do."

"Do you know why I stayed away?"

"What would you like to hear from us?" Ted asked, his brow furrowing. "I feel a little like you're baiting us. We have always only wanted for you to be happy, Ward. Correct me if I'm wrong, but we have always believed that you stayed in California because you were happy there. You liked your life there. Is that not so?"

"If you thought I was happy there, if that was the one thing you wanted for me, then why didn't you ever come see for yourself? You just—" He broke off, bombarded by the emotions that were rising to the surface inside of him. "You just—"

"We just believed you, Ward," his mother said, her voice gentle, but sad. "And you never invited us."

Ward stared at her, the words hanging in the air between them like a roiling storm cloud. He'd never invited them? Never? But he had. Surely, he had.

"You made it clear that you wanted a life of your own," Ted said. "We didn't want to intrude or assume that we had any part of that. You continued to come home to see us, and you seemed satisfied with that, so we decided that we needed to be okay with that, too."

"I invited you," Ward countered. "I asked you to come out for my opening ceremonies."

"I had surgery that week, remember?" Rachel's hand slipped under the table, and Ward knew she was resting it on her abdomen. She'd struggled with endometriosis her whole adult life, and her pregnancy with Ward had been a miracle. That was why he was an only child; it wasn't because his parents hadn't wanted more.

He'd forgotten how sick she'd been that whole month, how she'd ended up in the emergency room in pain so acute, they'd hospitalized her. Ward hadn't come home. They'd assured him she was being well cared for, and that they understood that he needed to be there for his business. She'd had a full abdominal hysterectomy soon after.

"I—I'm sorry. I forgot." Ward's face burned with shame. "That wasn't the only time, though," he insisted, racking his brain for specifics. "I invited you for Christmas at least a few times. I know that."

Rachel smiled and nodded. "I suppose you're right. I think we were just afraid of being in the way. And we never wanted to get in the way of your happiness."

He wanted to snap at her, to tell her that, of course, he was right. But his memories sifted and sorted and shook out until he remembered more clearly what his 'invitation' had consisted of. "I can't come home this year, Mom. I've got too much going on. But you're welcome to come this way if you want. I'll be pretty busy, but there are plenty of things you can do to keep yourselves entertained around here." He wouldn't have considered it an invitation, either.

"We should have come," Ted stated, sitting straighter in his chair. "You're right, Ward. We should have come. I'm sorry we never did. We'll have to change that this year, right, honey?" He looked at Rachel for confirmation.

"Absolutely," she agreed.

Ward sighed, feeling more and more like a spoiled, resentful child, and he didn't like it one bit. "I'd like that," he finally said. "I should have told you that I wanted you there. I'm sorry if I never did."

"We love you, Ward. All is forgiven." His mother lifted a questioning gaze to his. "Was there more you needed to tell us? To say to us?"

Ward nodded slowly, wondering if perhaps he was completely off the mark with the rest of his assumptions. There was only one way to find out. Communication, as his father had said that day that Ward had walked in on him watching his Hallmark movie. People need to communicate more.

"I feel like you think my life, the life I've worked so hard to build out there, is expendable. That I can just walk away from it all without blinking an eye. Recommending me for that job, Dad? If that doesn't make me feel like you think so little of what I've accomplished, I don't know what does."

"We have never thought little of what you've done, Ward," his father countered. "That's *why* I thought you'd be such a good fit for the job. At least one of the reasons why. I know how you jump in with both feet and stick to your guns, come hell or high water. I know that whatever you put your mind to, you see it through. I know you're here right now, here with us, when you would like nothing more than to be on the other side of the continent, doing your own thing. That you're here because you're going to see us through this difficult time. It's who you are."

"We would never have asked you for so much, Ward," his mother chimed in. "You have given above and beyond anything we could have dreamed you'd do for us this past year. We thought—we were hoping," she amended. "That you were beginning to enjoy being back here. You seemed to settle back in with your friends so quickly. People around here love you so much, Ward." She made a tsking sound and batted her hand in front of her like she was trying to knock her words out of the air. "That sounds like pressure from me, and that's not my intent. We just thought that maybe, just maybe, if you saw there were options here...." Her voice trailed off, and Ward saw color bloom on her cheeks.

"We thought if you had good options to consider here, if you knew you could move back without getting stuck trying to salvage my floundering business—which you've somehow managed to do, anyway." Ted smiled gratefully at him. "If you had a good job offer waiting for you here, we hoped that coming home might be something you'd want to reconsider."

As careful as they were being, Ward could hear the agony of waning hope in their voices. It just about broke his heart.

"Forgive us, Ward," his mother said. "We love you, and we're so proud of you. No matter where you call home."

"I feel—" He broke off, his own words catching him by surprise. "I feel," he repeated under his breath. "Me. I. I feel." His words faded to a whisper, and his eyes drifted shut. Somehow, without him realizing it, everything in his life had become about how he felt. Not about how his parents felt, and certainly not about the way he made *them* feel.

He hadn't wanted Rochelle to leave him, not because he still loved her, but because he didn't like the feeling of being rejected.

He certainly didn't want Johnny and Rochelle hooking up, even if it made *them* feel happy. It made him feel cuckolded.

And then there was Penny. He was angry at her for what she felt about his relationship with Rochelle. He wanted her to set aside those feelings and accept what he said as truth, even when the evidence was stacked against him.

For years, now, he'd been drifting around on his little storm cloud of his feelings, all the while dumping deluges on the people around him without even considering how they felt.

"What about your business, Dad? What would happen to it if I took that job? And how would you feel, knowing I'd chosen it over St. James Mobile Boat Repair?"

"Listen," Ted began, his face growing serious. "I want to be transparent with you. I would love nothing more than to pass it down to you, but only if you want it. I would never want it to be a burden to you. If you think you'll take it over one day, then I'll do my best to hang onto it until you're ready. But if you're not interested in it, if it's not an option you'd ever consider, just tell me. Please, just tell me." He glanced at his wife, who was nodding right along with him. "After last year's scare with your mother, I realized on a whole new level how precious you both are to me. I don't want to miss out because I'm holding onto something I don't need."

"I'm fine, Ward," Rachel said, smiling over at him. She must have seen the flash of fear in his eyes when his father spoke about her illness. "I'm healthy and whole."

His father continued. "But if you don't want it, I'm going to sell and retire early. There have been offers over the years, and I've kept them in the back of my mind, just in case." He tapped his right temple.

This was not at all how Ward had seen this conversation going, and yet here they were, having gone the circuitous route to end up with all his questions answered.

"I have something for you," Ted said, getting to his feet and crossing the kitchen to the refrigerator. He took a large envelope down from the top of it and returned to the table with it. "This is for you," he said, sliding it toward Ward.

It was the same envelope Lysha had tried to give him almost a month ago now. This time, he drew it toward him, opened the flap, and pulled the stack of papers out.

"Why don't you spend some time looking that over." He looked Ward square in the eye, and said, "Would you do that for me?"

His father rarely asked him for anything.

He could do this for him.

An hour later, Ward made his way down the hall to his parents' room. Their door stood open, and he realized they'd left it that way so that he'd feel free to come talk to them if he needed to.

He tapped on the door frame to let them know he was there. His mother was already in bed, sitting up against the headboard, a novel in her hand. "Come in, Ward."

His father stepped out of the adjoining bathroom, his toothbrush in one hand, a tube of toothpaste in the other. "Come in," he echoed.

"Hey, Dad. Do you have a copy of the contract Lysha offered you?"

Ted ducked back into the bathroom and emerged a moment later, drying his hands on a towel. "I do. In fact, I have it right here." He crossed to his bedside table and pulled open the drawer in it. He pulled out an envelope just like the one Ward's proposal had come in. "Is there anything I can help you with?"

Ward smiled and took the packet his father held out to him. "I've been doing a little thinking. A lot of praying—"

"So have we," his mother interjected.

"And a bit of... well, devising. I've come up with another option."

"Show us," his father said, turning to offer his wife a hand. She was already pushing back the covers and getting to her feet.

WARD STEPPED OUT ONTO the front porch and made his way to his favorite chair. The lights across the water drew his attention, and this time as he studied them, he wondered if he'd be able to see the lights of his parents' house, of Hazel's house, from over there.

He glanced over at the guesthouse, hoping to see a light on in the upstairs bedroom, but the second-floor windows were all dark.

What would Penny think of his plan? Would she approve? Would she be happy for him?

He pressed the heel of his hand over his heart the way he must have done a hundred or more times since she'd asked him to leave. He was sure if he looked in the mirror, he'd find an ugly bruise there.

He pulled his phone from his pocket, tapped in three small words, and pushed send before he could change his mind.

Then he dialed Johnny's number. When his business partner answered, Ward said, "I have a proposal for you."

23
Penny

I MISS YOU. PENNY stared at the words on her phone screen for the thousandth time.

I miss you.

Those three little words had carried her through the hectic week she'd spent at her aunt and uncle's home. They'd buoyed her up as she loaded her mother and all her things into the back of her car.

I miss you.

They'd stirred up the tiny ember of hope that she'd been secretly harboring in the back corner of her heart as she made the long drive back home.

Home. It had never rung so true inside of her before. Home.

Hazel hurried down the front porch steps to greet her, Juno and Claire right behind her, and the three dogs right behind them.

"Welcome home, Sweet Pea." The older woman hugged her quickly once Penny was out of the car, then she and the others stood back as Penny circled the car to the passenger seat to help her mother out.

"Hey, Mom. We're here. Do you remember Hazel?" Penny looped her arm through Judy's and led her around the front of the car to introduce her to the three women, but the dogs had other plans. All three of them hurried up to Judy, welcoming her with sniffing noses, wiggly butts, and wagging tails.

Judy brought both hands up to her cheeks in surprise, then burst out laughing. A moment later, she dropped to the ground, cross-legged, and welcomed Jimbo and Delilah onto her lap with snuggles and kisses and belly rubs and giggles. Murtagh circled the group once, twice, then licked her face, making her squeal with delight, and returned to Hazel's side.

Penny covered her mouth with one hand and swallowed hard at the tears that threatened to well up. Claire and Juno came up and put their arms around her on either side, and the three of them stood back, watching as her mother fell in love with the loveable little furballs.

"Did you give Miss Judy your stamp of approval, Murty?" Hazel asked, crouching down to stroke the dog's head affectionately. Then she, too, lowered herself a little gingerly to the grass, and sat down facing Judy, only a couple of feet between them. Murtagh sat on his haunches beside her. When Judy finally noticed her, Hazel smiled and waved. "Hello, Judy."

"Hi, Silvia." The rest of her words came out a little jumbled, but Penny thought she understood. Before she could translate for Hazel, the older woman responded.

"Oh, yes. They're mine. But they sure like you." She pointed at Jimbo, then Delilah, introducing the two little dogs in Judy's lap.

"Hi, Silvia," Judy said again.

"Hi, Judy," Hazel replied.

"Who is Silvia?" Juno asked as the three of them started unloading the car.

Penny explained to them about Judy's history at Autumn Lake. "She's the reason I started coming here," she said, hoisting a heavy canvas bag onto her shoulder.

"I remember her," Claire said, pulling a suitcase from the trunk. "That was the day we met, Penny. You and your mother came to my shop and spent the whole afternoon with your heads together, talking and giggling like schoolgirls over different books. I didn't want to interrupt, but I was so glad when you finally asked me for help."

"That was a good day." Penny remembered it well. Her mother had still been herself most of the time, and it had seemed like she was soaking up every experience as though she were storing the happy times up. They'd taken several pictures that day while they wandered up and down the boardwalk, stopping in at shops and cafés along the way. Later that week, Penny had picked up the photos she'd had printed at a nearby drugstore, and the two of them had talked about each one, labeling them with names, dates, and something special about each one. "Mom said you looked like

Cinderella that day. You were wearing a blue dress, and you had a blue ribbon in your hair. I remember it so clearly."

Claire beamed with pleasure. "That's right. I love that dress. Call me if you decide to bring her to my shop. I'll run up and change into it. See if it triggers any memories for her." Claire lived in a gorgeous two-bedroom apartment directly above her bookstore.

"That would be so cool. I will." They carted their first load inside and up the stairs to the bedroom that shared the bathroom with Penny.

"Oh my goodness," Claire exclaimed from Penny's room, where she'd taken the suitcase she was carrying. "Look at this, Penny. Hazel put a vase of sweet peas on your dresser. I just love that she calls you that."

Penny and Juno came in through the connecting bathroom to ooh and ahh over the green glass vase with the colorful bouquet of sweet peas. They were lovely flowers, with their ruffly petals and long, slender green stems. Penny brushed her fingers over the flowers, then picked up the vase and brought it close so she could smell them, breathing in the fragrance that always reminded her of Hazel. "I don't know what I'd do without her. She's like my fairy godmother." She peered at her friends over the tops of the flowers.

"I think she feels the same way about you, Penny," Claire said.

"I second that. She looks forward to you coming every year, girlie," Juno told her. "But this summer, she needed you. She *needs* you," she amended.

On their way back downstairs, Penny finished explaining why Judy called Hazel Silvia. "The reason my mom wanted us to come here was because she had these memories of this place from her youth. For a few years, she and her parents came to Autumn Lake with another family, the Pontiers, who had three kids: Silvia, Rita, and Hector. Mom had a massive crush on Hector."

"And she thinks Hazel is this Silvia person," Juno surmised.

"Apparently, yes. She actually started calling her Silvia the last time she came—gosh, seven years ago now." Penny stopped on the stairs on their way back down and pressed her hand to her chest. "The human mind amazes me, you guys. She can't remember who I am half the time, but she takes one look at Hazel and remembers who she is, at least who she is in her mind. She's not Silvia, of course. But she's Silvia to my mom. The fact that she remembers anything at all so clearly is nothing short of a miracle." Her voice cracked, but she smiled right through it. "I think this might just work. I can hardly believe it—talk about miracles—but I think we can make this work for all of us."

"Thank you, Jesus," Juno murmured behind her.

"Amen," Claire exclaimed. "Amen to that, girlie."

It took a little convincing to get Judy to come inside, but once Juno helped Hazel to her feet, and the dogs scrambled off Judy's lap to follow her, Penny was able to get her mother to do the same. In the kitchen, the five women set about getting a meal prepared. Judy set the table, mixing and matching utensils, placing drinking glasses at some places and not at others, and draping the napkins over the silver candlesticks in the middle of the table, but Penny didn't bother going around and putting things to right. Her friends would figure it out just fine.

"It's going to be like a scavenger hunt." Claire declared with a delighted smile when she saw the table.

The other women from the Garden Variety Lovers Club were joining them for supper, and although Penny had worried about having so many people descend upon them their first day there, she'd decided to let things play out the way they did. She didn't need to be embarrassed by her mother's behavior, nor did she need to pretend that everything was all right. She was among friends, and it would be good for them to know firsthand what Penny and her mother dealt with on an ongoing basis.

Judy, however, seemed to be on her best behavior all evening long. Although her words ran together and most of the time, no one really understood what she was trying to say, she remained pleasant and engaged. She seemed to really enjoy just being a part of the group of women, laughing when they did, leaning in when she wanted to contribute, and patting Hazel's hand on multiple occasions. It was a loving, familiar gesture that tugged at Penny's heartstrings. Her mother was a hand-patter; she always had been, and Penny hadn't realized how long it had been since she'd seen her mother do it.

In a moment of silence, Judy sat forward and asked, clear as day, "Where is Hector?"

Hazel, already knowing the stories, having heard them when Judy, herself, had told them, touched Judy's cheek to get her attention. "He'll be here soon. We just have to wait patiently for him."

Judy studied her for several moments, her brow furrowed, as if trying to process what she'd just said. Finally, she nodded. "Okay."

To the rest of them, Hazel said, "My mother suffered from dementia, and in the olden days," she said with a chuckle. "They used to tell us to correct them. To help them not be so confused by telling them the truth. But with my mother, the truth actually made things worse for her. In her mind, what she thought was the truth. When I'd contradict her, it scared her. So I started telling her what she wanted to hear. It wasn't like spoiling a child."

"Hi, Silvia." Judy patted Hazel's hand.

"Hi, Judy." Hazel took Judy's hand and just held it. "I always saw it as a comfort measure. A way to ease her mind. It wasn't cruel, either. I wasn't lying to her. I was responding to the truth in the world she lived in."

"That's what they tell us to do nowadays. Did you know that?" Penny asked, watching Hazel interact with her mother. It really was remarkable how calm Judy was; she was usually much more agitated after the sun went down.

"I think I must have heard that somewhere. At least, that doesn't surprise me."

"You were and are wise beyond your years, Miss Hazel," Liz said from her seat at the other end of the table.

"Well, thank you, Lizette." Hazel always called Liz by her full name. She thought it was the most delightful name in all of Autumn Lake. Turning to Judy, she said, "Tomorrow, we'll go sit on the dock and wait for Hector, shall we?"

For dessert, Hazel had made a lemon poppyseed loaf with silky lemon drizzle icing. While Juno dished it up onto pretty little dessert plates, Penny made coffee. "You should be doing this," she said over her shoulder to her barista friend.

"It's time for you to stretch your limits, girlie." Juno bumped hips with her as she passed with a few loaded up plates. "It's a season of change. Of growth. Isn't it exciting?"

It was, indeed, thought Penny. And try as she might to not allow it, her thoughts moved to Ward. What would he say when he learned that she and her mother were moving to Autumn Lake? Would he be happy for her?

No one had brought up the subject of Ward St. James that evening. At least not so far. Which didn't bode well, she thought. If the news had been good, or even hopeful, surely, one of them would have let it slip. But their silence on the subject led her to believe otherwise.

I miss you. His text must have been an isolated moment of weakness. Of guilt, maybe.

"We serve a mighty God, ladies," Hazel said, drawing Penny's attention to the woman seated at the table. The coffee was just finishing brewing, and Penny replaced the carafe with a mug to catch the last little bit, put the carafe on a tray with half a dozen mugs, and took them to the table.

"That we do," Juno agreed.

"A mighty God who sits up high and sees down low," Hazel continued.

"Amen, sister," Addison whispered.

"He sees this right here, this circle of hearts." Hazel gestured around the table at each woman there, ending with Judy. "He knows our every need and He meets those needs as He sees fit. Tonight, my lovelies, I'm so glad He saw fit to bring you to my table." She smiled at Penny. "To what is soon to officially become *our* table, right, Sweet Pea?"

"I will not cry," Penny declared, blotting her eyes with her napkin. "Not again. At least not right now. I don't know how to thank you, Hazel."

"Oh, silly girl. You already are just by saying 'yes' to me. I'm weary of being alone. I'm exhausted by the longstanding worry of what I'm going to do with this place when I can no longer take care of it." She shook her head and said with a dry laugh, "What I'm really tired of is having to clean bathrooms and bedrooms after guests who don't think twice about the mess they leave behind."

Hazel's proposal had been for Penny to bring her mother back to Autumn Lake with her to spend the rest of the summer at the guesthouse. "Let's see how we all do together," Hazel had said. "I think we might be able to manage both your mother and this guesthouse if we work together as a team, Sweet Pea." With Hazel's experience caring for her own mother, and Penny's willingness to pour herself into getting the guesthouse back up and running like it once had, they'd agreed that they'd make one heck of a team.

"We'll find our rhythm," Hazel said, reaching over to take Judy's hand. "We've got time."

"Don't you have guests coming next week?" Candy asked. "Is there anything we can do to help you prepare?"

Hazel grinned. "Not anymore, we don't. My guests were potential buyers. I called to let them know that The Garden Gate Guesthouse is off the market."

When the meal ended, and Judy's eyelids began to droop, the little dinner party broke up, and together, Penny and Hazel helped Judy get settled in for the night. She had a new medication that was supposed to help her sleep better at nights, and with all the upheaval of the past few days, she was exhausted, anyway. Hazel had done a wonderful job of child-proofing the Jack and Jill bedrooms and bathroom that connected them, and Penny hoped they'd all get some much-needed sleep tonight.

Once her mother was resting peacefully, Penny tiptoed out of the room, her trusty baby monitor in tow. She'd gotten one a few years ago when Judy's sleep patterns started changing, and it had become a necessity for her peace of mind. Her aunt and uncle used one as well, but somehow, they'd not heard Judy get out of bed that night. It wasn't their fault or their negligence; things like that just happened sometimes.

Penny wasn't surprised to find Hazel sitting out on the front porch, dozing on her swing, Murtagh snoozing beside her with his head on her lap. Delilah and Jimbo had made themselves comfortable in the loveseat, almost as though they knew she'd be joining them and had just been warming her spot for her.

Penny settled in between the little dogs and tucked her legs up under her.

"Have you heard from Ward, Sweet Pea?" Hazel's question caught her by surprise, especially after the evening during which it seemed that everyone was specifically avoiding any mention of him.

"Um... no," Penny began, then thought of the text. "Only a short text on Saturday letting me know he was thinking of me. Nothing important." It had been important to her, but to him, it probably meant very little.

"Then it seems to have fallen to me to fill you in on what I know. Not because I'm a gossip, mind you, but because I love you, child, and I will not have you be put in a position where you're caught unawares. You've had enough of that for a lifetime this month."

"I—I don't like the sound of this." Penny's voice shook. She picked up Delilah and held her close, turning away when the dog tried to breathe in her face.

Hazel got straight to the point. "Ward is going back to California this week."

"He is?" Penny's heart jackhammered erratically inside her ribcage. "Has he—when does he leave?" Was he going to go without saying goodbye to her? And why had he texted *I miss you,* if he was going back to California, to that... that Rochelle woman? Had he texted Penny by mistake? Had that message been intended for Rochelle?

"I believe he goes tomorrow. Early. I'm sorry, Penny. I was so hoping that he'd reached out to you to let you know personally."

"Is he coming back?" The question sounded so pitiful, she knew, but she'd hoped—oh, how she'd hoped—that his *I miss you* had meant that there might be a future for them. That maybe he'd heard she was moving to the lake, and that he'd be here waiting for her.

She'd hoped against hope.

"Rachel told me that he has several irons in the fire out there that need to be dealt with. She says he wants his father's business, which is such a burden off their shoulders, but when he'll return to take over for Ted will depend on how things unfold out on the West Coast." Hazel looked past Penny toward the house that sat across the inlet. "She didn't say much more than that, I'm afraid."

An ache so intense, Penny found it hard to breathe, pressed in on her until she thought she might be crushed beneath the weight of it. "I thought..." She didn't know how to put all that she was feeling into words. "It's only been a few weeks, I know, but I thought—I thought there was something real between us. Something worth making changes for. I guess I was secretly hoping that my move here might make his move here more of a possibility."

Hazel smiled and nodded. "I did, too, darling girl. I did, too. And don't let anyone tell you that time is the determining factor in love. Three weeks, three days, three years. If you know, you know."

"Listen to you." Penny let out a pitiful little chuckle. "Hashtag IYKYK."

Hazel smiled cheekily. "I learned that from Candy yesterday. She was showing me around the website and said it in response to something I said. I thought it was both cute and true." Hazel pointed at Penny. "We women—and men, for that matter—need to learn to trust our instincts more. God has given us the wisdom of the ages. All we have to do is ask for it."

"Lord, how I need a little of that wisdom," Penny said, lifting her face heavenward

After several minutes of silence, Hazel spoke again. "In all the good romances, be they novels or movies, when all seems lost, there's always a grand gesture. That act of courage, the leap of faith that brings the two lovers back together."

Penny eyed her curiously, wondering where on earth she was going with this. "The grand gestures. Yes."

"That's what I'm praying for, Sweet Pea. The opportunity for a grand gesture. Whether it's you who gets the opportunity or him, doesn't matter. I just wanted you to know that's what I'm asking the good Lord for you and Ward."

"I don't know whether I should thank you or run scared," Penny said with a sad laugh.

"Just keep your ears and eyes open for now. You can thank me later."

Just then, the lights on the St. James porch flashed on and off, on and off, on and off.

Hazel looked at Penny, one eyebrow lifted in challenge.

"You want me to go over there and talk to him? He's leaving in the morning."

"He's not gone yet." She held out her hand toward Penny. "Give me that monitor. I can keep an eye on your mother."

24
Ward

"D**ID YOU HEAR ABOUT** our Shiny Penny?" Alex's question had rung in his ears like a gong, snapping him out of his reverie, but it was what his friend said next that had replayed over and over in his mind for the past few hours. "Sounds like she's moving in permanently with Hazel. She brought her mother today. Isn't that something?"

How was it that Alex knew something so important about Penny? Ward had heard she'd gone home to handle some trouble with her mother, and he'd tried hard not to take it personally that she hadn't bothered to tell him about her departure herself. But there was still the issue of his California life between them, and until they talked it through—until he had answers for her that he still needed to get for himself—he could understand why she hadn't unloaded her altered plans on him. From what he'd heard from Juno, she was coming back eventually, once she got things sorted out with her mother.

"She's moving here?" he'd asked Alex, wondering if he was misunderstanding. Ward was out with several friends at Patsy's Pizza Parlor for his last night in town.

"Moving here. Making Autumn Lake home." Alex said each word slowly, as if Ward had trouble understanding. "Like you should do, my dude."

Ward grimaced and shook his head, but he didn't speak. He wished he could talk about what his plans were for the near future, but he didn't know how it was all going to work out, and he didn't need the rumor mill spreading supposition as truth. He was leaving for California in the morning. When he'd be back, he had no idea, but he hoped it would be sooner than later. And he desperately hoped Penny would still be interested in what he had to say when he did return.

Now he sat in his favorite chair in the dark, feeling like a creeper, watching the two women conversing on Hazel's front porch. He should flash his lights, so they'd know he was there, but he waited a few more minutes, soaking up the sight of Penny in her pretty pink dress, trying to burn the image of her into his retinas.

Finally, he rose, stepped inside the foyer so he wasn't standing under the porch bulb, and flashed it on and off three times. Then he headed back outside and dropped into the chair again. Across the way, Hazel waved, and after a few moments, Penny got to her feet and went inside.

Apparently, she didn't like the idea of him sitting over here watching them.

"Well, she's gone inside, and Hazel doesn't seem to mind," he muttered to himself, sinking a little lower into the chair. "So I don't have to go anywhere."

But ten minutes later, he saw Penny re-emerge from the house, a book in her hand. Instead of sitting back down on the loveseat, however, she marched past Hazel and down the porch steps. Once on the lawn, she turned on a flashlight, and as he watched, she made her way down the driveway and out onto Shoreline Drive.

"She's coming here," he said out loud. "She's coming to see me."

His heart thundered into overdrive, and he lurched up out of his chair. He pulled open the front of his shirt and took a quick whiff. He'd showered after work, but it wasn't unheard of to go into a pizza parlor smelling like pine and balsam and come out a few hours later wearing eau de garlic and cheese. Fortunately, Ward had driven home with his windows down, and he'd been sitting out on the porch for over an hour. "I'm good," he told himself.

He felt so awkward standing there, his arms just hanging uselessly at his sides. He needed something in his hands. His phone? Good grief; no. That was what had caused all the trouble between them in the first place. Was there a flower close by he could pick for her?

"Don't be so desperate," he berated himself, linking his fingers behind his head in frustration. He turned in a slow circle, looking around the porch for anything that might make him feel a little more prepared, more in control of the situation.

Then he stopped. It wasn't about how he felt. "I'm such a slow learner," he moaned softly. He wanted to be what Penny needed him to be tonight. And if that meant he had to simply wait to find out what she needed, then that's what he'd do.

So he made his way to the bottom of the porch steps and started down the walkway. The moon was out tonight, and even though it wasn't full, it was high and bright in a clear sky, and after sitting in the dark for so long, he could easily see where he was going.

He'd meet her in the middle, he decided. In fact, it should have been him taking the initiative. If he picked up his pace, he could meet her a whole lot closer to her place than his. He'd be walking her back home, regardless.

It didn't take long before she realized he was coming her way. She stopped in her tracks and waited for him; her flashlight pointed right at him. He lifted a hand to shield his eyes as he drew closer, and she lowered the light, so it was directed at the ground.

"Hey," she said in a hushed voice. He couldn't tell if she was breathless from the walk or because of him.

"Hey, Miss Penelope Anderson. How are you?" He squeezed his eyes shut briefly. What a banal first question to ask the woman he'd not spoken to in far too long.

"Better than I've been in a while," she said. "I heard you're going back to California in the morning."

He didn't hesitate. "I am. I have a break-of-dawn flight out of Evansville. In fact, I really should be in bed already, but—" He broke off, not quite sure how to finish that sentence. *I couldn't sleep because my mind is too full of thoughts of you? I couldn't stop wishing things were different between us? I love you and I want to figure out a way for us to be together?* Good grief. He cleared his throat and shoved his hands in his pockets.

"I—I brought you something," she said, holding up the book in her hand. She didn't give it to him, though. "A going away gift. It's a romance novel."

"A romance novel?" Even as he said it, he found he wasn't really surprised. He'd seen what she read. He'd even gone over to Claire's to look up the author of the book she'd been reading that first day at Juno's. Destiny Baudelaire. Claire had told him he should read the author, that he'd enjoy the books, but he hadn't been convinced.

"I know you saw inside my bag of books when you hauled them off Hazel's porch and threw them in my trunk." She paused, and he took the bait before he recognized it for what it was.

"I didn't—"

"Gotcha," she said, the moonlight bright enough for him to see her crooked smile.

"Fell for it again, didn't I?" He wanted to say that he'd fallen for her, and that he'd keep falling for her again and again and again if she'd let him.

"You did, indeed," she teased. "Anyway, you saw inside my book bag, so you know what I read. But I thought you might want to know why I read them." She brought the novel to her chest and sort of hugged it. He could see that the front cover was a little tattered, the edges of it worn. A well-loved, often-read thing, he realized. "This is one of my favorites. I've read it every year around my birthday, and it makes me laugh and cry and long for the kind of relationship the two main characters end up with. Every time. It never gets old."

"You sound like my father," Ward said, hoping she remembered about his Hallmark channel fixation.

"I'll take that as a compliment. I love your father, Ward."

"I do, too." This was the weirdest conversation he'd had in as long as he could remember—barring the one with his dad about romance movies—but he was in this for the long haul. He wanted to know where it would lead next.

Penny finally handed him the book, but when he started to open it, she put her hand over the cover, preventing him from doing so. "I hope you'll read it, Ward. For me."

"Of course, I will." He wanted to cover her hand with his own, to lift it to his lips and press kisses on her knuckles. He wanted to trail kisses up her arm, to feel the heat of her skin against his lips, to nuzzle her neck and breathe in the fragrance of her hair. He wanted to press his mouth to hers, to crush her against him and kiss her until she melted into him—

"Ward?"

"Yes?" She was looking at him with a curious expression on her face. Had he missed something during his little speed fantasy just now? *Focus, man.*

"Don't make promises if you're not going to keep them."

Ward hesitated before responding. Was she baiting him? Was this a trick? Was she setting him up to say something that would get thrown in his face later?

"I just mean that if you tell me you're going to read it, then read it."

"I'll read it," he repeated, this time more vehemently. "I'll start reading it tonight."

She gave him a small smile. "And maybe when you're finished with it, you can call me so we can talk about it."

"I'll finish it, and I'll call you when I do." She was asking him to call her. She was trusting him to take a precious piece of her with him back to California, and she wanted to hear from him again.

Penny lifted her hand off the book and said, "Open it. Carefully. At about the middle."

Ward turned the book in his hands and let the book fall open to a spot where something had been tucked into it. A flower encased in what felt like wax paper. He held it up, and she took it from him, opening a flap on one end and pulling the flower out to show him.

"It's a sweet pea," she said. "Hazel calls me Sweet Pea because of my initials. My full name is Penelope Eva Anderson." She tucked it back into its envelope and handed it back to him. "It's for you. To remember me by."

He didn't need a pressed flower to remind him of her. Or a book, for that matter. But he was deeply moved by the tender, thoughtful gift. "I'll read your book, Penny," he told her again. "And I'll be thinking of you the whole time."

She chuckled softly. "Hopefully, you'll be thinking of the storyline, because you know I'll be drilling you on it when you call."

"And you know I'll be calling when I finish it." He reached toward her; he couldn't resist touching her, just one more time.

Penny released a sound so soft, he almost thought he'd imagined it. But then she stepped forward and pressed herself into him, hugging him gently around the waist, her face buried in his chest.

Surprised, but oh, so relieved, Ward's arms went around her, and he held her against him as they rocked ever so slightly under the moonlit sky. He rested his chin on top of her head and said a silent prayer of thanks for these tender moments between them.

"I miss you, too," she whispered against his chest, then she pulled away and stepped back just out of his reach. "I'll wait for your call, Ward."

He walked her back to Hazel's house—it would now be Penny's house, too; he realized—where Hazel still sat on the porch awaiting Penny's return. He didn't touch her again, but all the way home, he couldn't stop thinking about the way she felt against him, held close in his arms.

25
Penny

Ward had been gone for almost three weeks. He still hadn't called. Penny understood that some people spent more time with their books than others, and she wanted to give him the benefit of the doubt. But it wasn't a big book. It wasn't boring. There was no reason she could come up with as to why he couldn't have gotten through it by now.

Unless, of course, he'd lost interest. In the book. In her. A DNF. "Did not finish," she said aloud as she stood at her window staring over at the little blue house where Ted and Rachel St. James were likely sound asleep.

Ward did text her every few days, but it was never in a way to generate any kind of conversation. It felt almost like he was checking in with her, but in a slightly poetic way.

I met a woman selling used books at a corner stand today. I thought of how much fun you'd have perusing her table.

At the grocery store today, I picked up a bag of lemons that smelled exactly like that Italian lemon cake we got for Hazel. It took me right back to her porch with you.

I took a young man and his father out in my boat today for a private fishing trip. The kid is dying. He has a brain tumor. I blamed my tears on the wind.

He hadn't sent a single *I miss you.*

Her mother was sleeping better than she had in years, waking up at a decent hour each morning in a good mood—most of the time—and ready to engage in whatever the day brought. Her favorite thing to do was to sit at the end of the dock in a lawn chair and wait for Hector. She'd take a notebook and a pencil with her, and she'd draw or make lists, both of which were completely indecipherable, or she'd help Hazel shell peas or snap beans. She was quite efficient at doing both of those chores.

Penny could hear soft snores coming through the baby monitor on her nightstand. Now that she was sleeping better, Judy was also sleeping deeper, and sometimes her snoring would wake Penny up in a panic. But for the most part, they were doing quite well.

Hazel, too, seemed to be blossoming under the knowledge that her future was a little better defined and a whole lot less alone. "You've brought my mojo back, Sweet Pea," she liked to say, and Penny didn't have the heart to tell her that the word usually referred to one's sex appeal.

The Garden Variety Lovers Club now met every other Saturday morning in the garden out under the shade of the pink-blossomed ornamental cherry tree. Addison had been able to get her shift changed so that she now had Saturdays off, altogether. The big news was that she'd met someone during her new hours, and she'd promised that the next time the ladies all got together, she'd tell them more about him.

Penny and Hazel had decided that they would temporarily close down the guesthouse for the remainder of the year. They were hiring Candy to help them with updating the parts of the décor that were outdated while incorporating what was vintage. She'd also oversee a remodel that included installing two new bathrooms upstairs, so each room had its own en suite. "We'll do a complete overhaul and when we open up next year, you'll see, Hazel," Penny promised, her anticipation contagious. "We'll be turning people away."

Penny had turned in her notice to the school, knowing she'd be leaving a position that wouldn't be difficult for the school to fill. There were many wonderful teachers out there desperate for work, and she was confident they'd have her replacement lined up well before the school year started.

She'd also sold their condo, and it was part of that money they were using to do the renovations. Penny had insisted in a conversation that had nearly turned volatile, but Hazel had met her match in Penny. Neither woman seemed to mind, either.

Penny turned away from the window. She wasn't very tired, but she knew she needed to try to sleep. She found herself often in a quandary with her mother. Now that she was sleeping better at night, Penny's tendency was to stay up later and get things done after Judy was asleep. The problem was that Judy also woke up at almost exactly the same time every morning now, and once she was awake, it was a lot like having a child. She was up and raring to go, and no amount of telling her to go back to bed would do.

Penny headed into the bathroom to wash her face and brush her teeth. When she finished, she checked once more on her mother, who was fast asleep.

She changed into her pajamas and dug in her nightstand for a book from her To Be Read pile, a pile she was finding time to plow through, now that she had help with Mom and no job she had to show up for without Judy in tow. Then she crossed to the window one last time, where she stood at the end of every night and said a prayer for Ward. She didn't bother turning off the lights; he wasn't there to see her staring at the St. James' house. Although, she hoped Rachel, or worse, Ted, never saw her up there at night. "That wouldn't be creepy at all," she muttered with a roll of her eyes.

Just as she was about to turn away for the last time, she saw movement across the way, and the St. James's front door opened. In the dark, it was hard to make out for sure, but she could have sworn it was Ward.

It had to be Ted, she thought. Who else could it be?

But it was almost eleven o'clock, and she knew they went to bed early over there.

And then the porch lights flicked on and off. Once, twice, and then a third time. She waited, breath held, for any other sign of life over there.

Then she saw it. Not on the porch, but on the walkway leading toward the driveway, a flashlight beam bouncing along to illuminate the path in front of whoever it was carrying it.

It was Ward. She recognized him in the breadth of his shoulders. She knew him in the curve of his neck, the way he held his head, chin up, when he walked. She saw him in the long, sure strides he took, past the van in the carport, down the driveway, and out onto Shoreline Drive.

"He's coming over here," she murmured under her breath. Her heart just about jumped out of her mouth. "He's coming over here," she said again, letting the curtain fall back into place and hurrying around the end of the bed to the closet. "He's coming over here." She said it one more time for good measure, pulled out a full-skirted, knit maxi dress, and slipped into it, leaving her pajamas strewn in a messy heap across her bed.

In moments, Penny was out on the front porch, waiting for him in the dark. She didn't want to worry Hazel by turning things on. She had the baby monitor with her, and she prayed fiercely that her mother would not need anything from her within at least the next hour.

Ward St. James had circled the inlet and was now coming up the lane toward Hazel's driveway. Penny sat down on the top step and wrapped her arms around her knees.

He crossed Hazel's lawn, then stepped into the narrow, flower-lined walkway that meandered up to the porch. In the dark, he hadn't seen her until he was almost upon her, and she stood slowly, looking down at him to where he waited at the bottom of the steps.

Ward had his phone in his hand. He held it where she could see it. He tapped the two and a photo of Penny in her favorite green sundress appeared on his screen, the name Sweet Pea above her head. In her pocket, her phone began to ring.

Ward said nothing as he brought his phone to his ear and listened. Penny smiled and pulled hers out. She swiped open his call. "Hello?" she said.

"I promised I'd call when I was finished." Then he hit the red "end" button and tucked his phone back into his pocket. "May I come up?" he asked.

When she nodded, he mounted the steps slowly until he stood before her. "Your book wasn't the only thing I finished," he said.

Penny wished he'd offer her his hand. She wished he'd say her name. She wished he'd open his arms and sweep her off her feet. "Oh, yeah?"

"Oh, yeah." He nodded, and even in the shadows, she could see the corners of his mouth lifting with humor. "I waited to call until I finished it all. The book. The sale of my business. Lining up my work here. Moving back home. It's all finished."

"So you called me. Today. Just now," she added.

"Just now. I got home from the airport about half an hour ago. I let my parents know I was home safe, and then I came straight over here to see you." He pulled her book out from a deep thigh pocket in the cargo shorts he wore and handed it to her. "Thank you for sharing this amazing piece of you with me."

"Did you like it?" she asked, desperately hoping he had.

He nodded slowly. "I laughed, and I cried a few tears, I have to admit. And I longed for the kind of relationship the two main characters end up with."

"Oh," she said, her throat tight with emotion. He'd remembered her words almost exactly.

Ward finally held out his hand, palm up, toward her, and she placed her hand in his. He threaded their fingers together and drew her a little closer to the edge of the top step so that they stood almost eye to eye. "Even more than that," he said, his voice just barely above a whisper. "I'm longing for a relationship with you, one that I believe could be even greater than the one in that book." He leaned forward and pressed his forehead to hers. "What do you say, Penny? I'm home to stay. Will you have me?"

Penny pulled her hand free and wrapped both arms around his neck, arching her body into his. "Yes, Ward St. James, I'll have you," she murmured, and then she kissed him.

Ward sighed against her lips, then swept her up against him, lifting her right off her toes, as he kissed her back, one hand slipping up her spine to cup the back of her head.

From inside the house, the sound of scrabbling claws on wooden floors told them they were about to have company. They pulled apart just as Hazel pushed open the screen door. The dogs ran past her to sniff at Penny and Ward, then down the steps and out into the night to do their business.

"You kids decent out here? I'm turning on the light."

"Hazel!" Penny put up a hand to shield her eyes from the sudden brightness overhead.

"What?" the older woman asked, acting all affronted. "I'm not the one kissy facing in the dark on the front porch." To Ward, she said, "Welcome home, Ward St. James."

Ward nodded and came up the last step to stand beside Penny. He put his arm around her and drew her up against his side. "I apologize if we woke you," he began, but Hazel waved him off.

"You didn't wake me. I was lying in bed praying about grand gestures." She pointed at Penny. "You can explain that to him after I go back to bed."

"I'll do that," she promised, smiling as the dogs came charging back up the steps and racing back inside, leaving the three of them standing in their wake. "Yikes, Hazel. Are they going to calm down enough to fall asleep?"

Hazel scoffed good-naturedly. "They'll be out cold by the time I get down to that end of the hall. I guarantee it." She started to head back inside herself, but stopped and let the screen door fall shut again. "I almost forgot. Tell me about this new job, Ward. But keep it short. I'm an old lady up past my bedtime." She lowered herself into one of the patio chairs nearest the door.

Ward pulled Penny over to the loveseat where she usually sat with the dogs. "Just the bullets, then." He held up one finger. "I sold my part of Blue Waters to Toby Trebler, my ex-girlfriend's father." He turned to Penny and added, "My ex-girlfriend, by the way, who is seriously dating my ex-business partner. She called that night to tell me herself so that I wouldn't hear it through the grapevine."

"Well, that sounds decent of her," Hazel quipped.

"It was. It is. She's a decent woman, but not the woman for me."

"I'm glad to hear that," Penny told him. "All of it."

Ward held up another finger. "I found a shop right on the lake that I'm going to see tomorrow. If it's what I'm hoping it is, then St. James Mobile Boat Repair is going to have a storefront again. Which means no office at the house anymore."

"How wonderful," Hazel said. "Oh, your mother will be so thrilled to get all of Ted's paper piles out of there."

"Yes, indeed, she will," Ward said, nodding emphatically. He held up a third finger. "And I made Carpe Diem a counteroffer by combining the two offers they made us. I will remain an independent contractor with St. James Mobile Boat Repair, but I now have a five-year maintenance contract with Carpe Diem, making them priority customers for me. My father can continue to tend to his loyal customers. The resort will have to find someone else to manage the employees, but I'm better with boats than people, anyway."

"You are so clever, Ward St. James," Penny said, poking him gently in the side. "My boyfriend is smart," she told Hazel, reveling in the way it felt to claim him as hers. She wrapped her arms around his waist and nestled into him a little more, resting her head on his shoulder.

"Oh, my," Hazel sighed, pushing herself to her feet. "You two are going to make us all a little squeamish with all your lovey-dovey stuff for the next several years, aren't you? I'm going to bed so you can start practicing now."

And that's exactly what they did.

26
Epilogue

The Fall Festival was everything Penny had hoped it would be and more. Everyone she'd met in Autumn Lake over the months since she'd moved there had welcomed her with open arms. Now today, she and The Garden Variety Lovers Club girls were all gathered around the Garden Gate Guesthouse's booth at the corner of Dahlia Drive and Camellia Court right in front of Juniper's Coffee Bar and The Cracked Spine. Both Juno and Claire had booths of their own outside their shops, flanking Hazel's with delicious treats on one side and delicious reads on the other.

Rachel St. James opted to share a booth with Hazel and Penny and Judy that year. Because of how sick she'd been, she hadn't had the time or energy to make such a big stock of her crowd-pleasing tomato jam. She'd brought enough to fill one table of jars that had almost already sold out.

Hazel was out wandering the festival with Judy, and Liz, Candy, and Addison had brought lawn chairs of their own and were 'helping' man the booth in Hazel's absence. In other words, they were indulging in the freebies Juno kept feeding them and fighting off fits of giggles that was a common byproduct whenever the six of them got together.

"Where is Ward?" Juno called out from where she was loading up a tray of individually wrapped pumpkin muffins. "I thought he said he was going to stop by this morning."

"He's got his shop open to the public today," Penny said, her voice ringing with pride for him. "He must be having the time of his life."

"I know his father is," Rachel said. She was all bundled up against the chill of autumn that had swept into town the week before. Fortunately, there'd been no rain in the forecast, and with the sun shining overhead and the leaves of the trees along the boardwalk turning all shades of red, gold, and brown, the day of the festival was turning out to be absolutely lovely.

Just then, Penny spotted Hazel moving through the crowds toward their booth. Judy was nowhere to be seen. Penny's breath caught as she moved around from behind the table, uncertainty filling her at Hazel's nonchalance. "Where's Mom?"

"She's fine, dear. She'll be here any moment. Here." Hazel pulled one of the folding chairs over and set it up front and center before their booth. "Have a seat. Catch your breath, Sweet Pea. Everything will be all right."

Suddenly, it seemed that the crowd parted, and Penny looked up to find Judy, her arm linked with Ward's, letting him usher her toward the three booths. When they stood in front of Penny, Judy smiled at her and said, "Hello, dear." She said the words as clear as the autumn day they were in.

Penny stood and gave her mom a quick hug. To her surprise, Judy returned the embrace, then stepped back and patted Penny on the cheek. "My sweet girl," she said, then spotted Hazel over Penny's shoulder and headed that way, greeting her with, "Hello, Silvia."

Then it was just Ward standing there, his shoulders relaxed, his laugh lines at the ready. He'd had a haircut, Penny realized, and she reached up to touch a strand that curled at the back of his neck. "I like your hair," she murmured, noticing how folks were beginning to gather around, more and more of them standing back and watching her with anticipatory smiles on their faces. "What's going on?" she asked him in a whisper. "Is everyone here with you?"

From behind his back, Ward brought out a single sweet pea with petals in a raspberry pink that faded to white. It was the most beautiful one she'd ever seen, especially this late in the season. "It's glorious," she breathed, reaching out to hug him in gratitude for such a treasure.

But Ward stepped back and dropped to one knee. Behind him, Alex was snapping pictures with a rather large, expensive-looking camera.

Penny suddenly knew exactly what was going on, and she almost laughed out loud at how long it had taken her to recognize the grand gesture that it was.

Ward reached into the inside pocket of his jacket and pulled out a black velvet box. He flipped it open to reveal a delicate white gold solitaire ring with a Marquis cut diamond. It was breathtakingly beautiful, and she was already nodding when Ward took her hand.

"Penelope Eva Anderson, my beautiful Sweet Pea, will you make me the happiest man in the whole wide world, but *especially* in Autumn Lake? Will you marry me?"

"Yes, yes, yes!" Penny threw her arms around his neck and practically fell against him in her exuberance as the crowd that had gathered burst into cheers and applause. In his desperate attempt to keep them both from tumbling backward, Ward dropped the ring box, but Ted was right there to pick it up. He brushed it off and handed it back to his son.

Penny let Ward stand, and then she let him slip the ring on her finger, and she even let him hand the ring box off to his father, before she launched herself at him again. Ward scooped her up against him and kissed her soundly, staking his claim on her in the grandest gesture of all.

Somewhere in the background, Penny could hear Claire quoting from one of her many favorite books, Victor Hugo's 'Les Misérables.'

"How did it come to pass that their lips met? How comes it to pass that the birds sing, that snow melts, that the rose unfolds, that May expands, that the dawn grows white behind the black trees on the shivering crest of the hills? A kiss and that was all."

Keep reading for a sneak peek of the next book in the Autumn Lake Romance Series, **The Apartment on Larkspur Lane.**

From the Author

Dear Reader,

Did you enjoy reading along while Penny and Ward sorted out their priorities in *The Guesthouse at Autumn Lake?* I have a special place in my heart for sisters, for mothers and daughters, for women's relationships in general, and I'm having a lot of fun getting to know the women who make up the Garden Variety Lovers Club. I hope you are, too.

I write heartfelt and wholesome Contemporary Romance, Women's Fiction, and some Christian Fiction, too. You'll find romance, friendship, humor, a little mystery and suspense, and lots of family drama in my books. And usually a four-legged or feathered friend or two.

Visit me at **BeckyDoughty.com** and check out my other books and series. **Subscribe to my mailing list** and introduce yourself – I'd love to meet you.

Where hope lives and love wins,
Becky Doughty

Excerpt: The Apartment on Larkspur Lane

Chapter 1

Jökulsárlón Glacier Lagoon, Iceland

~ ~ ~

Addison stood as far away from the group gathered on the beach as she possibly could while still staying within hearing range. The sky overhead was just beginning to shift and sway, hints of iridescence coloring the edges of her vision. She narrowed her eyes in a futile attempt to bring into focus the muted kaleidoscope sky. It wouldn't help, she knew, nor would it hurry things up, either. The aurora borealis refused to dance across the sky on command, and if the film crew huddled around their tripods and insanely expensive equipment wanted to catch the light show on camera, they would have to wait until the capricious Northern lights were good and ready to make an appearance.

She hunched her shoulders a little higher around her ears, burrowing the lower half of her face deeper into the fur-lined hood of her parka. She breathed slowly, trying not to steam things up too much, which would only turn the fur into tiny slivers of ice that poked her in the face. Her teeth chattered and her voice shook as she let out a nasally, "Brrrrr." She rolled her eyes at the noise. "You sound like a cold sheep. If there even is such a thing." She often conversed with herself on these excursions.

Across the way, no one seemed to have noticed her withdrawal from the group, but that was exactly the way she wanted it. She only wished she could withdraw all the way off this bitterly cold island altogether. Preferably, without anyone noticing, and even more preferably—did that even make sense?—somewhere warm and cozy and... well, homey.

But of course, eventually, someone would need something that wasn't readily available to them, and all eyes would turn to search for her. *Addison, would you be a sport and grab me another memory card, please? Addie, darling, my macro lens is in my other bag. Can you hunt it down for me? Hey Addison. Since you're not doing anything right now...*

That was the real issue, wasn't it? Somehow, she was always the one with nothing better to do than to be at the beck and call of those who actually did have something to do.

"I believe there are many cold sheep during shearing season."

Startled, she spun around, both hands up in front of her in a straight-out-of-the-movies martial arts pose that had to look as ridiculous as it felt. She blurted out, "I'm karate!"

Addison squeezed her eyes shut for just a moment. *I'm karate? Really?* Then she thought better of it and snapped them open again. She'd learned early on that closing her eyes didn't make the bad things disappear.

The beam of her headlamp illuminated a bulky man-shape standing a few feet from her. He squeezed his eyes shut against the light, then turned his head slightly to avoid it. "Sorry, sorry. I didn't mean to startle you." He slowly brought both arms up at his sides in an I-come-in-peace posture.

The guy kinda looked familiar, but then, it could be just the beard. It seemed most of the men she'd met on this trip sported them. It probably had something to do with the wind chill factor and the potential for frostbitten chins. *If I had a beard, I wouldn't have to breathe shallowly into my fake fur.* The ridiculous thought had her shaking her head to clear it.

"I mean, I know karate. I can do karate," she amended, narrowing her eyes in what she hoped was a fierce expression. Although, of course, she'd already lost any credibility she might have otherwise had. *I'm karate.* Was it possible that she hadn't said that out loud?

Besides, even the karate she could remember from her childhood lessons was rendered completely ineffective by the copious layers she wore. There was absolutely no way she could do a roundhouse kick in her puffy, knee-length coat. Maybe if she just kept shining her light in his face, he'd be too blind to attack her.

But his expression confirmed her suspicions; she looked about as threatening as she actually was. Like a shivering fluffy pillow with a scowl.

Addison squared her shoulders. Lifting her chin a little, she said, "Sorry. I didn't mean to...." She made a few chopping motions with her hands, then grimaced, mortification creating a warm flush up her neck. "I'm—I'm going to go back. Over there." She pointed over her shoulder at the photographers on the beach. "I'm sure they're wondering where I've gone."

She was sure they weren't wondering any such thing, in fact, but this guy didn't need to know that.

Diamond Beach in winter.

Iceland in December.

At midnight.

What on earth was she doing there? Again.

Addison shoved her hands into her pockets and sent the guy a dismissive nod, barely able to meet his gaze. But before she could turn and flee, he lowered his hands to his sides and shrugged. "I know a place nearby that serves hot coffee."

That brought her up short. Hot coffee. She pressed her lips together and her gaze swung back and forth between the man and the group she'd come with. Oh, there was plenty to be had down the beach in the middle of that melee, but she was still trying to work up the courage to wade in again, now that she had finally broken free.

"It's good coffee, too. Not just hot." His slight Icelandic accent made the short sentences sound lyrical.

"Where?" Addison narrowed her eyes at him, her light once again forcing him to turn his head. "Sorry," she said, tipping the beam up a little. She could still see his face, but at least she was no longer blinding him. But she couldn't recall seeing any restaurants or cafes—any structures at all, in fact—within miles of where they were.

He shrugged again and pointed at the small contingence of vehicles parked close together some distance away. "In my van."

Addison rolled her eyes so hard that her head bobbed in a circle, too. "Nice try, buddy." How desperate did he think she was? She took one decisive step away from him.

"I also have *kleinur*. Both plain and dipped in chocolate," he added, wiggling his brows at her.

Like offering candy to a child, she thought, surprised to find that she was actually considering his offer. The classic Icelandic fried dough treat was one of the many delights to be experienced on the island. Not too sweet, crispy and flaky, perfect for dunking in hot coffee.... She eyed the van parked just behind the one she'd come in. Presumably, he was part of their group. "Dipped in chocolate?"

He smiled, his mustache curving up at the corners of his mouth. "Dipped in chocolate," he confirmed.

Addison turned back to study him again. The glint in his eyes told her he knew he was getting to her. What was she thinking? "I'm sorry," she said, shaking her head. "Who are you? I mean, did you come with us?" She gestured vaguely in the direction of the photographers.

"I am one of the drivers, yes. My name is Gunnar. I am Gunnar Ólafsson." He started to offer her his hand, then seemed to think better of it. He was attractive, she decided, in a winter wildernessy way. He had kind eyes, and as far as she could tell, under the facial hair and the bright red beanie pulled down over his ears, he was probably close to her age.

She was nothing, if not polite. "Hi, Gunnar. I'm Addison. Wedgewood," she added quickly, not missing the curious tilt of his head. Was it her name he didn't get? Maybe because in Iceland, a surname typically ended in *son* or *dottir*? She drew his attention to the group on the beach with a thrust of her chin. "Those are my parents. Carl and Vivian Wedgewood."

"I already know who you are," Gunnar said, his eyes crinkling in a smile that was starting to grow on her. "You obviously have not noticed me before now, but I noticed you already." He tipped his head toward the parked vehicles. "Hot coffee. *Kleina*. A warm car. How can you resist this?"

Addison was waffling, and she could tell that he could tell.

"I have music…" He drew the word out in a singsong lilt and shimmied his bulky shoulders a little. "How about Of Monsters and Men?"

It was so utterly and completely cliché, his suggestion of the popular Icelandic band. Addison couldn't bite back a smile. "Are you suggesting them because you listen to them or because you think I listen to them?" she asked.

Once again, Gunnar shrugged. "If you want to hear them; that is all that matters."

Addison hedged just a moment longer, the pull of the coffee and *kleina* making her mouth water. Finally, she capitulated. "I need to tell my mom where I'll be. In case she needs me for anything."

"She already knows," Gunnar said a little sheepishly. "She is the one who told me to find you."

Great. Just great. So the guy wasn't hitting on her at all. He'd been recruited by her mother to babysit. To feed and entertain her. Addison couldn't decide whether to be grateful—she was, indeed, cold and hungry, after all—or offended.

"Wasn't that nice of her," she said dryly.

"Yes," Gunnar agreed, seemingly oblivious to Addison's sarcasm. "A good mother always looks out for her children." He gestured again toward the van. "After you."

The biting wind had picked up a little in the time it took them to reach the van, and by the time Addison was settled into the passenger seat with a thick wool blanket draped over her lap, she was more than grateful to both her mother and Gunnar. The blanket had been his suggestion when he noticed that her teeth were chattering.

"From here, we can watch the lights just fine," Gunnar told her, nodding his head toward the view out the windshield. "I think it is more pleasant this way, don't you?"

"Absolutely," Addison agreed, watching with anticipation as he opened the large console between them and withdrew a thermos, two insulated mugs, and a brown paper bag.

"I'm sorry. I don't have cream or sugar. Just strong, black coffee."

"That's not a problem for me," Addison assured him. The smoky, robust aroma that wafted into the air when he unscrewed the lid of the thermos had her salivating. She peeled off her heavy wool gloves so she could hold the mugs for him to fill.

Several minutes later, fortified by the midnight snack, Addison settled a little deeper into the bucket seat and sighed contentedly, both hands wrapped around a second cup of coffee. She was starting to feel her toes again. "Thank you," she said, turning to look at the man in the driver's seat. "You might have just saved my life, you know."

"Really? So I am a hero now?" Gunnar winked at her from over his own cup.

For whatever reason, this guy made it easy for Addison just to be herself. Maybe it was the bizarre setting—although that was nothing new for her. Growing up as the only child of her famous photojournalist parents, Addison had borne witness to parts of both the world and humanity that most people never even knew existed. Winter in Iceland was no commonplace thing, but it wasn't even close to the wildest place she'd ever been.

Gunnar's smile was warm and friendly, and Addison nodded. "My hero." If she didn't know any better, she would have mistaken her behavior for flirting with the man.

"So tell me," Gunnar said when the silence between them started to get too loud. "Are you a photographer, too?"

Addison snorted softly and shook her head. "I'm the kind of camera operator who takes pictures from a moving car. They're always blurry and so nondescript that even I can't remember what the picture was supposed to be of."

He laughed out loud at that. "No. Surely not. The daughter of the world-famous Wedgewoods?"

"You've heard of them, then? Before this trip?" Addison asked. Not that she was exactly surprised. Her parents had been in the business for over three decades, and their names were credited with innumerable images and articles in countless forms of media around the world.

"Of course," Gunnar said matter-of-factly. "It would be difficult to find a home in Reykjavik that doesn't have at least one copy of *Edge of the World* on a shelf." The book was an awe-inspiring collection of photos captured during multiple visits to Iceland over the course of several years.

Images of food, culture, the convergence of ancient and modern lifestyles, and the ever-changing landscape that made up the southwestern part of the island.

"Of course," Addison echoed, but not without a measure of pride in her tone. "I've always secretly wondered if I was adopted. I mean, I don't have a single artistic streak in my body." She tugged on a strand of her straight, dark brown hair that she kept trimmed just past her shoulders. "I look nothing like either of them. They're both blonde and beautiful and otherworldly, you know?"

"Otherworldly?" Gunnar said it like he didn't know what the word meant.

"Like creatures from another realm." Addison gestured out the window at the star-spattered sky that was beginning to vibrate with swirling shafts of blues and greens. "They belong in places like this. They thrive on the hunt, the pursuit of the next fantastic beauty on 'this round of green, this orb of flame,' as Lord Alfred Tennyson would say." She took a sip of coffee and looked away, feeling suddenly dull and lacking in substance in the long shadows cast by her glorious parents.

"And you are not otherworldly?"

"Oh, Gunnar." Addison sighed and shook her head. "No. I'm not otherworldly at all. I am *this* worldly. I'm a homebody. A put-down-roots girl. I am not a pursuer, a chaser of anything. I don't want to sleep in a new bed every night. I don't want to wake up wondering what side of the planet I'm on. I don't want to eat things I can't pronounce or go places where important things are lost in translation." She broke off, realizing she was beginning to rant. She pointed at the mug she held and shot him a suspicious look. "I'm talking way too much. Is there truth serum in this coffee?"

Gunnar chuckled. "Just Arabica beans; I promise you." He studied her for a few moments, then said, "So tell me something else, then." His expression had lost some of its joviality; was that concern she read there instead?

"What do you want to know?"

"If not this," he began, making a broad sweeping gesture with one arm. "Then what is it that you do want?"

Addison didn't even hesitate. "I want to wake up in my own bed and eat the same boring breakfast every morning. I want to feed my cat, water my plants, and do the crossword puzzle in the newspaper that gets delivered to my door every day. I want to check for mail in my own mailbox, and I want to drive to and from my nine-to-five job five days a week in my own car." She pressed her lips together to keep from listing even more things she wanted, lest she sound too pathetic, even though she knew it was unlikely she'd ever see this man again. *I want to be seen,* she didn't say aloud. *To be known. To belong. I don't want to be the new kid, the stranger, the alien, ever again. I don't want to fade into the background until I completely disappear.*

"What is your cat's name?" Gunnar asked after a few moments.

"My cat? I—I don't have one."

"But you said you wanted to feed your cat..." His words trailed off, and his brow furrowed in question.

"I know, I know." Addison waved a hand dismissively. "I meant that I wanted to do normal things that people do every day. Things that take place at the same time in the same place again and again and again. Dependable. Constant. Predictable." She sighed resignedly. "Boring."

"Do you—um..." He hesitated, then proceeded to ask the question anyway. "Do you have any plants?"

Addison shook her head. "I don't have any plants. Not a single one." She chuckled softly. "I'm pretty pathetic, aren't I?"

"No, no," Gunnar insisted. "It just seems to me that the things you want aren't so difficult to come by. Why don't you have a cat? Or a plant?"

Addison grimaced. "Promise you won't laugh?"

"I promise," he was quick to assure her.

"Well, I've never had either one. I don't know the first thing about taking care of some other living thing. I'm—I'm afraid I'd do it wrong. I mean, I suppose it's okay if a plant dies under my care, but a cat?" She shook her head. "It's probably better if I just keep it all in my imagination."

"Hm."

"What does that mean?" she challenged, feeling slightly chastised by the simple sound.

"If this is not what you want, then why did you come? I mean, it doesn't sound like a very pleasant way to spend your holidays. Your mother said you were staying in Reykjavik through Christmas."

Addison nodded slowly. "It's the only way I can see my parents. If I come to them."

"Ah. I see." His gaze shifted away from hers and she recognized immediately the look in his eyes. He was feeling sorry for her.

"What about you? Is this—" She gestured broadly the way he had earlier. "Is all of this what you want?"

Gunnar didn't hesitate, either. "I love it here. It's wild and vicious and intense and beautiful, and of course, the people here are all so attractive, yes? Like gods and goddesses."

"Well, of course," Addison agreed with a grin.

"But seriously, this is home to me," Gunnar continued. "Johann—the other driver. Have you met him?"

"Yes. I rode here in his van."

"Of course. He and I have been operating private excursions like this one for many years, and I wouldn't want to be doing anything else with my life right now."

"Wow." Addison sighed dreamily as she let his words sink in. The colorful northern lights continued to swirl and sweep across the sky, casting a surreal greenish tint over everything. "I wish I could be that certain about my own life."

Gunnar slid his stocking cap off and ran his fingers through his shaggy hair, drawing Addison's attention back to him. He really was an attractive man, she acknowledged. He had a broad forehead above a strong brow and clear blue eyes that made her think of the crystal blue chunks of iceberg that crowded the shores of Diamond Beach. His nose was long and straight, his mouth was quick to flash a smile, and the beard, although long, looked neatly trimmed, soft, and well cared for. She wondered what it would feel like to run her fingers through it.

"Does your beard keep your face warm?" she asked to derail the direction her thoughts were headed.

Gunnar grinned. "Why yes, it does." He reached up to scratch just under his jaw, then ran his fingers down the length of it in what seemed like a semi self-conscious manner. He caught her watching his movements and paused. "You want to touch it?"

She shook her head quickly. "No. Goodness, no," she insisted, far too adamantly than necessary. "That's all right."

Gunnar's soft chuckle had her burying her face in her cup again.

Keep reading Addison's story in **The Apartment on Larkspur Lane: Autumn Lake Romance Book 2.** It's available in print, ebook, and audiobook, and you can find it at **Becky Doughty Books** or any of your favorite online bookstores.